HOME TO HILLDALE
Hilldale Series - Book 2

D1176615

Pat Jaeger

Home to Hilldale
Hilldale Series Book 2
Published by Grand Circle Publishing, LLC
P. O. Box 513
Kanab, UT 84741

ISBN: 978-0-9982022-0-4
Christian suspense/thriller/crime
Printed in the United States of America
Year of first printing: 2016

COVER DESIGN: Harvey Nazareno Bunda
http://www.harveybunda.com
AUTHOR PHOTO: Sharon Dalton

Dedication

Survivors all: Paul John, Dianne, Joshua, Danny, and Peter, you survived your mother's craziness with grace, kindness, a loving spirit, and a quirky sense of humor. Love you more!

Acknowledgements

Two of the characters, Mary Johannsen and Sue Miles, entered their names and won the contest to be written into this novel. They chose to be a good or bad character, and as chosen, I've enjoyed working them into the plot. Thanks ladies!

Launching a new novel is like raising a child: it takes a village! I'm so grateful to God, the Father who's given me grace and mercy. Though MS may slow me down, it hasn't stopped me! For that, I give You the glory.

I used my deceased mother's name, Mary Ethel Harmon, and though she wasn't an English teacher, my namesake character has my mom's sweet, spunky, kind nature. Miss you Mom.

Russell Jaeger, husband extraordinaire, thanks for letting me read this story out loud to you, and for your generous comments and insight. Without your encouragement and unconditional support, for kindly overlooking the forgotten meals and mentally-absent-while-writing times, these stories would remain in the computer. Love and blessings to you.

Dorothy Rowden, you're not just a loving sister, you are an awesome editor! Your help, suggestions, encouragement, and prayers are invaluable. Love you right back!

Dianne Solberg: terrific daughter; healing massage therapist; and talented writer; thank you for all your help, for listening with wisdom and encouragement, for your thoughtful critiques, and for your unfailing support. I love you, young lady.

Peter and Brandy IraLilly Fay, you wizards with computers! What a blessed mom I am to have you helping me get beyond my cyber-phobia! Your patience and love helped me through several crises. Love you, kids!

Heartfelt thanks to my awesome business manager and beta reader, Amy Bertling. Thanks for helping me enact (Purely for reality's sake—really!) the various scenes. You give selflessly to all your family, friends, and yes, strangers. You live your faith. Love you, dear lady. I still think you're one of my kids.

Thanks go out to my faithful beta readers: Vicki Gares, Lois Sapp, Roger Theide, Paula Yancy, Keralee Oblad, fellow novelist, Carol Edwards Denekas, and anyone else who participated but didn't get your name back to me in time for publication. You are greatly appreciated!

Katie Book, PA, thank you for answering my questions on the arduous journey to become a physician's assistant--you're one of the best!

Dotty Manns, thank you for once again letting me use your café in my story. Hartsburg, Missouri is blessed to have you living there.

Sonya Kimball and Desiree Lathim, ladies in charge of Fredonia Senior Center, thank you for keeping Russ and I fed, for keeping us laughing, and for keeping us in line. You two ladies are a dear blessing to us, and to all who dare to enter.

A special thank you to Liz Adair and the Red Rock Writers who have so graciously taken me in with encouragement, sharing the writing experience with helpful critiques, insightful lessons on the art of writing, lots of laughter, and kindness. Liz your help has been an invaluable gift. Blessings to you all.

Home to Hilldale
Hilldale Series – Book 2

Pat Jaeger

Grand Circle Publishing, LLC

PROLOGUE

Stirring her oatmeal, she watched as weatherman Al Roker interacted with the jubilant crowd. Her morning ritual—the TODAY show. A smile skittered across her lean face and set a constellation of freckles into brief movement. She loved this part of the show: the laughter, the joking, the happy faces, people waving signs declaring birthdays, anniversaries, holidays. Families who vacationed together. Longing stabbed through her.

Scraping the oatmeal into a chipped bowl, she filled the hot sauce pan with water, leaving it in the sink to wash up after school. Her hip against the counter, she reached for her cereal and blew on the first spoonful of the bland gluey mess. Watching the antics and happy faces, she wished she could crawl through the small television screen and pick a laughing person with a kind face. She imagined herself wrapped in their joyful hug, imagined being welcomed into their happy family.

Then she saw him.

The bowl dropped from her hand, hit the worn linoleum, and shattered, splattering its contents and tiny shards of glass at her feet. She never noticed. The flickering screen held her captive. Her heart twisted. Her stomach threatened to spew its meager contents. She cried out, quickly slapping her hand over her mouth--*the neighbors might hear*!

He pointed at her. The camera panned past him across the eager crowd, then back, and there! There he stood. Silent, a smile on his face that oozed evil, his eyes stared right at her, as though he could see her through the television. For a brief instant, he inserted himself in front of the people around him, pointed his finger, cocked his thumb, and made a shooting motion. His smile widened. The camera slid past him, back to the happy faces, the waving signs.

As it panned back across the crowd, she searched the screen. Gone. But, she knew where he was going. He was on his way here, on his way to kill her. Her breath burned in her chest as panic tried to seal her lungs, making her lightheaded. Heart pounding, pushing her blood and adrenaline into flight mode, the rushing blood made helicopter sounds that thumped in her ears.

She grabbed her backpack as she dashed from the tiny kitchen into the bedroom. Racing through the apartment, she dumped schoolbooks, notebooks, pencils, pens, a baggie housing her peanut butter and jelly sandwich out on the worn living room carpeting. For just a moment, regret slowed her down. A month until graduation. Fear pushed her regret aside and she continued down the hallway.

In her bedroom, she stuffed her few belongings into the cheap canvas backpack, then ran to her mother's bedroom where she went to the lone chest of drawers. Pain squeezed her heart. Her panicked mind made it difficult to think.

She reached beneath the scrambled assortment of undergarments in the top drawer and found the cigar box tied with a battered turquoise ribbon. Into the backpack it went, nesting down into the few items of clothing she owned. Blood pulsed in her head, nearly blinding her, but she hurried back down the hallway where she scooped the fallen sandwich from the floor. In the bag it went without breaking her dash back to the kitchen.

She stepped over the glass-spiked glob of oatmeal, reached to the top of the corner cabinet and lifted down the chipped sugar bowl with the sunflower lid. Pulling out her meager stash of money, she pushed the folded bills deep into her jeans' pocket.

At the refrigerator, she crammed the nearly full peanut butter jar, the half-loaf of white bread, an almost empty jar of grape jelly, and a jar of sweet pickles on top of the clothing. Placing a butter knife, spoon, fork, and the last plastic trash bag into the backpack, she forced the zipper closed and raced out of the apartment, never looking back.

New York. Two days, maybe three—no, two. He'd travel fast. He was coming. He'd find her and then—blanking out her thoughts, she ran down the three flights of stairs and out onto the sidewalk where no one noticed her fear. She stopped. Which way? Where could she go? Her chin jutted forward. Her decision made, she turned and headed south, moving at an even, purposeful pace. Somewhere south she knew there was a place her mother called home.

"But now faith, hope, love, abide these three;
but the greatest of these is love."
1 Corinthians 13:13 (NASB)

ONE

"Get your hands off me, you scum-sucking, bottom feeding, piece of—uh—Sheriff. Hey, I wasn't doing nothing."

Lund County Sheriff Daniel Halloran's dusky face broke into a smile. "Double negative young lady, meaning you *were* doing something. Gave yourself away!" He grinned and tried to look stern at the same time.

Nineteen-year-old Gordie Bently, who'd entered the convenience store with the sheriff, stared, sky-blue eyes wide, his mouth open in wonder.

The girl, who looked to be about Gordie's age, wore baggy gray sweats and a black, hooded jacket, much too big for her. A battered, bulging, thread-bare backpack rode her back, its weight digging into her shoulders. *Too many clothes for a warm day in May*, Dan observed to himself.

Gritting her teeth, lips pursed in anger, the girl scowled up at the sheriff and the young man standing next to him. Her hair, a flaming riot of red tangled curls, fought a stained, but still vivid purple headband for freedom and won, tumbling down below her narrow shoulders, the bright store light sparking fire from the red-gold strands. Her narrowed eyes glared at the two men.

"Fine, Mr. English Teacher, *sir*," she growled. "I haven't done *anything*, and you can just keep your hands off me. You touch me…I scream." Her chin jutted forward.

The girl's lioness-colored eyes had a black ring outlining each tawny-gold iris, and when she

1

focused her eyes on Gordie, he sucked in his breath letting it go with an audible *whoosh.* Her fierceness crackled like static electricity in the air around them.

"Yah, so what you staring at, *retard?*" she snapped at the open-mouthed teen.

Golden brown freckles tracked across her face, including her high forehead. All-in-all, the girl was an eye-opener, her fierce attitude somehow making her appear more vulnerable.

Gordie gulped and answered, "Your hair! You look like an angel!"

She rolled her eyes toward the sheriff. "He for real?"

"For real," Sheriff Dan assured her, "only, he's not mentally handicapped. He's probably smarter than the two of us put together—he just doesn't flaunt it, young lady."

The red-head snorted. Shrugging, she grabbed Gordie's hand and stuck his broken, twisted fingers in her mass of curls, "I'm no angel, *retard,*" she said, as she glowered at the sheriff, "but the hair is real."

Dan Halloran gave her shoulder a slight shake, frowning. "All right, miss, that's enough from you. We don't use the *r* word around here—ever," he said, leveling a stern look at her. "Looks to me like you want to pay for that sandwich you stuffed inside your jacket, or you were about to put it back in the cooler, correct?" His dark eyes bored into hers.

He'd worked through most of the night when one of his deputies had called in sick, but now he was off duty, tired, and in no mood for this young woman's sass.

He and Gordie had just come back from breakfast at Dotty's Cafe and his plan was to deliver the young man back home, then head for his own place and some much needed sleep. Still in uniform, he decided to take care of this young woman himself rather than call Dick Banner, the Hilldale police chief. She hadn't stolen the sandwich—yet, he reminded himself.

A look of panic swiftly crossed her face before settling back into surliness. Dan guessed she was broke and hungry. Before he could offer to pay for her food, she snarled at him. "Yah, all right, copper, don't get bent out of shape." Reaching into her jacket, she pulled out a roast beef and Swiss cheese sandwich and replaced it inside the cooler.

Copper? Dan nearly laughed out loud. *Must like old movies.*

Surprised by sudden movement, he saw Gordie snatch up the sandwich, grab a bag of chips from a nearby shelf, pick up a cold carton of milk from another cooler, then head toward the cashier.

Once the items were paid for, the young man carried the plastic bag of food back to the girl, who waited with a puzzled expression. Handing the bag to her, Dan watched a huge grin spread across Gordie's badly scarred face, and fury spread across the girl's. *This was going to get interesting.*

Yellow fire sparked from her eyes. "Don't need your charity," she growled, shoving the bag back at the young man, her face flushing deep scarlet.

Gordie looked genuinely confused. "Charity?" he stammered, looking at Sheriff Dan, then back at the angry girl. "Ain't—I mean, it isn't charity, ma'am. I wanted to be able to say I bought lunch for an angel!" As he laughed with true delight, the girl looked from him to the sheriff at her side, the smart-aleck mouth gone for a moment.

"Sure he's for real?" she questioned, her eyes staring into the sheriff's, looking to see if she was being mocked.

Dan nodded. Taking the bag from Gordie, he handed it back to her. This time she took it, though reluctantly.

"Where you staying?" Dan asked, casually herding her and Gordie out the door toward his maroon Silverado.

"I got a place to stay and I'm going to get a job." Glancing at Gordie she said, "Thanks for breakfast and probably lunch, too. I owe you." Her voice went soft for a moment, and flicking her hair over one shoulder, she lightly punched his arm.

The young man smiled and replied, "You don't pay for gifts, silly. Even a *retard* knows that!" Turning his back on her, Gordie climbed into Dan's pickup closing the door behind him.

Dan studied her stunned face and laughed.

"Told you," he said.

"Yah, so maybe he's got a brain in that ugly head. What did he do, run into an acne epidemic?" Trying to tuck unruly escapees beneath the headband, she backed away from the sheriff.

"Not acne," Dan replied tersely, his face turning sad. The girl had the grace to blush, then shrugged, still backing away.

"Yah? Tough! Not my problem. See you around—not!" She took off across the convenience store's parking lot and headed toward the highway leading into Hilldale. Shaking his head, Dan walked around his truck.

The two men watched until they saw her turn left toward Neely's Cafe. Dan had an idea she was headed to see Carter Neely about a job, and he wanted to get there first. Hopping into the driver's side, he drove up the back street to the rear of the cafe, pulling into the delivery area where he parked. Gordie and Dan hurried in the back door, just in time to hear voices up front at the lunch counter.

The two men moved through the kitchen, and peeked through the window in the swinging door. Carter Neely stood stacking mugs on the shelf next to one of the two coffee makers, glanced over the girl's shoulder at the sheriff and the young man. Dan shook his head and put his finger to his lips. Carter frowned, then focused his attention back on the mugs and the fast-talking girl's words.

"I'm a good worker and there isn't anything I won't do—sweep, mop floors, wash dishes, wait tables, clean toilets—anything. I'll start at minimum wage until you see how hard I can work. You won't be sorry, Mr. Neely, I promise."

Carter Neely looked helplessly at Dan, then back at the girl.

"Listen, young lady, I can't hire you. I don't need..." His voice faltered as the sheriff shook his head, mouthing for the owner to give the girl a job.

"Fine, okay," Carter sighed, "but you can't wait tables until Tina, she's the head waitress, well, she's the only waitress, says you're ready, got it? You can clean up, maybe help me in the kitchen—part time. You ever cook on a grill?" he asked hopefully, giving the sheriff a *you-owe-me* look. Satisfied, Dan and Gordie slipped out the back door and drove away before the girl could see them.

"We didn't get her name!" Gordie said, looking at the sheriff.

"Shoot! You're right, we didn't." Dan laughed, surprised that he'd forgotten to ask her. "Reckon we'll find it out when we visit Neely's tonight." He grinned at the young man happily nodding from the passenger's seat. The girl itched his memory, but he couldn't figure out why.

"I'm going to call her Wanda," Gordie said, staring out the window. He couldn't get the image of all that fiery red hair out of his mind. She was the most beautiful girl he'd ever seen, and thinking about her made him feel strange inside.

"What if that's not her name?" Dan asked.

"Don't matter," Gordie said, "she calls me *retard* and that ain't—isn't my name!"

They drove in silence, Dan staring at the county blacktop ahead, and Gordie just staring, his mind wandering places he rarely allowed it to go. For the first time in his life, he found that his scarred face embarrassed him. He never really thought about it much, never looked in a mirror until he moved into his first foster home. What he saw surprised him—even shocked him a bit—but he got used to the furtive glances and outright staring of outsiders. It never bothered him, until now.

Miss Molly, Sheriff Dan's wife, had made arrangements for his face and deformed fingers and shoulder to be operated on, but he'd put off the procedures, somewhat fearful of the outcome. What if he came out looking worse? But now? *Maybe I better get started on the operations,* Gordie thought, watching the familiar cropland and pastures roll by without actually seeing them.

The girl hadn't avoided looking at him, and she hadn't stared like he was a freak the way some folks did. She hadn't flinched, or looked away from his face, even though she'd called him the *r* word, and she hadn't acted disgusted when she took his deformed hand and put it in her hair. He shivered.

Most folks wouldn't touch his hands. Gordie could still feel where her fingers had wrapped themselves around his wrist. His skin tingled. What a strange girl, and she really had a mouth on her! He smiled to himself.

"What?" Dan asked.

"That girl, Wanda, she sure can sass can't she? Whew! I thought she might scorch us there for a minute!"

"That she can. I don't think she's from around here. You hear the way she says *yah*? Sounds like she's from up north, maybe Minnesota or Wisconsin. Wonder where her folks are? Seems a bit young to be hiking on her own.

Could be a runaway, though why anyone would run away to Hilldale beats me. Too small a town, and too many folks know each other. A runaway wouldn't be able to hide very well, at least, not for long. It doesn't look like she's just passing through, getting that job at Neely's. Wonder where she's staying."

The sheriff in him knew something was wrong with the girl's situation, and he planned on making it his business to find out just what that something was.

*****

Dan and Gordie arrived at Muley Burger's farm just outside of Tilson, Missouri. They saw the eighty-four-year-old farmer sitting on his porch swing, his young Coonhound, Cootie II, sleeping at his feet, and Beauty, the pup's mother, draped across Muley's lap. His gnarled fingers worked the hound's old scars left by the same bull whip that Bobby Lee Bently had marked Gordie's face and body with. Dancer, Gordie's Doberman, leapt off the porch and raced up to the Silverado, dancing in circles on his hind feet, barking a joyful welcome to his beloved master.

7

"Howdy," Muley called from the porch, working the loose skin around the Black and Tan's neck. Groaning happily, Beauty shifted so he could get better coverage.

"Hey, Papa Muley, you ain't—shoot—aren't going to believe what Sheriff Dan and me saw in Hilldale at the convenience store."

Gordie, petting Dancer as he headed toward the porch, could barely contain his excitement, bringing a broad grin to the wrinkled, gray-whiskered face watching him.

The love the old man felt for the teen glowed in his eyes. Nearly two years ago, this young man had given Muley a reason to keep on living after Arden Wickem, Sr. shot him and left him for dead, then killed the boy's mother and his step-grandfather.

Watching the boy and his dog, Muley recognized again how blessed he was, surviving the shooting and having Gordie, the boy's critters, Danny, Molly, Obed Martin, and Billy Sumday, in his life. Contentment radiated from him.

Still in the Silverado, the sheriff leaned down and locked his pistol in the safe installed under his truck seat. Climbing out of his pickup, Dan removed his uniform shirt and leaving it across the back of the seat, he crossed the driveway and climbed the porch steps sinking down on the top one, nestling his back up against the post. The morning sun had warmed the wood and it felt good to just sit, soaking it up.

"Going to Neely's tonight, ain't we?" Muley asked. "Being Thursday and all, I didn't start nothing cooking. Reckon Billy's gonna meet us up town. Said he's riding that pathetic pile of bones he calls a horse. Give it some Shawnee name I can't even begin to pronounce. A woman warrior, no less! Seems a Kickapoo ought to use a name from his own tribe, but he says he has great respect for this here gal. Don't look like no paint horse I ever saw, much less a warrior, pitiful thing, all splotchy where the hide's laid bare." He shook his bald head setting his fringe of fine, too-long, white hair drifting in a circle around his neck and ears.

Gordie hopped up on the porch dancing from one foot to the other.

"'Course we're going to Neely's, Papa Muley. Don't matter if Sheriff Dan has the rest of the day off, it's Thursday and you always go to Neely's on Thursday. I'm coming with you." His face split in a huge grin.

"What about your music lessons?" Dan teased.

The young man countered, "Called off for the summer. The director and the choir are going on tour to Europe. I didn't want to go with them, so I don't have lessons again 'til September."

"What you so all fired up about, lad?" Muley asked, curious at the boy's unusual excitement. Normally easy-going, the young man hopped around the porch and the two men like a frog on a hot griddle.

"We saw us a girl in town," Gordie started, a blush quickly staining his neck and cheeks, spreading to his ears.

"You that excited about a girl?" Muley interrupted, surprised.

"Papa Muley, you ain't never seen nothing like this girl in your whole wide life," the boy said, his eyes round with the memory of her. "Shoot, I forgot and said *ain't* again," he groaned.

"Never you mind, boy. Ain't nothing wrong with *ain't*. You get to talking too fancy and I might not be able to understand you." He laughed at the young man's crestfallen face. "Go on now, cheer up, you're doing just fine with your lessons, lad. Don't get yourself down about it. Now tell me about this here girl that's got you so riled up."

Listening to the men's banter, Dan stretched out his long legs and laced his fingers behind his head, shifting to a more comfortable position on the step.

"Think he might be in love, Muley," he drawled, his eyes drifting closed, his body shedding the tensions from a hectic night of paperwork and chasing drunks racing their pickups down the center of the county road.

Shaking his head, Gordie laughed, "I don't know what being in love is, Sheriff Dan. Well, if it's like you and Miss Molly getting married, I ain't in love, but she sure is beautiful. Papa Muley, she looks like an angel with fire in her hair." His voice grew hushed.

"Ma used to tell me about Gramma Sarah's best friend, Wanda, who had red hair. She said it was the most beautiful sight she ever saw, the sun shining on that hair, sending out sparks. I used to try and picture it, but now I know just what it looks like! And she's got gold-colored eyes!" Breathless, he stopped for a minute.

"Your gramma's friend or the girl? Who's got gold eyes?" Mulcy asked. "Get on with your story, lad." The old man's eyes glittered with mischief.

Gordie sank cross-legged to the porch floor, his dog settling beside him. "The girl! The girl has golden eyes." He shook his head at the interruption.

"Sheriff Dan caught her stealing—leastways I think she was stealing a roast beef and cheese sandwich. I don't think she has any money. She's going to work for Carter Neely, and I hope we'll see her tonight."

"Ha! So that's what's got you all worked up. A red-headed girl working at Neely's, eh? Well, by golly, we'll just have to take a gander at her tonight, won't we. Say her name's Wanda and she's got a head full of red hair?" Muley asked, a frown of elusive memory creasing his forehead.

"Well," Gordie hesitated, "I named her that. We don't rightly know her real name, but I'm going to call her Wanda. She calls me *retard*!" He laughed.

Muley scowled. "Don't like that kind of name-calling," he spoke, fiercely protective of the boy he'd come to think of as a beloved grandson.

"She don't mean it Papa Muley. You'll see. It ain't—isn't like she believes it, it's just her way of acting tough. She isn't though—tough, I mean. Got one smart mouth on her, though, don't she Sheriff Dan?" He looked to the dark-skinned man dozing in the warm sun.

"Hmmmmm," Dan murmured, not opening his eyes. "That she does."

"Reckon I'm going to put on my barn clothes and go milk Kissie." Gordie said. "She and her calf will be ready to head out to pasture, then I'd best take me a bath and get ready," He jumped to his feet startling Cootie II and Dancer. Petting them until they relaxed again, the young man headed for the screen door, disappearing inside. The two older men could hear him singing to himself as he went up the stairs.

"Might early to get ready to go out tonight, ain't it Danny?" Muley looked concerned. "Land sakes, the boy's sure taken with that gal you all saw in town. You know who she is?"

"Nope. Don't know her, but, she seems a bit familiar to me. I haven't figured out why—never saw her before, and we forgot to ask her name. Guess that mouth and all that red hair gave us brain freeze." Dan laughed.

"I don't think she's from around here. It sounds more like she's from up north, maybe Minnesota. Reminds me of that woman who called about giving Neva Sue a ride the day she disappeared from the hospital—that woman who lived up near Duluth."

Dan thought about Gordie's mother, Neva Sue, who had been murdered a couple of years ago. The lawyer who had murdered her had also shot Muley and Cootie, killing the old Bluetick Coonhound, and nearly killing the farmer.

"S'pose she's a runaway? Seems a mite familiar to me, too, Danny. That name Wanda the lad give her...."

"Strange, isn't it? I think Gordie's talking about Wanda Harmon, old Willie's widow. There's something about the girl, that's for sure. If she's a runner, I hope to find that out," Dan replied. "She's got a reason for being here and I'm guessing she isn't going anywhere just yet, seeing as how she took a job up at Neely's." He sat up and stretched.

"Speaking of Neely's, you said Billy's coming up on that old paint horse he got from Betsy DeGroat? Surely not the one she took from that fella that had all those beaten and starving horses up near Rocheport? I can't imagine that poor old thing going a mile, much less ten."

The old man set the swing in motion. "Yep. Had her three weeks now, and she looks a good bit better. Still see her ribs and she don't cotton to no one but that old Kickapoo. Even Betsy had a heck of a time trying to get her out of the trailer. Billy, he up and walks right in there and sweet talks her real quiet, backs her out of the trailer, and she commences to follow him like a dadburn pup. Beats all I ever saw, 'cept that boy upstairs. He's got that gift, like Billy."

Dan wasn't sure it was such a great idea for Billy Sumday to ride the horse into town and back, but if the Native American thought it was okay, it was probably okay. Billy knew his animals, especially horses, and Dan trusted the Kickapoo's judgment.

Shrugging, he stood and stretched. "Got to get home and look after Snoozer, clean a sink full of last week's dishes, grab a long hot shower and a few hours' sleep, and then I'll meet you and Gordie at Neely's."

He yawned, scratched the dogs behind their ears, gave Muley a quick hug, then headed down the stairs toward his pickup. He smiled and waved good-bye as Gordie headed out the screen door and down the porch steps. The teen whistled as he made his way across the driveway toward the barn.

*****

That evening, the three men joined Billy Sumday, Obed Martin, and two of Sheriff Dan's deputies, Randy Carter and Jeff Springer, at Neely's Cafe. The men often met on Thursday nights for supper, catching up on the local news, and the easy conversation of men who've known each other most of their lives. Billy and Obed, both in their eighties, sat drinking icy bottles of soft drinks, and helping themselves to the iron skillet-roasted peanuts and pretzels Tina Sapp served before their meal. Gordie, seated between Muley and Billy, suddenly went still and sat up straight in his chair, a blush staining his ears and neck. The older men followed the direction of his gaze, their voices fading into silence.

*****

Balancing a tray loaded with glass soda mugs, Juanita threaded her way through the tables to behind the lunch counter where she quickly stacked the mugs inside the freezer. Turning, she noticed the table of men staring at her. One of the men at the table was that sheriff who'd caught her trying to steal from the convenience store, and the boy that'd been with him. Quickly lowering her eyes, she headed back to the kitchen. Shame flooded her face.

The boy smiled and waved at her, trying to get her attention. Ignoring him, she hurried through the swinging door to the safety of the large sinks filled with dirty dishes and hot sudsy water. She'd mocked the boy for his looks. Cringing at her own behavior, she thought of the many times she'd been mocked for her wild mane of red hair, and her splattering of freckles that stippled her arms and face.

Wishing she could stay in the kitchen the rest of the evening and avoid the boy's attention, she knew that would be impossible. She had a job to do, and do it she would, no matter what. With a sigh, she pulled on heavy rubber gloves, plunged her hands into the hot soapy water, and began scrubbing the dishes and silverware, dropping them into the hot bleach-laced rinse water. Tears threatened to spill over her flushed cheeks.

Not normally a weeper, Juanita grew impatient with the mood swings that had taken over lately. What in the world was wrong with her? Why did it matter to her that the boy she'd made fun of

14

understand that she didn't really mean it? Whenever she felt threatened, she found herself slipping into her tough, street-girl persona. She knew what it was like to be the butt of cruel jokes and unkind words, and yes, she thought sadly, she wanted the boy to know she was sorry.

TWO

Eddie Felton half-listened to the truck driver, his mind focused on his plan. He figured they would be in Minneapolis early the next morning. With any luck, he would surprise Juanita before she left for school. A smile twisted his mouth looking more like a grimace. He'd surprise her all right. His hand slid to his pants pocket checking again for the small baggie he'd purchased, just for her.

Like her mother, once he got her hooked on heroin, she'd be putty in his hands. *Won't have to fight her like before*, he thought touching the healed scratches on his neck. And when he tired of her, needed to move on, well, like her mother, he'd give her a little help falling asleep—forever asleep. Again, he smiled. Wouldn't be long now. That little spitfire would get what was coming to her.

He must have dozed off. Felton gazed out the bug-spattered windshield and heard the trucker keying his CB mike. "Yo, bandoleros, got your ears on? Coming west on 94, any Smokies rolling? The coop open? Come on."

Eddie listened while other truckers checked in identifying the mile markers where state troopers were last spied, and letting the driver know the weigh station a few miles ahead was open for business.

"Gonna delay us a bit, buddy," the trucker said, glancing at the man riding in his passenger seat. *Scary dude*, he mused, focusing back on the interstate and the heavy morning traffic.

"How far into the city are you going?" Eddie asked.

"Going north on 94 to Broadway. Where you want me to drop you?"

Eddie thought for a moment. "Broadway's fine. I'm headed for Lowry Avenue, but I'll thumb it there. It isn't that far."

Nodding, the driver exited the interstate toward the weigh station where he queued up behind several semis pulling various kinds of trailers. They inched forward until the Minnesota DOT gave them the green light to move on.

THREE

Juanita IraLilly Edmonds woke up early, her legs and lower back aching from the long night of standing at the sink doing dishes, and helping Carter Neely at the grill. She'd surprised herself, and him, at how quickly she'd caught onto working with the deep-fryer and grill, happily relieving him at one or the other, in between washing the tray-loads of dishes and glasses she and Tina Sapp brought back to the kitchen.

Good thing this place doesn't have motion sensors or video security. She sighed, heading for the women's restroom. She'd been up a few times during the night—unusual for her. Standing in front of the full-length mirror anchored to the wall next to the sink, she studied her slight figure. Running her hands over her abdomen, she felt a tingle of fear at the slight protrusion. She'd have to keep wearing her big tee shirts to hide the swelling as long as possible.

Mr. Neely would be in soon. She'd best clean up and hide until he unlocked the place, pretend she'd just come in; he'd never know the difference. It had been nice, sleeping in one of the booths, covering herself with her sweatshirt jacket, her bundle of belongings making a pillow. She'd been pretty comfortable, and for the first time in a very long time, Juanita felt safe while she slept.

The trip from Minneapolis to Hilldale, Missouri had taken her a lot longer than she'd anticipated, using her food and money resources far too quickly. She'd resorted to stealing food when she could, had picked up a tee shirt, jacket, and sweat pants from a clothesline somewhere in Iowa, and more than once, she'd had to use the large trash bag to help keep her dryer than she'd have been without it. It had also provided her ground cover when she slept outside, giving her a slight barrier against the damp ground. Getting to Hilldale had been slow going, but she'd made it, and that gave her great satisfaction—and hope.

Her stomach growled. Grinning at herself in the mirror, she quickly washed her face and hands, then pulling and twisting her unruly red mane into a large bun at the back of her head, she tucked the ends inside the center, knotting it in place. Last night she'd washed her hair with hand soap, and it felt wonderful to have it clean. Used to the snide remarks about how she looked, she stuck her tongue out at the reflection of herself, shrugged off her dark thoughts, and smiled.

Working for Carter Neely meant eating. On a regular basis! The man positively pushed food at Tina and her, and never charged them a dime for it.

Said it was to keep them from fainting on the job, but Juanita saw past his crusty exterior and knew the man was a pushover. She'd have to be careful not to take advantage of him—not too much, anyway.

Hearing the scrape of the lock at the back door, she scurried from the restroom and hid in the utility closet. When Mr. Neely opened the front dining area up, she'd sneak into the kitchen and act like she had just arrived at work. She stood in the dark listening to the owner singing to himself as he made his way up front. Suddenly she went cold. She'd left her jacket and her meager belongings wadded up in her backpack on the bench in the back booth. Groaning inwardly, she waited for her inevitable discovery.

*****

Carter Neely passed the utility closet door and stopped. A ragged backpack and black sweatshirt jacket lay in a pile on the back booth bench. *The new girl, Juanita,* he thought. Seeing the depression in the old bench cushion, he figured she'd let herself get locked in last night, and had slept in the dining room. Quickly he moved toward the front door. If she was watching him, he didn't want her to know he suspected her of being in the cafe.

He wondered if she'd taken anything. The money lay locked in the safe, but he always left a cigar box of change under the counter and she'd had to break a fifty for Tina earlier last night, so she knew it was there. Checking, he saw the usual hundred in small bills still in the box. Mentally chastising himself, he realized she probably wouldn't still be here if she had stolen the money.

Frowning, he heard the back door open and slam shut, heard her voice call out to him, and then she walked into the main room as though she'd just gotten to work. But Carter saw the tiny spark of fear in her eyes as they darted to her belongings then back to him, and he felt his heart melt. The kid was probably homeless and had nowhere else to go. What the heck did he care if she slept in the place, as long as she wasn't stealing from him. And by the look of things, she'd done some cleaning on her own time. She probably didn't think he'd even notice it. Carter reckoned he could do worse. Deciding to pretend he knew nothing about her situation, he called back to her.

"Hey, Juanita, you left your stuff here last night. Tuck it in the back closet where I keep the towels and stuff. There's room on one of those shelves. Don't forget it tonight when you go home. I can't be responsible for your valuables!"

The girl stood just inside the dining room doorway and studied his large angular face, his kind brown eyes. Her expression softened and for a moment he thought she would cry, but with a shrug, she gave him a cocky grin and said, "Yah, sure. Sorry. I'll move my stuff right now. When's breakfast? I'm starving!"

Shaking his head as he headed back to the kitchen, Carter Neely growled something under his breath about kids being bottomless pits, never getting enough to eat. Juanita trailed behind him, chattering away. She couldn't see it, but the cafe owner was grinning from ear-to-ear.

Re-entering the kitchen, he stopped, taking in the spotlessly clean floor tiles, and the big stainless steel sinks gleaming beneath the bright fluorescent lights. It must have taken over an hour just to scrub the greasy tiles. This kid was going to be okay, Carter smiled to himself as he turned on the gas burners beneath the grill.

Once the breakfast customers began arriving in earnest, he asked Juanita to help him at the grill and deliver the plates of food he cooked up. The teen left the dishes in the sink and stepped over to the grill and took one of the order slips from Carter's stack. Quickly cracking two eggs onto the well-oiled grill, she reached over and dropped four slices of toast into the toaster. Turning back to her side of the grill, she took up her spatula.

As she stared at the eggs sizzling and staring back at her, her stomach lurched and she ran for the sink. Carter quickly stepped over to rescue the eggs and placed bacon, toast, and home-fried potatoes on the warm plate. Stepping to the service window, he placed the food beneath the heat lamp and slapped the bell, calling out the name on the order to let them know they could pick up their food. Tina didn't work mornings, and most of his customers knew the routine and didn't seem to mind retrieving their food for themselves.

He turned to see Juanita rinsing her mouth and flushing the sink, running the garbage disposal, then sanitizing and scrubbing the sink. Her face was pale and sweat beaded her forehead.

"Sorry, Mr. Neely, I couldn't make it to the restroom," she said.

"Told you to call me Carter. What's up, kid?" Carter asked, concern gentling his voice.

"Just hungry, maybe. I dunno," Juanita mumbled, not looking her boss in the eye. She wondered if he would fire her when he found out her secret. Just when she thought her life might be getting on track.

"What sounds good, honey? Eggs, sausage?"

Her stomach roiled at the suggestion of eggs. She thought a moment then answered, "A fish sandwich with dill pickles, like McDonald's, and a chocolate shake!"

Startled, Carter Neely burst out laughing. "Fish sandwich? Ice cream? For crying in the soup, girl, that isn't much of a breakfast." And then he knew.

Without another word, he stepped over to the large freezer, opened it and removed a fish cake, dropped it in the deep fryer and started on the next breakfast order. Pregnant! He knew the signs, and he'd stake the cafe on it. Not only homeless, the girl was going to have a baby, and it looked like she was all alone. Well, not if Carter Neely could help it. Besides, he thought he had a pretty good idea why the teenager was in Hilldale.

FOUR

Eddie Felton gazed up to the third floor of the ramshackle apartment building. Not much had changed since he'd helped Sarah Elaine overdose. He'd had to leave in a hurry when the cops had come sniffing around, but it looked like the same scene he'd left three months ago, only the spring thaw had arrived.

Garbage lay scattered in stinking piles around the perimeter of the cracked and eroding foundation of the four-story building. Ripped black plastic bags oozed their rotting contents. Fast food wrappers fluttered and drifted, catching in the chain link fence, or if lucky, they rode the spring breeze over the barrier and escaped to whatever lay beyond. *Dump,* he hissed, spitting on the first of three steps leading up to the entrance.

The girl had probably headed to school already. He knew only a few weeks remained before she graduated, and he knew she was determined to do so. The only time he could remember her missing classes was when she found her old lady dead, overdosed on heroin and cheap whiskey. Wasn't anything Sarah Elaine loved better than her drugs and booze—not even her teen-age daughter. Made it all the easier for him.

Taking the stairs two at a time, he tested the handle of 304. Locked. Shaking his head at the foolishness of the useless lock, Eddie jiggled the handle while leaning his weight against the door. As usual, it popped without much effort. Entering the apartment, he quickly closed the door and relocked it so Juanita wouldn't suspect anyone waited inside for her. He yawned and looked around at the mess. A neat freak to the point of annoying him, it was unlike the girl to leave the place like this. A suspicion began to nag.

Walking through the living room and down the hallway, he picked up papers—homework papers. Pens, pencils, and textbooks were scattered along the hallway nearly to the back bedroom. There he found drawers pulled out and emptied of their once meager contents. He strode into Sarah Elaine's room. The top dresser drawer gaped, and after a quick search, the one thing Felton found missing was the cigar box that held the only items left from Sarah Elaine's life in some hick town in Missouri. The kid would never have left the box behind; it held her mother's few good memories from her folks' farm.

Juanita was gone.

Fury flashed through him like ignited gunpowder. He kicked the dresser sending it to its side where the drawers tumbled out, spilling their shabby contents across the faded carpet. Back in the kitchen, he reached for the sugar bowl sitting on the counter. Empty. Viciously, he threw it against the wall, nodding at the satisfying crash that sent splinters of cheap ceramic flying. She'd taken her money and fled. From the looks of the dried mess on the floor, he figured she'd been gone awhile. Cursing, he wondered how far of a head start she'd gotten.

He should have never let her see him on the TODAY show. Yes, he wanted her spooked. He relished the terror it must have caused her when she turned on her favorite program and there he was, looking right at her, pointing at her. She knew he was on his way back—that he was coming back just for her. With Sarah Elaine's death ruled an accidental overdose, he felt safe returning to the apartment, knowing the girl hadn't told on him. He missed her. She should have known he'd never leave her for long. She should have known running away wasn't going to stop him. She was his, and he'd find her. No matter what.

Slowly, methodically he pulled the pitiful collection of mismatched dishes from the cupboards and sailed them across the small room into the wall. When the shelves were empty, he wrenched the doors from their hinges and threw them into the debris on the linoleum floor. A mild sweat prickled his face.

Picking up the television, he ripped the cord from the outlet, lifted it above his head, and tossed it through the kitchen window where he heard it shatter three floors down. Satisfied, he stomped out of the apartment leaving the front door ajar. Just in case he was wrong and she hadn't left town yet, it'd give her something to think about. But Eddie Felton knew Juanita was gone. And he had a pretty good idea where she was headed.

Leaping down the stairs two at a time, he crashed through the entrance door knocking a young woman off the top step to the concrete sidewalk below. Her groceries flew in disarray around her. Too bad he didn't have time. She was good looking and would have been entertaining, but he had business to take care of. Kicking a head of lettuce against the fence, he gave the fallen woman a smile that caused her to scoot backwards away from him. Laughing at her fear, he moved down the sidewalk and headed south.

FIVE

Carter Neely made a quick phone call watching the kitchen door to make sure he wasn't overheard. When he finished, he hung up and smiled. After nearly a week of sleeping in the cafe, if he didn't miss his guess, Juanita would have her own room tonight. Whistling as he went back to the kitchen to prep for his lunch regulars, he sent the teen out to clean the tables and check the ketchup bottles, making sure they were ready for the noon crowd.

Juanita finished preparing the tables, then came back through the kitchen door and picked up a tray of coffee mugs she'd cleaned, taking them back to the dining room where she stacked them on the shelf next to the coffee machines. Returning for the tray of glass soda mugs, she stacked them in their place on the shelf next to the plastic pitchers. When she went back to the kitchen for the clean silverware to wrap in napkins, Carter Neely looked over at her.

"You act like you know what you're doing, young lady," he complimented her.

Shrugging, Juanita smiled. "It's not too difficult to figure out where this stuff goes, Mr. Neely." She blushed with pleasure at the compliment.

"Carter," he corrected her, grinning back. The lunch regulars, everyone from farmers, local businessmen, high school students, and seniors out for the day, came in for Friday's lunch special—tater tot casserole or grilled tilapia, with their choice of three sides, or their hamburgers, fish baskets, chicken fingers, and fries—lots of fries. Carter served the waffle-cut fries and changed his oil often, so they were always crisp on the outside, tender on the inside, and always tasted fresh.

The afternoon rush settled into a trickle then came to an end. Tina, who worked the eleven-until-two, then the six-until-ten weekday shifts, finished cleaning off the last of the lunch debris from the tables. She lifted the tray and started for the kitchen. The front door opened and Mary Harmon walked in, stopping just inside to let her eyes adjust from the bright sunlight to the cool dimness of the cafe. Setting her tray of dirty dishes back on the table, Tina smiled broadly and walked over to the elderly woman.

"Coming in for a late lunch, Miss Harmon?" she asked, taking the older woman's arm, leading her to a clean table where she settled her into a chair.

"Yes dear, I think I will. And how is your young athlete, Richard, Tina?" Mary asked. At seventy-five years old, Mary Harmon knew most of the people living in the area, and having taught English Literature at Hilldale High School for forty-five years, she knew many of her past students'

25

children and grandchildren. Tina was amazed at how she kept all the names in her head. Giving the elderly lady an affectionate hug, she straightened up and grinned.

"He's doing great. Coach wants him to be starting center this year." Pulling her pad from her apron pocket, she asked, "What can we get for you?"

"How about a half order of Carter's wonderful fries, a small salad with a wee bit of bacon and a smear of blue-cheese dressing on top, one chicken finger, and a nice cold glass of water, please." Smiling, she winked at Tina. "These are all no-noes except the salad and the water, of course, but I'm walking so that should make up for whatever's in the rest I'm not supposed to have, correct, dear?"

Tina laughed and nodded. "I like your thinking," she said as she scribbled a few notes on the order pad. Mary Harmon reminded Tina of a small brown sparrow: tiny, busy, and with eyes bright and full of mischief. She'd been many of the student's favorite teacher, including hers.

"Oh, and I'd like that new girl working in the kitchen to bring it to me, if that's all right with you, dear?" Miss Harmon smiled up at her, brown eyes full of innocence.

Surprised and wondering how she knew about Juanita, Tina nodded and turned to see her boss walking over to them.

"Miss Mary!" Carter grinned, bending to give her a light kiss on her cheek. "Thank you for coming. I don't think you'll be disappointed."

Tina looked at the two of them, and hands on hips, she said, "Hey you two, what's going on here? Am I being replaced?"

"Nah, honey," Carter wrapped his arm around Tina's shoulder giving her a hug. "Juanita needs a place to stay and I just heard Miss Mary is looking for someone to help her around her place. She's willing to trade room and board for house- and light yard-work." The owner of Neely's looked smug.

"Well aren't you something, Carter Neely," Tina smiled up at her boss and long-time boyfriend. "If I didn't know you better, I'd be looking for your angel wings!"

They laughed and Carter returned to the kitchen with the loaded tray of dirty dishes. Preparing Mary Harmon's lunch, he looked over to where Juanita rinsed, washed, and re-rinsed the pile of lunch dishes, stacking them in the drainer where the scalding water quickly evaporated. *Have to give the kid credit, she's not afraid of work,* he thought.

"Hey, Juanita," he called over to her from the deep fryer where he carefully drained the half order of fries and the single chicken finger. "Take this lunch out to the customer at table four. I don't think there's anyone else out there, but you can't miss her—little old gal with a big smile."

After removing her rubber gloves, Juanita picked up the tray of food and headed out the kitchen door, looking for the customer her boss described. She saw her at the table near the lunch counter talking with Tina, and walked over to the two women, carefully lowering her tray to the table. Giving the elderly lady a quick hug, Tina headed to the kitchen.

Mary Harmon looked up at the teenager and smiled. "Why thank you, young lady."

"No problem, ma'am," Juanita smiled back, setting the warm plate of fries and chicken on the table. She felt herself blushing under the woman's scrutiny. Lifting the salad, she placed it next to the glass of ice water.

The old lady reached out and lightly touched her arm. "Do you do yard work, dear?"

Flinching at the unexpected touch, Juanita's forehead wrinkled, her chin jutted forward. "Excuse me?"

"Well, I need a young woman to help me out at home, or it's off to the nursing home for me. Carter said you were a good worker, and he thought you might be interested in exchanging room and board for a bit of house- and yard-work. I have to promise not to take you away from him, though. Don't you think it would be a lovely arrangement, dear? Mind you, I have two cats and they're quite the pests."

The girl stared down at the woman. "You want me to come live with you and help you out at your house? You don't even know me! Mr. Neely doesn't know me. I've only worked for him five-and-a-half days. What if I'm a thief—or something?" Juanita stammered, incredulous at her good fortune, but fearful of it at the same time.

"Why, my dear girl, I've taught young people all my life, and I believe I'm a fair judge of character. Wasn't I the one to say that James Baytree—well, never mind about that. Besides, I've known that boy all his life, and if Carter Neely vouches for you, that's good enough for me. Would you like to try it out for a bit, and if it doesn't work out for either of us, we can split, as you young folks say!" She giggled like a schoolgirl while Juanita sucked in a deep breath.

"Ma'am, as long as it's okay with Mr. Neely, I'd really like to give it a try. When do you want me to start?"

Nibbling on a waffle fry, Mary smiled up at her, "Right after work, dear. Do you have many things to carry? I can fetch you in my car, if you tell me what time you're off work."

"I—no, I don't have that much and I've only just started here so I don't really have set hours. I'll have to talk to Mr. Neely."

Mary Harmon wiped her fingers on her napkin and patted her mouth. "Fine dear. Carter has my number. You could hop back and ask him now, or call me later. I don't live very far from here, well within walking distance, but if you have a lot to carry. . ." she hesitated.

Laughing, Juanita replied, "Nope, I really don't have a lot to carry, and I'll go ask Mr. Neely while you finish your lunch." Without further words, the young girl grabbed the tray up from the table and bounced out of the dining area, breezing through the kitchen door. Excitement lit her pale face, setting her freckles aglow. She had a place to live! Her own room in exchange for work, the old lady said. Juanita couldn't believe her good fortune. Her plan might work out after all.

*****

That evening, Carter Neely dropped Juanita off at Mary Harmon's home. Miss Mary wasted no time leading her through the compact rambler, while she carried her backpack and her jacket, the only possessions she owned. The retired teacher walked before her explaining where everything was. The room that would belong to her was second in a series of three bedrooms, with a bathroom just across the hallway from her door.

Painted in a pale peach color, the bedroom walls held paintings of peaceful country scenes. The double bed offered four pillows, and a beautiful quilt lay across the top. In the center of the bed lay a huge gray-and-black striped cat. It watched the girl enter the room and studied her with unblinking, round, yellow eyes.

"Now, Ornery!" gently scolded Mary, "this young lady will be occupying this room until she tires of us, so be nice. Where's your sister?" Smiling at Juanita she said, "He doesn't take to new folks well. I'll take him with me when you're ready to settle in for the night." Looking around, she continued, "His sister, Calico Cliff Kitty, should be close by. They're never usually far apart."

Reaching across the bed, the teenager held her hand out to the cat. He pretended not to see it, but his eyes closed, then opened in a slow blink. Taking his time, Ornery stood, stretched his long, thick body out to its full length, and pushed his head beneath the outstretched hand. A purr, sounding more like a growl, radiated from the giant animal, and Juanita scratched the broad, silky head.

"Well, my stars!" exclaimed Mary Harmon, surprised. "I do believe he's taken to you, young lady. I've never seen him do that before—a very good omen, indeed."

Miss Mary patted Ornery, then ran her hand lovingly across the quilt. She explained that she had pieced and hand-quilted the blanket while she waited for her fiancé to return from Korea, where he'd served during the 1950 conflict. The quilt blocks were cut from her old dresses, and a few of her fiancé's worn shirts, then sewn together, as they were to be sewn together in marriage. The blocks were made up in the shape of fans, and the colors were soft from years of use. Juanita wanted to ask about the fiancée, but the sadness in the old woman's eyes and voice stopped her. Leading them back out of the bedroom, Miss Mary continued the tour to the end of the short hallway, ending at the master bedroom. It had its own bathroom. Juanita grinned. That meant that *she* had her own bathroom.

Miss Mary, as she instructed Juanita to call her, finished the tour and fixed them each a slice of cinnamon-raisin toast for a snack. When finished, they cleaned up the kitchen together.

"Good night, Miss Mary, and thanks," Juanita blushed and shrugged, "for everything." Mary smiled and shooed the young woman from the kitchen. Juanita headed for her bathroom where she found shampoo and hair rinse, shower gel that smelled like Lily-of-the-Valley—she read that on the label as she'd never even heard of the flower before—on a shelf built right into the wall of the shower. Delighted, Juanita soaked beneath the steaming water, lathering and scrubbing her long hair twice. Stepping from the tub, she wrapped herself in a huge, pale yellow terry towel, marveling at the soft fluffy pastel-colored towels stacked neatly on the shelf in the narrow linen closet behind the bathroom door. Next to the towels a set of baby blue, light cotton pajamas lay folded with a note that had her name printed on it. They fit her perfectly.

Sighing happily, she went in search of Miss Mary, to thank her for the bath items and the new pajamas. She found her in the living room, sitting on a couch, looking through a stack of photo albums. Closing the album in her lap, she laid it on the coffee table and stood up and smiled at Juanita.

"How about a nice glass of milk and an oatmeal cookie before bed? I'm going to have a cup of chamomile tea. Would you rather try that, dear?" she asked the weary girl. Following Miss Mary to the kitchen, Juanita said, "Thank you, Miss Mary, but the cinnamon toast filled me up. No tea, but I'd love a small glass of milk, if that's okay?"

"Of course, dear. Let me get it for you." Mary poured their drinks and took a cookie for herself. They sat at the table, both women quiet, but content. When Juanita finished drinking her milk and rinsing her glass, she offered to do the few dishes left in the sink.

"Not tonight, dear," Mary said. "You head to bed. You've had a busy day, why not start helping me tomorrow?" Juanita nodded, grateful she could go to bed. Once again, she wished her new landlady goodnight and headed for her room.

When she entered her doorway she was pleasantly surprised to see Ornery, along with Calico Cliff Kitty, comfortably ensconced in the center of her bed, quietly studying the new creature in their lives. Leaving her door ajar, just enough for the cats to come and go, she stood for a moment surveying her room in the soft light of the bedside lamp. The lovely peacefulness nearly overwhelmed her.

Her room. Tears sprang to her eyes and she swiped them away with the back of her hand. She promised herself she would work hard to earn the wonder of living with Miss Mary. This all seemed too good to be true, but she felt so tired, she let all her thoughts of fear, sorrow, and loneliness go, thinking only of the double bed with the lovely fan quilt and soft pillows waiting for her.

Crossing to the bed, she tumbled beneath her covers and curled into a protective ball around the new life inside her. She felt the cats cuddle up against her back, their loud purring giving her a sense of security. For now, she and her child were safe.

*****

After washing up the dishes, Mary returned to the living room, picked up another photo album from the stack on the coffee table, and settled herself at the end of the couch. Leaning back against the soft pillows, she propped her feet on the book-covered coffee table.

The house lay wrapped in silence except for the cherry-wood mantle clock that had belonged to her grandmother, Mamie Sapp. The rhythmic ticking soothed her. Listening, closing her eyes for a moment, she remembered when she was a child frightened by the fierce Missouri storms with the sky-splitting lightning, the booming thunder, how her grandmother rocked her, holding Mary in her arms. She would listen to the clock mimicking her grandmother's steady heartbeat. Shaking loose of her memory, Mary returned to her task, sadness welling up, as the memories flipped by, page-by-page. One day before Juanita's child was born, she'd have to tell her about Ronald—and about her secret.

Time slipped by. Nearly midnight. Yawning, she closed the last yearbook from the stack she'd brought to the couch and laid it aside. Removing her glasses, she rubbed her eyes, weary from the hours of looking through her collection of photo albums, and Hilldale's yearbooks, marking the pages she wanted for later use. Sorrow etched lines about her mouth, and the retired schoolteacher leaned back against the cushions, remembering.

She had photographs of her niece, Sarah Elaine, at all the family reunions, birthday parties, vacations, and the photos from her classes at school. Seeing her as a young, happy teenager in the

33

yearbook pictures, made it more difficult than ever for Mary to understand what had caused her niece to run away, ending up on the streets of Minneapolis, refusing Willie and Wanda's plea to come home.

Sarah Elaine must be dead for her daughter to be here on her own. And Juanita was Sarah Elaine's daughter. Mary saw the resemblance in the child's face and mannerisms. Why, the girl jutted that chin out just like her Grandmother Wanda when she was nervous, or didn't like what she was hearing. Laughing softly, Mary switched off the lamp on the end table and closed her eyes against the bright overhead light.

Carter Neely, having grown up with Sarah Elaine, warned Mary that he thought Juanita might be her niece's child, and he felt sure she was going to have a baby. After seeing the girl this afternoon at the cafe, she agreed with him, at least about it being Sarah Elaine's girl.

And there was the birth certificate her sister-in-law received in the mail all those years ago. Except for her grandmother's chin, red hair, and freckles, she looked just like her mother. What had happened to Willie and Wanda's daughter, Mary wondered?

She would stake her life on the fact that Juanita's arrival in Hilldale was a purposeful act on the girl's part. Mary believed she came to find her grandparents. Poor child wouldn't know that Willie died a few years after Sarah Elaine ran away. But Wanda still lived on the old Harmon family farm, located nearly fifteen miles out of town, and Mary intended the child would meet her grandmother, but first, she needed to win Juanita's trust, and then they'd have to break through Wanda's self-imposed isolation. Mary knew she had her work cut out for her.

She stood and stretched her lower back. *Getting old isn't for sissies*, she silently teased herself, grimacing at the twinge of pain that shot through her right knee. Turning out the lights, she moved down the hallway toward her room, stopping for a moment outside the sleeping girl's door. Seeing a soft glow, she pushed the door open, noting the bedside lamp had been left on. The girl lay sleeping peacefully, the cats curled next to her. Ornery looked up over Juanita, his eyes wide and unblinking, then he shifted himself to a more comfortable position against the sleeping girl's back, his sister nestling up against him. The felines seemed to know Juanita needed their attention, and Mary felt grateful for their acceptance of her.

Offering a short prayer for her great-niece, she made her way to her own bedroom. After a quick wash-up, she donned her summer nightgown, pulled her covers back and climbed into bed. It felt good to stretch out and pull the light-weight quilt up to her chin. As sleep slipped up on her, Mary whispered in the darkened room.

I've got your granddaughter here, Willie. She looks just like your Wanda and Sarah Elaine, stubborn chin and all.

SIX

The June sky held benign clouds drifting on a light summer breeze. Eddie Felton drove the Escort, windows down, south along Highway 63. Three weeks of searching, and still no trace of Juanita. And then, just after lunch at a truck stop outside of Waterloo, Iowa, the kid behind the counter recognized the picture Eddie showed him. He remembered her because he thought she stole some food, telling Eddie he let her go without challenging her. He said she looked scared and hungry.

Alone. Elated, but forcing himself to look sadly grateful—after all, he was supposed to be the girl's father—Eddie thanked the kid, slipped him a twenty dollar bill which the kid magically made disappear, and continued south. At least he was headed in the right direction, he congratulated himself.

Just after ten, he took the exit that led into Hilldale, Missouri, pulled into the convenience store's nearly empty parking lot, and killed the engine of his bargain beater he'd picked up in Zumbrota, Minnesota. The cash came from several stops along the way south—a few pool games he'd hustled, a few drunken businessmen who'd lost control of their wallets, unsuspecting old ladies who'd just visited an ATM. Money came easily to him and he never tried to make a big score—that would have put too much heat on finding him. As it was, the police reports would all have different descriptions of him, because over the years of hustling, Eddie had learned that diversity was his best weapon.

Hilldale. He had a good feeling about this little town. Close to Jefferson City and Columbia, he remembered Sarah Elaine gloating about applying for scholarships at the University of Missouri, in Columbia. She'd talked about shopping with her mother in Jefferson City. This dinky burg qualified: close to the two cities, it appeared to be a very small town, and it lay just off the highway. He wished he'd paid more attention to her whining and sniveling memories, but they'd bored him. Hilldale? This could be the hick town she had missed so much. Maybe his luck was turning.

Inside the brightly lit store, he smiled at the bored young clerk. The woman's short, spiky, black hair looked like a rat's nest with its pink, green, and blood red streaks. Her wary brown eyes brought a smile to his thin lips. Easy prey. Walking up to the cash register, Eddie set his cup of coffee down on the counter, then slowly sauntered over to the meager selection of sweet rolls left in the clear plastic case.

"These things look old enough to vote," he said, keeping his voice friendly.

"Nobody's forcing you to buy them, mister," the woman said, yawning to let him know he bored her as much as her job did.

Eddie made his selection and walked back to the counter, feeling the girl's eyes watching his every move.

"Got a motel in this town?" he asked, knowing it was unlikely. He pulled a small wad of bills from his pocket. "I'm beat and looking for a place to crash." He paid her with a fifty-dollar bill, letting her see the other fifties on top of the roll of cash. Interest sparked in her dark eyes, and a lazy smile curled up her full lips.

"You got to be kidding, right? Hilldale? A motel? Gimme a break! There's Lolly Sapp's Bed-and-Breakfast just south of the town square, but you need a reservation to get in there. Closest places around are in Columbia or Jeff City." She smiled as though it pleased her to be giving him bad news. Eddie smiled back at her. He knew how to play this game.

"No fun to be had around here, either, or I bet you'd be there, not here. A pretty girl like you could have her pick of studs fighting each other to get the privilege of your company." He caught her eyes and held her gaze with his, putting his best *lonely-guy-with-money-to-spend* look into his. "I just bet you could show a fella a good time." Still holding the roll of bills in his hand, he watched her expression change from bored to interested.

Handing him back his change, she let her fingers brush slowly across his palm, looked back up into his eyes and smiled. "You going to be around long?"

"Depends," Eddie said, leaving a twenty on the counter, slowly pushing it toward her. The girl left it sitting there and rolled her eyes toward the security camera behind her. With a slight nod, he retrieved the bill, adding it back to the roll before he slipped the money into his pocket. "So, what time do you get off? Someone picking you up, or you drive yourself? I'm thinking about taking a nap in my car, maybe wait around awhile."

The girl studied his face while Eddie watched her make her decision, keeping his own expression neutral. She shrugged.

"I usually walk when the weather's good. I rent a mobile home in that park you passed when you came off the highway. Got a spare bedroom, nothing fancy but it's clean. I suppose you could rent a room from me for the night, get yourself a shower and some sleep. How long you staying?" She repeated, raising a well plucked, black-penciled eyebrow.

"Like I said, that depends," Eddie drawled. "You rent out your spare bedroom often?" His laugh was soft, inviting.

"Just when someone interesting comes along. By the way, my name is Cassie, Cassie Calloway. What's yours?"

"Jeremy Blade. Very pleased to meet you Cassie Calloway. I'll take you up on that room. How much?" Eddie started to peel another fifty from the roll, but she stopped him. Rolling her eyes at the camera again, she reached under the counter for her purse, pulled a key that dangled from a short chain attached to a small bottle opener, and handed it to him.

"We'll settle up when I get home," she said, her voice full of promise. "This is your lucky day, Mr. Jeremy Blade. You'll find some sandwich makings, and beer in the fridge. I went shopping today. Help yourself. I'll put it on your tab." The young woman laughed, showing a pierced tongue.

Getting instructions from Cassie, Eddie headed out the door and across the parking lot to his Escort. *What a piece of work*, he thought as he climbed into the station wagon and started the engine. *Well, she made the perfect base for his hunt. Gotta love them understanding women, Elton John sang about. His lucky day, indeed. He'd keep this broad happy long enough to find Juanita, then bye-bye Cassie.*

SEVEN

Juanita woke up, fear pounding in her chest. Gasping for breath and forcing herself to awaken fully, she sat up on the edge of her bed. Ornery and Calico Cliff Kitty sat up, startled, then slowly curled back into sleep. Trembling, she hugged herself and stood up. She was in her room at Miss Mary's.

Reigning in her breathing, she headed for the bathroom.

In her dream she'd been running, looking behind her. She'd tripped and fallen. Footsteps came closer and closer, and she'd looked up into the face of Eddie Felton reaching down for her. Shivering, Juanita closed the bathroom door, turned on the light, and looked into the mirror at her pale reflection.

"He's not going to find you here!" she whispered to her image, eyes wide with remembered terror. "He doesn't know about Hilldale. Mom said she never talked about Missouri with anyone but me. I'm safe here." She tried to laugh at herself, but the fear still lingered, sour in her mouth. "Get a grip," she scolded the girl in the mirror. With that, she finished up and headed back to bed. But the image of Eddie Felton's face popped up each time she closed her eyes. Curled into a ball, she snuggled with the cats, comforted by their large furry solidness and rumbling purr.

Dawn began to seep through the peach-colored curtains. Juanita got out of bed, dressed, and left the house. Walking to work in the early dawn gave her a sense of peace after her nightmare. Inhaling the morning air, her fear faded as she arrived at Neely's Cafe. She walked to the back entrance where she used her key to enter, smiling to herself. Two keys: one for Miss Mary's, not that she locked her house very often, and one for the cafe. And she'd only been here a little over a month. She felt a sense of belonging, the way Carter Neely and Miss Mary seemed to trust and genuinely care about her. A fierce protectiveness swept through her. No matter what, she promised herself, she would never betray their trust. Never.

Juanita held the brass key for a moment before putting it back in her pocket. Carter Neely had given it to her the third day she'd worked, acknowledging that she seemed to beat him to work in the morning, and as he'd closed her fingers over the cool metal, he'd admonished her with a twinkle in his eyes.

"Young lady, you're in charge of morning prep until I get here. I'll get to sleep an extra fifteen minutes, and for an old guy like me, that's a blessing." He'd laughed and turned quickly away pretending not to notice the stunned look and the tears that sparkled in her eyes. Juanita believed he knew she had been sleeping in the cafe, and yet, he'd still given her a key.

Flipping on the kitchen lights, she moved to the grill and turned on the burners to pre-heat it. Next came the burner under the deep-fryer before she went into the bathrooms and dining area, to make sure they were clean and ready to receive the morning customers. Satisfied with the condition of the rooms, Juanita headed over to the coffee machines behind the lunch counter and filled them with fresh grounds, poured a pot of water into each machine, and tapped the switches to the *on* position.

It would take several pots of coffee to wake up Hilldale, and she felt a satisfaction that it was her responsibility to get it ready for them. The sound of the water heating up and trickling through the fragrant grounds into the glass pots comforted her. In the dim light, she took in the dining area, breathed in the fresh brewed coffee smell, and sighed shaking off the residue of her nightmare. She unlocked the front door for the early coffee drinkers, and headed back toward the swinging door leading into the kitchen.

"Not here," she reassured herself out loud. "He'll never find me here."

Back in the kitchen, Juanita took sausage patties and bacon from the refrigerator. She laid them neatly on the hot grill, her thoughts turning to the kindness and acceptance of the elderly lady she'd moved in with. After a month without snide comments about cutting her long, unruly hair, about wearing something other than worn out jeans and baggy tee shirts, and not a word, or disapproving look, about the tattoos that vied for attention amongst the freckles along her slender arms, Juanita felt herself relaxing.

As far as the teenager knew, Miss Mary never invaded the privacy of her room, leaving her to care for it herself. She had a place to live, two jobs she enjoyed, and before long, she knew she'd find her grandparents. Maybe sometime later she could go to GED classes to get her high school diploma, but for now, she felt satisfied with her life.

Juanita wished her mother could see her. Would she be proud of her? Her mother had told her a little about her grandparents. In one of her drunken and drugged stupors, through gushing tears, she'd talked about her folks and their Missouri farm, and at ten-years-old, she began to listen closely. The next seven years brought little more information, but every scrap offered went into the girl's memory. She had a dream.

Juanita had never known her father, he'd taken off before she was born, and she'd never met or talked to her grandparents in Missouri. An old wedding photo of William and Wanda Harmon, along with a snapshot of a woman and a smiling little girl, lay in the cigar box her mother had kept her few memories in. As far back as Juanita could remember, it had always been just her and her mother, and of course, her mother's nasty boyfriends. The drug-and-alcohol induced fog her mother lived in, kept her from worrying about what was happening to her daughter, and if she did worry, she was always too high, or drunk, or both, to rescue her.

Sadness drifted over Juanita like morning mist drifting on the river. Mentally shaking herself, she pushed the memories aside, pulling her thoughts back to her job. Carter would be in before long, and she prided herself on leaving him as little prep work as possible. She measured out pancake flour, then measured the oil, eggs, and milk knowing the amounts by heart. Dribbling just a touch of vanilla into the mix, she gently stirred the batter.

Here she was in Hilldale, so close to finding the only family she knew of, and Miss Mary was her connection. Juanita believed she must be some relative, after all, her name was Harmon. Humming softly, she smiled. Her life was looking up. She finished prepping just as Carter pushed through the back door, yawning.

"Coffee! I need coffee," he growled, grinning at the young girl frying sausage at the grill. Juanita laughed and handed him the spatula.

"You handle the grill, I'll get your coffee and see about refills out front. There's a few early birds—one is the sheriff, so I let them in. Hope it's okay?" She looked nervous.

Patting her shoulder, Carter smiled. "There's a few that like to come in and get started on their coffee before they eat breakfast. You did good, kid. Keep it up and I might have to give you a raise!" Juanita studied his face for a second, then hurried out of the kitchen before she burst into tears. No one had ever treated her as though she had any value, and the pain of walls breaking down in her heart made her want to cry out loud.

She brought Carter his coffee, then refilled empty, or near empty, mugs out in the dining room. Carter set several plates under the warming lights and slapped the bell. Juanita returned the coffee pot and quickly moved to retrieve the plates of food.

Dan Halloran sat nursing his hot cup of coffee watching the new girl deliver the heaping plates to a table of three men. The tray she'd stacked them on looked heavy, but the girl handled it like she was used to it. She smiled, nodded at something one of the men said, and after serving them, she headed back to the coffee machine, picked up the full pot of fresh brew and walked back to their table.

The defensive wariness was all but gone from her face, and this young woman, who looked quite pleased with herself, was a remarkable change from the angry teen he'd first met in the convenience store a bit over a month ago. Knowing who she was, and guessing why she had come to Hilldale gave him a sense of gratitude that it appeared to be working out for her.

As she turned from the men, he caught her eye and held up his near-empty mug. She headed his way.

"How's it going, Miss Edmonds?" It wouldn't hurt to let her know he'd found out her name, and he'd learned much more—more than he was willing to let on to just yet.

"Great, Sheriff. See, I told you I'd get me a job and a place to live!" Her chin thrust forward, one hand went to her slender hip, and she gave him a triumphant grin. "Mr. Neely and Miss Mary even trust me with keys! What do you think of that?"

"I think I'd be watching the piggy banks," Dan teased her, grinning to let her know. She glared at him, opening her mouth to fling back a retort, then noticed his expression and joined in the laughter.

"Yah, and I guess I deserved that one, Sheriff Halloran."

"Sheriff Dan will do, and I'm really happy for you, Juanita. Looks like Hilldale got lucky the day you came to town. Hope you're thinking of staying around awhile. Miss Mary and ol' Carter might sorely miss you if you decide to wander off. Oh, and a certain young man I know would pine away something awful, even if you won't give him the time of day!" He smiled as Juanita blushed.

To think someone would miss her—for the good things she did! Indifference or anger, or—well other stuff—that was all she'd ever known. Coming to Hilldale felt like coming home, something she'd always dreamed about, but never thought she'd feel. Wonderful and scary at the same time. She pushed the thoughts aside and filled the sheriff's cup, and with a smile she let him know she hadn't taken offense at his teasing. Two tables and a booth needed cleaning up. That was her job, and with a grateful heart, Juanita IraLilly Edmonds turned her thoughts to the tasks ahead.

Dan watched her return to the kitchen and wondered at the life the girl must have known in Minneapolis. He'd found out that her mother had died from an overdose of heroin and alcohol, and that it was Juanita who'd found her early one morning about five months ago. There'd been a boyfriend who'd disappeared right after the mother's death; a guy named Felton. Sarah Elaine's death had been ruled an accident, so he'd never been investigated.

Carter Neely told him he suspected the girl was going to have a baby, and Dan's heart ached for the teenager. But if anyone could help her, Carter, Mary Harmon, and her grandmother, Wanda Harmon, could and would. Dan wondered what Juanita planned on doing with her child. Would she want to keep the baby, or go for adoption? The sheriff thought he might give Arden Wickem a call up in Independence. He and his wife ran Heartland Adoption Agency which doubled as a home for unwed mothers, and had once been owned by Arden's father. Maybe Arden and his wife, Linda, would have some insight on how to proceed with Juanita's situation. Shaking his head, he sipped his coffee and looked up as the door opened and a stranger walked in.

The man sat down a few tables away and looked around the dining area as though casing the place. Strange that his perception of the man went there, Dan thought, but it was true. The way the guy studied the people at the tables and booths around him gave the impression he was looking for someone. One more person to keep on his radar, he chided himself.

Dan laid his money on the table, including a generous tip for Juanita, and placing his Stetson on his head, he made his way past the stranger. Nodding to him, he took a good look into the man's face before he left the cafe and walked uptown to the Lund County Sheriff's Department.

*****

Eddie Felton watched the sheriff stride out the door into the morning sunshine. He didn't like the way the black man stared into his face, as though he thought he might recognize him, or maybe he was planning on looking him up in his wanted bulletins.

Scowling, his appetite gone, his mood turning foul, Felton pushed back his chair, stood and walked out of the cafe. As the heavy oak door closed behind him, the kitchen door swung open and Juanita walked through.

Phooey! she said under her breath, seeing the door close. *Guess he doesn't know the routine about ordering breakfast at the window. Maybe he didn't see Carter's sign. Must not be from around here.* Shrugging, she went behind the lunch counter and started a fresh pot of coffee. Picking up the one that had just brewed, she headed over to the dining area.

EIGHT

Gordie woke up with a headache. Rubbing his temples, he sat up in bed and looked out his window. The sun wasn't up yet. Keeping quiet, he crawled from beneath the covers and dressed in his barn clothes. He'd get Kissy milked and walk her and her calf to the pasture, practice his singing scales and vocal exercises out in the open field where he wouldn't wake Papa Muley, then head into the farmhouse and get breakfast ready.

Moving down the stairs, he took his boots up and headed out the screen door to the front porch steps. He sat and put his boots on, lacing them up and tying them in double knots, just as his mother had taught him as a small boy. A sudden ache arrowed through him and he caught his breath. After her murder two years ago, Papa Muley had asked him to stay with him at the farm to help out.

Gordie knew they were helping each other: he needed a home for himself and his animals, and Papa Muley needed someone to help out with the heavier chores on the farm and keep him company. Along with Sheriff Dan and his wife, Molly, and Billy Sumday, the farm work went quickly, and the repairs that were long overdue, were getting caught up. Gordie felt happy and loved.

He walked across the yard toward the barn. Dancer loped over to him and nudged his hand, begging to be petted. The young man laughed as he knelt before the Doberman and gave him a thorough petting. Then, with a final pat to the dog's head, he continued toward the barn.

A stabbing pain hit him in the temples and Gordie stumbled, falling to the ground. Dancer whined and licked his master's still face. Eyes wide open, Gordie shuddered, a picture flashing before him. The red-headed girl he called Wanda stood before him, while a black roiling cloud welled up behind, its evil threatening to engulf her. Tears rolled down her cheeks as she handed a wailing newborn to him.

Gordie struggled to pull himself from the scene. He felt Wanda's tears on his face and heard the infant crying. When his eyes cleared, he saw Papa Muley leaning over him trying to help him sit up. The old man's tears fell on the boy's face while Dancer whined and cried, nudging the boy with his nose. Gordie shook his head trying to clear it, and holding onto the work-worn hand, he pulled himself up, breathing deeply to dispel the fearful image he'd seen.

"I'm okay, Papa Muley. I think I must have tripped or something. I'm okay," the teen repeated, as he rubbed his temples, trying to massage the dull ache away.

"Lord have mercy, lad, you scared the dickens out of me! My ticker's going ninety-mile-an-hour! Old Dancer here commenced to barking and carrying on so, I thought the world come to an end right here in the driveway. Let me have a look at your noggin, lad. Might of hit it on that hard clay, maybe knocked some marbles loose." Muley's face twisted with concern, his faded blue eyes wide with fear, tears still spilling over onto his wrinkled cheeks.

Gordie laughed. "For crying in the soup, as Mr. Neely would say! I'm okay. My head is fine. I'm sorry I scared you, Papa Muley. I got to get the milking done and turn Kissy and her calf out to pasture, but I'll come in directly and get us some breakfast. You go on and see if you can get a little more rest until I get back in." He hugged Muley who returned it, neither shy about doing so.

Nodding, Muley gave the back of Gordie's head one more look, and satisfied there appeared to be no damage, he headed back to the house, followed by the Coonhounds who joined Dancer to see what all the excitement was about. The boy watched the old farmer until he was settled in the porch swing, his hounds surrounding him, then he and Dancer continued to the barn.

Shadows filled his eyes. The laughter left his face, replaced by worry. *Something mighty wrong with Wanda*, he thought. Soon as his chores were finished, and he'd gotten Papa Muley's breakfast, he'd head into Hilldale and have his breakfast and maybe even his lunch at Neely's Cafe. Gordie knew the girl needed protecting, and he knew that the dark cloud meant something really bad stalked her. He didn't know why he couldn't get that girl out of his head, or out of his heart, and he believed it was up to him to keep her safe.

Pulling the barn doors open, he relaxed at the soft sounds Kissy welcomed him with. After giving her grain, he headed over to the deep utility sink, filled the stainless steel bucket with warm sudsy water, and carried it to the milking stanchion where the cow stood patiently chewing feed. He washed, rinsed, and dried her bag and teats, then milked the front half of her bag, leaving the back half for the calf. Her calf. A baby! Wanda was going to have a baby. But why had she tried giving the newborn to him?

Leaning his forehead against Kissy's warm flank, he finished his milking, covered the pail and put it up on a near-by shelf. Taking up the halter rope, he led the old cow and her frisky calf out to pasture, closed the gate behind them and returned to the barn for the milk.

A baby. Gordie reckoned his life sure took a turn the day he laid eyes on that red-headed, sassy angel. Grinning, he headed into the house to put the milk away and get Papa Muley's breakfast going. He had a lot to do this morning if he was going to make it to Neely's for his own breakfast.

NINE

Dan Halloran sat back in his chair and tossed the report he'd pulled from his fax machine back on his desk. He'd read through it twice, studying the blurred photo, and what he'd read left him feeling uneasy. Sipping his lukewarm coffee, he reached for one of his receptionist's homemade applesauce cookies. Soft and chewy, they nearly melted in his mouth, and the blend of their natural sweetness with the bitter coffee made the balance of flavors just right. Vicki knew how to bake, and Dan knew how to enjoy her offerings.

Swallowing the last of his third cookie, he let his mind go back to the report on his desk. He didn't believe in coincidences. The stranger who walked into Neely's this morning was one Edward Francis Felton, age forty-seven, served a smattering of jail time over the years for petty theft and scamming, current address unknown. His last known address appeared to be where Juanita and her mother had lived. The report showed no job, only disability income from a work injury eight years earlier that couldn't have paid all the man's bills. Dan wondered, *what did the guy do for money? Jobs on the side that paid him cash? Living off the women in his life? He'd heard through the grapevine that Cassie Calloway had taken in a stranger, rented him a room. Felton?*

He believed the man was a hustler, and he believed Felton was the stranger who'd walked into Neely's this morning, most likely looking for Juanita. It was no coincidence the man showed up in Hilldale not long after the girl arrived. Did she know he was here? If not before, she would now, after him eating at Neely's this morning. But why hook up with Cassie Calloway, if it was Felton who moved into her place? A place to stay, to lay low? Maybe he was the person Juanita was running away from—because the sheriff believed the girl's arrival in Hilldale was no accident. He wondered if this Felton creep drove her to find refuge with her grandparents. But, according to Miss Mary, Juanita hadn't tried to contact them. Did she know her grandfather died years ago? She didn't even appear to be looking for them. Confusing business.

He reached for the coffee pot behind him and poured the last of the strong brew into his mug, mixing it with the now cold coffee. Picking up the last cookie on the plate, he pushed back and put his military-style boots up on his desk. Chewing the cookie and sipping his coffee, his mind mulled over various scenarios that reared themselves. None of them were good.

Pinching the crumbs from the plate and carefully moving them to his mouth, he leaned over and retrieved the fax. Re-reading it, he wondered again how Sarah Elaine got her drugs. The illusive Mr. Felton? And what did he want with Juanita? Did she know something about her mother's death that the police didn't know? Dan reckoned he'd best keep a close eye on Hilldale's newest visitor. His cop instincts were buzzing. If he didn't miss his guess, trouble had come to town. Billy Sumday would call it *Windigo*—the evil one. Dropping his feet to the floor, he forced his attention back to his paperwork.

Finishing all the reports on his desk, he signed the last one and carried them out to his receptionist's office.

"I'm headed to Neely's for lunch. Want me to bring you something back, Vicki? Your cookies really are worth a lunch. Carter's got pork roast with all the trimmings today."

Smiling, Vicki's round cheeks turned pink. "No, but thanks anyway. I'm always baking for the boys and just bring in the overflow to the office. Baking is my therapy, but you can see where it gets me when I eat it all!" She laughed and then blushed a deeper shade of red, her eyes sparkling. "Besides, umm, Randy is bringing in a pizza with the works to share with me. Sheila said she'll take the desk for half-an-hour so we can eat in the break room."

"Randy Carter?" Dan asked, surprise widening his eyes. Randy Carter, one of his deputies and a good friend, had gone through a very rough divorce three years before, and to Dan's knowledge, had not dated once since then. And he hadn't said a word to Dan about dating Vicki. He'd have to check this out.

Her husband had passed away after his pickup slid off an icy embankment five years ago. Vicki had come to work for the sheriff's department not long after that, trying to keep her two young sons and herself in their home. Dan and Billy Sumday helped with repairs on her house and made sure the boys had a good Christmas, and any school supplies they needed. It wasn't the same as having their dad around, and his heart went out to them.

"Hey Vicki, that's great. Randy, eh? Reckon you can fatten him up any? The guy's so thin you could thread him through a needle." He laughed.

"Sheriff Dan!" Vicki said in mock horror. Then smiling, she said, "I'm working on it. He does like my baked goods, especially my chocolate swirl cheese cake. He's been over a few evenings for supper and gets on real well with the boys. He even came to Nathan and Benny's soccer practice last week." Tears brightened her eyes. Looking up at Dan she whispered, "Do you think I'm being unfaithful to their dad?" Worry wrinkled her forehead. Dan shook his head.

"Ben would want you and the boys to be happy. He would never want you to mourn him and stay alone the rest of your life, now would he? He wasn't that kind of guy. Shoot girl, he loved you all so much, and I know he'd want the best for you."

Vicki nodded, wiping the tears that slipped down her cheeks. "My head knows that, but sometimes my heart doesn't get caught up right away. Randy, well, he's the first fellow that's shown interest in the boys and me. He's so kind, you know?" Again, she looked up into Dan's eyes.

"Couldn't tickle me more to see the two of you together. Keep me posted, young lady!" With that, Vicki grabbed up the jangling phone, and the sheriff left the building. *Randy and Vicki, eh?* He felt pleased that two people he cared very much about might be finding love and healing in their lives.

TEN

Cassie yawned, rolled over and sat up. She'd have to get herself ready for work or she'd be late again. Getting fired wouldn't be good for her finances. She sighed thinking how low her bank balance was. Maybe Jeremy would come through with some of that money he carried around in his pocket. He'd been so quick to offer it the first time she met him, but once he moved in, he'd never offered her a dime.

He'd kept her awake into the early morning hours, and then when she'd told him she had to get some sleep, he'd gotten all huffy, climbed out of bed and had gotten dressed. He'd stomped out the door, slamming it behind him.

What a jerk. To add insult to injury, she'd watched as he'd taken her car instead of his station wagon. *Better pay me something for the gas he's using. How do I always pick the losers and users?* She'd fallen asleep hoping he'd locked the front door. This close to the highway, any creep could come along and do who-knows-what to her.

Now, awake but feeling sluggish, Cassie pulled herself up and ran her fingers through her gel-stiff hair. She needed a shower. The June afternoon looked hot and she was glad she worked inside with air conditioning. Seeing her car parked next to Jeremy's, she wondered where he'd gone after he left her. She turned on the shower, stepped under the hot water, and let it wash over her.

ELEVEN

"Leave the child be, Mary. Don't meddle. If she wants to come to me, she's got to do it on her own, no one forcing her to come. I'll wait. Don't push her. She might run off like Sarah Elaine." Wanda Harmon's voice cracked, then went still.

Mary scolded back, "My goodness, Sis, the way you talk, you'd think I've never worked around children. I'm not going to push Juanita into coming to see you. She's here with me, she's safe, and Carter Neely's given her a good job. I suspect the girl is working through a lot of things in her head right now, and I intend to give her the time and space to do that. I just wanted to warn you she's here. Don't want you dropping dead when she comes to your door, you stubborn old woman!" As she continued, Mary's laughter softened her words.

"Wanda, she's beautiful. So full of life and dreams and hopes, like we were once. Be kind when she comes, for her sake as well as your own. Love you, Sis." She listened to Wanda snort and hang up the phone. Shaking her head, she sighed. Two stubborn women. Trying to get them together would be a real feat, but Mary felt up to the task. Willie would be grateful, Juanita needed family, and Wanda needed her granddaughter. Smoothing her hair back and tucking stray strands into the bun, she headed for the kitchen. A tuna sandwich with a few slices of fresh cucumber sprinkled with black pepper sounded good.

TWELVE

Eddie Felton drove Cassie's car out of the town square and kept to the speed limit as he headed out of town toward the mobile home park. *One horse, no-action town. Well, you bunch of hayseeds, you'll see some action, I find that kid here.*

Then, as if thinking about her conjured her up, Felton saw Juanita walking down the sidewalk heading toward town. He drove Cassie's car to the next block, turned the corner and slowly re-entered Main Street. She never noticed him behind her. He pulled the car off the road and watched her until she turned right, just before the one-way street for the town square began. Felton crawled back onto the road and drove up to the turn in time to see her disappear into a small, neat rambler, three houses down from the corner. *Gotcha!* he smiled, his face twisting into a cruel mask.

With every ounce of his being, he wanted to push his way into the house, force the girl into his car, and get out of this lame town, away from the nosy sheriff, away from the whining, boring Cassie Calloway.

He could grab Juanita and head back to Minneapolis where he knew a lot of places he could hide out until he disposed of her—one way, or another. His brain screamed at him to fulfill his raging passion. Worked into a near frenzy, he parked the car at the end of the block and studied the house and the area around it. Anyone watching? He couldn't tell, and being near noon, it was too easy to be spotted.

Within just a few minutes, Juanita left the house and headed back toward the main road. He caught his breath. As he watched, she turned away from the town square. Again, he followed her, making sure she didn't spot him. When she came to the cafe, she walked to the alley behind and entered through the back service door. *She works there!* Sweat beaded his forehead. What if she'd seen him the morning he'd come in for breakfast? What if she'd made a scene in front of the sheriff!

He forced himself to calm down, forced his rage back under control, and forced his passion to the back of his thoughts. He knew how to wait. He knew how to plan. His time would come, and when it did, he would make his move. Still trembling, he gripped the steering wheel. He still had time before Cassie went to work. The lazy brat was probably still asleep. No problem. He knew how to wake her up.

THIRTEEN

"That there girl don't belong in Hilldale, Danny, let alone traipsing into church alongside a decent lady like Miss Mary. What's that old woman thinking, bringing a trollop like that into her home, and worse yet, a place like my folks' church? Why, my Pa helped build that building back in eighteen-and-ninety-four." Obed Martin chewed on his bottom lip and pulled at the dirty tuft of hair sticking out of the top of his head, like the horn of a unicorn. Dan Halloran winced and shook his head. Gordie sat silent, staring at the table top.

"Well, ain't it the truth, boy?" Obed stared at the sheriff. "You seen them markings all up and down her arms, like she was some dadblamed sailor.

57

Don't look like she combed that mop of hair for a month, and if that weren't enough, she come waltzing into church dressed in everyday wear. Same clothes she wears here! Don't that beat all? Don't even have the decency to dress a little for the Lord's house." He lifted his icy bottle of cream soda and took a long pull.

Dan quickly changed the conversation, and just in time. Juanita walked up to their table with their orders and carefully set their plates of hot food in front of them. The men grew quiet. She looked around at them and then smiled at Gordie.

"Hey, how's it going?" She asked, her voice uncertain.

"Good," Gordie responded and blushed. Dan quickly spoke up, giving the teenager time to recover.

"This looks mighty good, young lady. You help Carter cook this up?" Dan smiled up at Juanita.

"I certainly did, Sheriff! Mr. Neely lets me help a little with the grill. I'm getting pretty good at it, too!" Grinning, she pointed to his double bacon cheeseburger. "I fixed your burger myself!" Her eyes glowed with pleasure.

"That'll make it extra delicious! Thanks." Nodding, Juanita headed back to the kitchen, missing Obed's rude remarks about how clean could their food be with her handling it. Dan responded, holding his anger in check. Looking at the old man's dirty fingernails, oily hair, and food-stained shirt, he raised an eyebrow, and lowered his voice.

"It appears that would be the pot calling the kettle black, so to speak, Obed. Don't you think you can cut the girl a little slack? She didn't arrive in town with much more than the clothes on her back. Looks to me like she's trying to fit in here, and working hard at it. Reckon we can all use a little kindness and forbearance in our lives."

"For—huh—what?" Obed scowled at the sheriff. "Speak English, boy. You think I'm being hard on that girl, you just wait 'til her gramma gets hold of her. Yep, I know who she is. Any fool can see she's the spitting image of Wanda Harmon and Sarah Elaine. Ol' Wanda's going to make the feathers fly!" He picked up his cheeseburger and took a big bite.

The rest of the meal was spent with Dan leading Obed into telling stories about himself, about how Obed rescued him from a frigid pool up on the Ridgeway bluffs. Dan knew the one thing Obed liked better than talking about other folks, was talking about himself.

When Dan and Gordie walked out of Neely's Cafe they were still chewing on the comments of Obed Martin. Gordie, silent through the entire meal except to speak to Juanita when she served them, finally looked up at his friend.

"Reckon he thinks that way about me but don't dare say so on account of you?" Sadness darkened his eyes, and Dan could hear the pain in the teen's voice.

"Hard to say, Gordie, but since Obed's gotten to know you, I don't think he even sees your scars, or thinks about where you came from." Dan wanted to hug the young man, assuage his pain. Gordie sighed.

"Well, it looks like Wanda has to stick around Hilldale awhile so Mr. Martin can get used to her scars. Might take a bit longer though, because most of her scars are in her heart."

As Dan and Gordie strolled up the sidewalk headed for the sheriff's office, Dan noticed Cassie

Calloway's car traveling toward the mobile home park. Cassie wasn't driving. The sheriff looked closer and recognized Edward Felton, and the man acted as though he never saw him, driving past without so much as a wave, or a nod.

Why drive Cassie's car? Trying to go around unnoticed? Folks were sure to take a second look at a strange vehicle in town. This creep most likely knows that, so he snoops around in a well-known car avoiding attention. Dan's hackles rose. His gut told him this guy was watching Juanita, and everything in him feared for Cassie, and the teenager.

"Gordie, see that blue Ford Focus that just passed us?" Dan nodded toward the disappearing car. Gordie looked up and watched the car as it continued down the road.

"That's not his car, it belongs to a local girl. I think the guy driving is looking for Juanita—your Wanda," Dan grinned at the young man before turning serious again, "and I think his intentions aren't very good. I think if he finds her, she's in real trouble. Whenever you're in town, watch out for her, okay? If you see anything you think isn't right, let me know. It's none of my business, but I'm going to ask anyway. Have you asked her out yet?"

Gordie blushed, gulped, and stammered. "Gosh, no, Sheriff Dan! She thinks I'm stupid, ugly. Why would a beautiful girl like Wanda go out with me? Besides, I don't really know anything about asking a girl out. What would I say? Where would we go? Who would go with us?" Moisture beaded his forehead and upper lip. "But I want to. I really want to."

The sheriff stopped walking and looked at the worried young man. He rested his hand on

Gordie's shoulder, and staring into his eyes, he smiled. "Son, you just find a quiet time at the cafe, or you get Miss Mary's phone number and call Juanita, and you ask her. As far as where you go, and who goes along—if anyone does—that's up to you two. Ask her.

"First though, I'd recommend getting to know her a little better. Could be lots of issues hiding in the background. So, you know, have more meals up here, try to engage her in conversation, see if you can get hints about what she's interested in, a little of her history. Never can tell, maybe she sings, too! Think you can handle that attitude of hers?" Dan laughed. "Don't forget the first time we met her. She really let us have it, didn't she!" It wasn't a question.

Gordie laughed, relief washing across his face. "She sure did, but she was scared and hungry. Her attitude doesn't scare me—I scare me! But, I want to help. I'll drive up here a few times a week, and I'll be here Thursday nights with you and the other guys, at least until the choir gets back from their tour." Hope softened his voice. "Will you help me? Sure is nerve-wracking, this courting thing."

"Courting thing!" Dan exclaimed with a hoot. "Gordie Adam Bently! You're thinking of courting this spitfire before you even know her? You're a braver man than I am. You know, courting is serious business."

The teen nodded, his expression one of total seriousness. "I've been studying up on it, and I know what it means." Blushing, he continued, "Sheriff Dan, I aim on marrying that red-haired angel someday. First I got to get me a real job, and a place to live, and insurance, and have a plan for our future, and..."

"Whoa!" Dan stopped him. "You're serious, aren't you."

"As a heart attack," the young man answered, his eyes steady on his friend's. "I just know it here, Sheriff Dan." He touched his chest. "She's the one for me. I knew it right away, the first day we saw her in the store. Maybe I don't know what the married kind of love is, but I believe I love her like nobody else. Besides, she's going to have a baby, and I'm going to help her take care of her little girl.

"I'll have money when I sell Grampa's farm, and I got some from that Mr. Wickem's estate on account of him killing Ma. I get paid nearly every time I sing at a wedding or funeral. I've been saving for college, but I don't think college is for me. I think I'm meant to sing and maybe farm some."

Gordie started walking again; Dan caught up. After a few moments the sheriff spoke. "You have been studying on this, haven't you. Sorry I laughed, but that girl tickles me. She scares me, too. And Gordie, that man I showed you a few minutes ago in Cassie's car? I do think he's after Juanita. He lived with her mother up in Minneapolis, and she ended up dead. Reckon we'll all have to start looking out for the girl, especially if you're determined to marry her."

Nodding, Gordie looked up at the man walking beside him. "She's going to have a baby, Sheriff Dan." Dan slowed his pace, choosing his words carefully.

"Yeah, Gordie, I know about the baby. What I don't know is, what's she going to do about it? Probably need to know who the father is before we get too involved in future plans. Could be, she'll be marrying whoever that might be. Could be, she won't keep the baby."

Gordie shook his head. "She'll keep her. I'm supposed to help her. I saw it in one of my spells Ma always called *angel taps*." He smiled and tapped the top of his head. "Ma said my guardian angel gives me a tap on the head once in a while and lets me in on a secret. She said to always take it very serious, and don't go blabbing it around. Said if God wanted everybody to know, He'd put it in the newspaper, or tell it up at Neely's." He eyed the sheriff. "You think I'm crazy?"

"Nope, I sure don't. You're sharp as can be, and I'd trust you with any secret I have. Besides, Billy Sumday does the same kind of thing—he seems to get inside information from somewhere—could be God, I reckon. You want to tell me about it?"

They were almost to the Lund County Sheriff's Department. Gordie stopped and looked at his friend. "Something awful bad is after her, Sheriff Dan. There was a terrible dark cloud behind her and she was crying, handing me a new baby girl. That's it. That's all I saw. I know it means trouble, and I'm supposed to help her." Looking down at the sidewalk and then back at the sheriff, Gordie's voice crackled with emotion. "You reckon I love her enough, Sheriff Dan? I mean, the way you love Miss Molly—the marrying kind of love?"

"Only you can answer that, son. Besides God, only you know your heart. If you think you love her, then you offer that up to the Lord in your prayers and ask Him to lead you, lead you both." Then he grinned. "Still think you're playing with fire with that girl!"

Gordie laughed. "She sure is worth any amount of trouble a body's got to go through, though. Under all that sassiness, she's got a right big heart. She just ain't—isn't ready to let folks know that, yet. Probably been broken too many times."

Patting the boy's shoulder, Dan thought of the life Gordie lived before he was rescued, and he marveled at the wisdom and gentle spirit radiating from this young man. He had every right to be angry, rebellious, to feel sorry for himself, yet here he was, worrying about a girl he barely knew, ready to dedicate his life to loving and helping her and her child. He wondered if he should discourage Gordie from getting involved. Something told him to back off and let the two teens work it out between themselves.

FOURTEEN

Mary Harmon returned from her bedroom dressed in her Sunday best. "Why, you're not ready, my dear. Aren't you accompanying me to church again? You're more than welcome, and I'd love to have you come along." She smiled at the young woman curled up in the corner of the couch, still wearing her pajamas.

Juanita snorted. "Yah sure! I was such a big hit." Offering her arms for inspection, she displayed the many crude tattoos one of her mother's boyfriends left her with. "The rest of your church folks get a look at these and they won't just throw me out, you'll be laughed—or bullied—right out of that place. You saw that old man staring at me last Sunday. Same way he looks at me when he comes to Neely's—like I'm dirt." She sighed. "Believe me, I know how this works. I tried it once and was told to go home and clean up, then come back. I wanted to ask that pastor at the door how I scrub these things off—but, it wasn't worth it—you know, trying to fit into their world. You best go on without me. I'll just mess things up for you, Miss Mary."

Sadness darkened her eyes to a tarnished gold. Mary moved to the couch and seated herself next to the girl. She took her hand.

"Oh, my! You mustn't worry about those old things. They're not your doing, my dear, and even if they were, it wouldn't matter." She gently traced the tattoo that snaked up Juanita's forearm. "Some Christians worry about tattoos and piercings because they were a symbol of slavery, and once the Lord sets us free—well—we're free! But sweetheart, once we're clothed in His righteousness, our Lord doesn't see any flaws in or on us—He sees us through His Son's blood, the reflection of His cleansing love. If Jesus doesn't care, what right do we have to judge how you look?

"When a person accepts Jesus into their life, into their precious heart, why, He throws all of their sins and mistakes as far as the east is from the west! He loves you, Juanita, and longs for you to come home, to find sanctuary in Him." Mary sighed, knowing that coming home for sanctuary might be a stumbling block for the teen. The poor child didn't really know where she belonged, and it seemed there hadn't been much safety for her at home. Mary's eyes grew tender with understanding.

"Really, dear, you mustn't worry about how you look on the outside. It's the inside that counts. Believe me, I know well how some church folks are. They'll judge the righteous just like Jesus turned over his Lordship to them. But, we're tougher than that, aren't we, dear? We have a king doing battle for us. A king who thinks we're worth dying for. No matter what those poor folks think—or say—they are wrong. You can be redeemed by the most wonderful Savior that ever lived, died, and rose again! The *only* Savior that rose again. Now, I shall be most pleased and most proud to have you accompany me, Miss Juanita IraLilly Harmon Edmonds!"

Juanita looked at the older woman, startled. "IraLilly? Harmon?" she gulped. "How did you know about the IraLilly and Harmon in my name? IraLilly is my gramma's middle name."

Mary laughed. "Young lady! You've lived with me long enough to know that I'm not a stupid old woman. I might be a bit foolish and a wee bit silly sometimes, but stupid I am not. You are my great-niece, my brother Willie's granddaughter. And yes dear, I know you are here looking for your grandparents—at least I believe you are?" She stopped speaking long enough to pat the surprised girl's cheek.

"Willie's gone. He's been gone about thirteen years now. But your Grandmother Wanda? She's alive and well, or at least last time I saw her she was. She rarely comes to town, and it's even rarer still for her to visit anyone. I've gone out to the farm a time or two, but she's never been the same after Sarah Elaine left, and Willie died. Took the starch right out of her. You are the spitting image of her, Juanita, and she loves you though she's never met you."

When the girl looked doubtful, Mary laughed. "Oh, yes my dear, she somehow got word from Minneapolis that Sarah Elaine had a baby, and she even got a copy of the birth certificate sent to the farm accidently—a God-ordained accident—so she knew about your birth and knew your name. Your grandparents longed for their daughter to bring her baby home. Every year Sarah Elaine didn't come back, Wanda grew more reclusive.

She and Willie would take trips when they could get away from the farm, head to Minneapolis looking for you two. After Willie died, Wanda never went back. She tried to get an address, but it seemed like your mother never stayed in one place for long and always gave the farm as her address—I suppose so Willie and Wanda couldn't find her. Mark my words, young lady, your grandmother has never stopped looking for you two to come home. You're here alone. Is your mother gone, dear?"

Juanita let her tears fall unchecked. Nodding, she wiped her eyes and nose on the tissue Mary offered.

"Drug overdose. I ran away before they could put me in foster care, or *juvie*. I've heard about those places. . . " A fierceness crept into her voice, "I'm not going to either one. I'm not." She thrust her chin out and clenched her hands into fists, pushing them deep into the couch cushions.

"Of course you're not. First of all, at seventeen, you're old enough to emancipate. Besides, you have a home right here with me, for as long as you want it, my dear. Once your grandmother finds you're here, she'll want you to live with her. Why, she'll near smother you with her love."

Juanita frowned. Mary said, "Don't you love her, and you've never met her? You've traveled a good long way, and what a difficult journey it must have been all alone, looking for your grandparents. I'd call that love of the truest kind, and it'll be no different with Wanda."

Mary gently pushed Juanita's fiery locks back from her face. She dropped her hand and cupped the girl's chin.

"So like her." Smiling, she patted the smooth, tear-dampened cheek. "Go on, get dressed, or come like you are, I don't care. I am very proud of you, and I will never be ashamed to be seen with you, my dear. Never. Don't you ever forget that."

Nodding, Juanita laid her head against Mary's shoulder and allowed herself to be held, to be hugged. Slowly, her body relaxed and her arms encircled her Aunt Mary's waist. Giving her a squeeze, she whispered, "I love you, Aunt Mary. Wait for me, okay?"

Without waiting for an answer, she jumped up from the couch and quickly went to her room to look for a clean pair of jeans and a cotton shirt. Mary Harmon stared after Willie's grandchild.

"Oh, Willie, see your granddaughter? Isn't she something, brother!" she whispered to the sun-filled room.

FIFTEEN

Cassie rang up the cup of coffee. The old man kept staring at her, and she knew what he was going to say before it came out of his mouth. Handing him his change, she returned his smile with little enthusiasm, waiting.

"Miss Red Feather, have you spoken with your grandmother lately?" Billy Sunday put his change in the front pocket of his worn carpenter jeans.

"You know I haven't, Mr. Sumday. Gramma doesn't have a telephone. And stop calling me Red Feather—it's Calloway. I don't want any part of the rez—no reminders." She scowled at Billy. Native American tradition taught it would be disrespectful to look him directly in the eye, but her stare came close enough he knew the scowl was for him.

Why did that old man have to come in here every week and torment her about calling her gramma up in Red Lake, Minnesota? Just because his wife and Gramma Ellen had been best friends, and just because he'd helped her get a new start in Missouri, didn't mean he had the right to interfere in her life. She left the reservation for a darn good reason, and it wasn't any of that old man's business, though she knew her grandmother had told him all about what had happened. She frowned at the man across the counter, trying to ignore his words.

"But you still wear your red feather, Cassie," he motioned toward her wing of red hair that streaked from her forehead, sweeping back behind her left ear.

"Real funny. Ha, Ha." Cassie snapped, wishing he'd go away and leave her alone.

"Oscar tells me that your mother has a cell phone and, as you well know, she lives right next door to your grandmother. In fact..." Billy dug into his jeans' pocket pulling out a scrap of notebook paper and handed it to the young woman behind the counter. "Just in case you lost the last paper I gave you, my son gave me Lillian's number again. I believe you'd like to talk to her and your grandmother and let them know you are doing well here?"

Cassie snorted and rolled her eyes, "I'm sure you and your son have filled Mom and Gramma in on everything I do. They don't need to hear from me." Her expression of annoyance brought a chuckle from Billy.

"Are you saying we're busy bodies, young lady?" He smiled. "If you are, you're one hundred

69

percent correct. Your Grandmother Ellen sends her love. Lillian says just come home."

"Right," Cassie growled, eyeballing the man who pushed through the door and headed toward her. "Listen, I have to work for a living, Mr. Sumday. Thanks for the phone number—again. I'll put this," she held up the paper, "where I put the rest of them." With that, she wadded it up and tossed it in the trash basket, a defiant look tightening her mouth, narrowing her eyes.

Sighing, Billy nodded. "Forgiveness isn't easy. I know you're angry, but your family loves you, and I hope you can find it in your heart to let go of the past. Ellen and Lillian thought they were doing what was best for you, Cassie. Let it go before it's too late.

"Enough of this old man's meddling, young lady. I enjoy our visits and don't want to spoil your evening. When you do talk to your grandmother, give her my love." Smiling, Billy walked out the door into the warm summer evening.

"Your coffee..." Cassie started, then, as she did every week the old man came in, she tossed the full cup into the trash, mumbling under her breath.

"What was that all about?" Jeremy Blade asked, dropping a paper-wrapped, jelly-filled roll on the counter. He set his cup of coffee down next to it and dug in his pocket for change. "Why'd you throw his coffee away? You could have given it to me."

"I didn't know you wanted it, now did I?" Cassie snapped. "That old man comes in every week just to annoy me, and I'm sick and tired of him. He thinks he knows me—he doesn't." Bitterness dripped from her words. Jeremy looked interested and she liked his attention.

"Sounds like a bed-time story to me," he purred. "Hurry home, sweetheart." Leaning across the counter he slipped his hand behind her neck and pulled her toward him planting a kiss on her lips.

"The camera!" Cassie protested pulling away. "You'll get me fired, Jeremy." Eddie looked startled for a moment, forgetting he'd given her an alias. He looked to see if she noticed, but she smiled and lowered her voice. "See you when I get off at eleven?"

"Maybe," he smiled heading toward the door. "I'm leaving my car for you, and taking yours. I want to check on a few things, and I don't want every gossip in Hilldale watching a strange vehicle."

"Put gas in it, Jeremy," she said. Then, not wanting to sound like a nag, she added, "Robbing a bank or something, you don't want anyone to notice you?"

"Or something," he countered pushing out the door, disappearing around the corner of the building. Only after he left, did she notice he'd left no money on the counter. *Digging in his pocket like he was going to pay. She'd have to shell out money for him—again.* Cassie watched the closed circuit television as he walked across the parking lot. Shaking her head, she moved to the end of the counter, retrieved several cartons of cigarettes and began to refill the overhead racks. *Up to no good,* she thought, anger stinging her heart.

In the shadows of the building, Billy Sumday watched the stranger Daniel told him about. Daniel was right. This man had the stink of *Windigo* all over him.

*****

Eddie Felton decided to walk, rather than take Cassie's car. The night was warm, but a soft

71

breeze kept it from being unbearable. He crossed the highway and walked along the side streets taking the long, circuitous route to his destination, keeping to the shadows as much as possible.

He hid in some untamed willowy-limbed bushes growing in a huge over-grown yard belonging to a senile old man. Across the narrow street sat the old lady's house, where he knew Juanita lived. He had followed the girl twice to make sure, and now he watched and waited until she came up the sidewalk and entered the unlocked door. Glancing at his watch, he read the faintly glowing dial. Ten-forty-five. Knowing Neely's closed at ten on weeknights, Eddie figured Juanita helped with clean-up and then walked home—to an unlocked house.

He shook his head. *How easy these small-town hicks make it for me.* Noting which window lit up once the girl disappeared inside gave him a pretty good idea which room belonged to her. Satisfied with his information, he stole from the bushes walking up the street to the corner where the streetlight illuminated him. Felton didn't notice the eyes that followed his every move.

*****

Obed Martin watched the man leave his yard. *Third time he's been here*, he mumbled to himself as he rubbed the stubble covering his chin. Disgust screwed up his wrinkled face, and he spat in the grass. *That there girl's bringing nothing but trouble to this town, and looks like she's bringing it right to Miss Mary's door. If Wanda don't come get her soon, that no-good trollop needs to be run out of town. Girls like her ain't got no place in Hilldale, no-sir-ee.*

He watched the stranger head out of town. Satisfied that he was gone, at least for the evening, Obed went into his dark house replacing his .22 rifle in the corner of the kitchen behind the door. By the light filtering in from the street, he fixed himself a glass of lemonade with a little extra sugar. Still not turning on any lights, he settled into his recliner, put his legs up, took a long swallow, and sat in the dark, thinking. Too many strangers were coming to his town, and with them came trouble. Obed didn't like it one bit. Not one little bit.

SIXTEEN

For the third time this week, Gordie sat in Neely's waiting for his hamburger and fries. But it was Tina who waited on him, never Juanita. Watching the girl as she moved in and out of the kitchen picking up dirty dishes, stacking clean ones behind the lunch counter, he swallowed—hard. How could his mouth be so dry when he was sweating so much, he wondered? Tina watched him for a moment.

"Hey, Juanita, will you take the lunch counter for a few minutes? I need to get caught up with these booths and tables." Nodding, Juanita picked up a tray of clean mugs and took them over to stack in the freezer.

Only the boy, Gordie, sat at the counter. Juanita smiled and asked him if he needed anything. Stammering and flushing to the roots of his curly black hair, he replied, "My lunch, please. And could I have a glass of water, please? Maybe a napkin, please? And..."

"Hold on there, mister—umm—Gordie, right? Enough with the *pleases*, and we'll take the rest one item at a time." Juanita looked at the boy behind the scars. He wasn't really a boy at all. She could see he was young, probably her age, maybe a bit older, but his eyes—he had really beautiful eyes, but they looked like they'd been around a long time, and seen way too much. Sadness hit her hard and she turned away hiding her emotions by gathering ice in a tall glass and filling it with water. When she set it on the counter in front of him, she smiled.

"Okay, got the water. What's the rest of that?" She laughed, and tapped his hand, noticing how quickly he hid the twisted fingers in his lap. "Lunch? You ordered it already?" When he nodded, she headed back to the kitchen to check on the order.

Returning with his food, she set his plate before him, moving the ketchup and mustard bottles within easy reach, placed two napkins in front of him, and asked him if he wanted anything else. Shaking his head, Gordie tried to eat, but the food stuck in his throat, like his words. Juanita decided to help him out.

"So, what you doing out today? You don't have a job?"

Gulping, swallowing a bite of burger, and taking a drink to wash it down, Gordie cleared his throat. "I don't have a job. I sort of have one, but I don't work. I mean...." He stopped, looking helplessly at the girl across the counter.

"You don't work, but you do? You have a job, but you don't? Well, I don't know about you, but I'm confused as all get out!" Stacking the clean glasses, she looked at him, "Do you drive? I wish I could drive. Even if I could, I suppose it'll be a long time before I can afford a car. Not that I'm complaining. Miss Mary—do you know her?" she continued without waiting for an answer, "Miss Mary lets me stay at her place in exchange for a few chores. My room is awesome! You should see it." She stopped. Blushing, she backtracked. "I don't mean you should see it, as in you should. . .Oh! Never mind. Seems like neither one of us can talk straight." Laughing, she wiped the empty tray off and stacked it beneath the counter.

Gordie studied her. "You can't drive? I have a car and the driver's manual, and I have my license. I could teach you—if you want." He looked away, then back at Juanita. Her golden eyes held his gaze, and her face took on a look of caution.

"You offering to teach me to drive, *re*—uh—Gordie? You drive?"

"I know you think I ain't too smart and all. I might be hard to look at, but I'm not stupid, and I sure ain't as mean-mouthed as you!" Gordie dropped his hamburger on the plate and stood to leave the lunch counter, fumbling in his pocket for money. Juanita quickly reached across and grabbed his arm.

"Wait, Gordie. I'm sorry, okay? Really, I'm sorry. I don't know why I act so awful." Tears sprang up and threatened to spill over onto her freckles. She held his eyes, refusing to look away. He saw the shame in them and sat back down.

Still holding his arm, Juanita spoke softly, "I've wanted to apologize to you since that first day I was so hateful. A lot was going on. Anyway, I really am sorry, and if you would teach me to drive, I'd love it! Would you really do that—after me being so darn mean?"

Gordie nodded, unconsciously chewing on a waffle fry. "Apology accepted. And I sure would teach you to drive. Anytime you say. I got chores at the farm most mornings, but the rest of the day is usually free—at least until the choir comes back from their tour."

"Choir?" Juanita asked, relieved that he appeared to forgive her.

"Uh huh," Gordie said, biting into his hamburger, suddenly hungry, the knot in his stomach untangling. "I sing with a choir in Columbia. Sometimes I sing for weddings and funerals, wherever I'm asked. I've been taking music lessons and writing some of my own songs." He stopped. "I'm talking too much, ain't—aren't I?" Juanita smiled at him.

"Yah, but it's kind of nice, Gordie. Better than earlier?" She laughed and grabbed up the coffee pot behind her. "I'd better get to work or I won't have a job. We'll discuss when's a good time to start, okay?"

From across the dining room, Tina Sapp smiled.

Twenty minutes later, Gordie walked into the sheriff's office, grinning from ear-to-ear. "I did it, Sheriff Dan! I talked to her." Out of breath with excitement, he plopped down in a chair and waited for Dan's response.

"Juanita?" he asked, teasing the boy, knowing full well she was the only girl Gordie would be so excited about talking to. "What did you two talk about?"

"Driving. I'm going to teach her how to drive! Don't that beat all? Me! Gordie Adam Bently is going to teach the most beautiful girl alive how to drive! Shoot, my heart is banging so hard it feels like it'll jump right out of my throat."

Dan laughed and leaned his elbows on his desk, resting his chin on his hands. He studied the boy across from him; it was good to see him so happy.

Standing, Gordie began to pace in front of the desk as he looked at his best friend. "Do you think I can do it all right? I mean, I don't want to do anything wrong, get her hurt or something."

"You'll do just fine, Gordie. Don't you worry yourself about that. Give her your manual and help her get her permit, and then take her out on the gravel roads where there's not much traffic, like you did. Bet she's a quick learner, just like you."

"Thanks, Sheriff Dan. You always know how to make me feel better. After Ma died, well, I didn't know what I was going to do. But you, and Papa Muley, and Uncle Billy, you're my family, and I'm awful grateful you are."

"Me too, son. You know you're loved, don't you?" Dan asked, his voice soft with emotion.

Nodding, Gordie looked at the man across from him. "I sure do. Do you?" he countered, grinning.

Laughing, Dan nodded and sent the boy on his way. "I have work to do, young man, even if some folks I know, don't," he eyed Gordie with mock severity. Then, his tone changing, he added, "We'll see you this evening. Billy is cooking up some roasted chicken with all the fixings. He and Muley invited Molly and me to supper. She's leaving tomorrow for St. Louis to start her Physician's Assistant classes. Before she leaves, she wants some hints on training that Coonhound you talked her into raising! He's two years old and still doesn't know how to tree a coon. Shoot, I think she likes that hound better than she likes me! I hold you responsible for that, young man."

"You know it ain't true, Sheriff Dan. Miss Molly loves you more than anyone. You're going to miss her, ain't you?"

Dan nodded, admitting he would miss his wife, but what he didn't admit was flashbacks of his former fiancée leaving him and never coming back. He was trying to trust God, but he knew he still had some work to do in that department. Gordie noted the sad look on his friend's face, and gave him a quick hug before he left the building. Dan watched him push out the door. The sheriff prayed Gordie's budding friendship with Juanita would turn out to be a good one—but with all the unknowns in the equation, he had his doubts.

SEVENTEEN

In all his wandering around the country roads, Eddie found the perfect hideout. An empty farmhouse west of Hilldale, abandoned by the looks of it, sat well off the main gravel road behind a windbreak line of poplar trees. A menacing wall of limestone rose high on the west side of the farm, blocking the afternoon sun. An old barn sat off from the house, and though the doors were barely hanging on their rusty hinges, with some effort on his part, he could hide the car inside, away from prying eyes.

Watching the place for the past several days led him to believe there would be little human interference. If he collected canned and dry goods, bedding, and cleaning supplies to store at the old place, give the kitchen and bedroom a good cleaning, he figured he could be ready to hide out there in a few weeks—at least by late July, early August.

An old hand-cranked pump squatted over a rock cistern, and after several minutes of cranking, the squawking turned to splashing. Rusty water gushed from the pump, plopping a small green tree frog into the old galvanized bucket. A few more revolutions and the water came clear and cold. Eddie cupped his hand beneath the flow and sucked up a mouthful. Perfect! If all went well, he and the world would be rid of Cassie Calloway and he would have Juanita all to himself. When the heat of the two missing girls died down, he and Juanita would head back north—maybe not Minnesota, the cops might look there—but north, maybe Canada, anywhere away from these nosy, small-town southerners who couldn't mind their own business.

His plan laid out, Eddie decided to take the next step. He needed Cassie to befriend Juanita, gain her confidence and get her to visit the mobile home. Once she was there, he would fix Cassie a drug cocktail she would never wake up from. And Juanita? Why, that sassy little redhead would be all his.

Hiding out in the old farmhouse, miles from anyone, he felt certain they would not be noticed, and if the kid wanted to scream? Let her! Who was going to hear her out in the boonies? Excitement coursed through him. A few weeks—maybe a month. He could keep up the facade that long, he cautioned himself. Play the game well and the prize would be his.

EIGHTEEN

Mary Harmon patted the cushion beside her. Juanita, tired from working the morning and evening shift at Neely's, collapsed next to her aunt and leaned her head against the back of the couch, groaning as her body relaxed into the soft cushions.

"Feels good to sit down," she sighed. "My back and legs hurt, and I feel like I could sleep for a week!" Turning her head toward her great-aunt, she smiled, shadows forming half-moons beneath her eyes. "What's up, Aunt Mary?"

"I've pulled out some photograph albums and some of the high school yearbooks, ones your mother's in. Would you like to see them?" Mary gazed at the weary girl beside her. She knew the child hadn't been to a doctor yet, and believed no one knew about the baby. In Mary's mind, it was time to stop the charade and get care for Juanita and her unborn child. Some very important, life-changing decisions needed to be made.

Surprised, Juanita sat up and studied Mary Harmon's face. "Pictures of Mom? When she was a kid? I'd love to see them. I wanted to ask you about pictures, but I'm kind of scared, too. Not sure why." She wrinkled her forehead and studied her hands, picking at her chipped nails. "Maybe because it'll hurt to see her—you know—different. I only remember her when she was an addict. I really think she loved me, Aunt Mary, but, drugs—they did a major number on Mom's brain, on her body.

"She tried to kick her habit once when I was twelve. That lasted about a week before she met one of her boyfriends who just couldn't wait to help her get reacquainted with the stuff. After that, she was worse than I'd ever seen her." Dark shadows slid across her eyes and she looked away.

"He wanted more than my Mom," Juanita's lips trembled, her chin jutted out. "Most of them did. The last guy, Eddie Felton, he really got her cranked up, and one night, about five months ago, they partied way into the night. I heard Mom crying, laughing, begging him for more heroin, coke, anything he had. Then she was quiet.

"The next morning, I was getting ready for school and I found her on the couch. She'd thrown up all over and messed herself, the floor—everywhere. I got a warm washcloth to clean her up, help her to bed. She didn't move." Tears seeped from beneath Juanita's lashes and rolled down her cheeks. Looking into Mary's eyes, she cried, "I couldn't save her, Aunt Mary. She was gone. Mom was gone."

Mary pulled the sobbing girl into her arms and rocked her, gently rubbing her back, kissing her forehead. "Cry, child. Get it all out. I'm so sorry you had to go through that all alone, my dear. It's over now and you're home. Hilldale is your home. You're loved here, and you will thrive here. You and your child. I have wonderful memories of your mother, and I'll share them all with you, so you can know the real Sarah Elaine. Your child can grow up knowing the good to balance the—well, the other things."

Juanita pulled back from Mary's embrace, her face blanching, her eyes wide with fear. "How did you know? About the baby, I mean. Oh, I'm so sorry, Aunt Mary. I couldn't fight him off—not any of them. I tried. I really did. When it didn't work, I just gave up, made myself go to sleep, pretend nothing was wrong." She placed her hand over the small swelling on her abdomen. "I won't be able to pretend much longer." Tears fell in earnest.

"I didn't know what to do. I didn't know where to go, or who to tell. I lied and told the police and the social worker they sent out, that I was going to live with my grandparents, and that I'd be leaving soon. They never bothered to check on me after that. I just kept going to school and waiting for the landlord to kick me out. The money I saved from odd jobs and babysitting was almost gone, and I—I stole food." She couldn't look at her great-aunt.

"Stories about what happens to kids in *juvie* scared me. Eddie Felton scared me. And then, I missed my monthly and I figured I was going to have a baby. That really scared me. I don't know anything about having a baby." Juanita stopped long enough to blow her nose and wipe her tears. Taking a deep breath, she snuggled closer.

"When I was around ten, Mom told me about the farm in Missouri. I found two pictures she kept in her cigar box. One is her folks, and I don't know who the lady and little girl are in the other picture. Gramma and Grampa looked so nice. I thought if I could find my grandparents they would help me. Then I got scared about that, too. What if they didn't like me, and made me give my baby away? Maybe I should. I'm so confused." Her sobs escalated as she burrowed into Mary's arms.

"We'll do this together, child. You hear me, Juanita? Together. You, your grandmother, and I. First off, you must go see Doc Ridley and make sure everything's all right. Don't worry about your job, dear. Carter already knows and he's not thrown you out yet, has he? You're too good a worker! Now, stop worrying, start remembering, you are not alone!" Mary softly tapped the girl's back, as she emphasized the words. "You are surrounded by family, folks who love you, and those who might give you trouble, why, they'll have to get through your grandmother, and your Aunt Mary!"

Chuckling, she handed Juanita the box of tissues and waited while she wiped her face. When she saw her sobs were little more than hiccups, she reached for the first album stacked on the coffee table. "We'll start with this one, dear. These are the first pictures ever taken of your mother. Pictures of when Sarah Elaine was born. My goodness, she was adorable. Willie and Wanda were so happy to have that child."

Opening the quilted album cover, the two women settled shoulder-to-shoulder. Juanita looked down into the faces of a smiling couple holding a chubby-cheeked baby wrapped in a handmade quilt. Awe-struck, she touched the child's face and through her tears, she whispered, "Hi, Mom."

NINETEEN

Doc Ridley moved from the exam table and made a few notes in the folder on the desk. "You get dressed, young lady, and I'll bring your Aunt Mary back. We'll go over what we know, together. That way, I won't have to chew my cabbage twice!" He laughed at Juanita's confused look. "Never mind. It's something us old fogies say. Do you want Michelle to stay and help you?"

Juanita shook her head. Doc nodded to his nurse and the two left the room, closing the door behind them. He found Mary alone in the reception area and motioned for her to follow him. They walked back to the only closed door where he tapped lightly.

"Come in," Juanita answered, her voice small, scared.

Doc moved a chair for Mary, then stood re-reading his findings. Clearing his throat, he smoothed his mustache and looked over the top of his glasses at Juanita.

"You are a bit over five months along, if my figuring is correct. Your last cycle appeared early in February, you said, and this is the first week of July, so we're in the ballpark. We're going to schedule you for an ultrasound, but from what I can tell, the heartbeat is strong, I feel movement, which is good. Are you feeling any little wiggles?" When Juanita nodded, he smiled. "Good. You're a bit underweight. I don't want you to gain too much, but a few pounds won't hurt you. These little critters take a lot of your nutrition. I've got some pre-natal vitamins for you to take home with you, and I'll have Michelle call you when we get an appointment for the ultrasound. Any questions?" He looked at both women.

"You can hear the heart beat already?" Juanita looked surprised.

"Yes, it's audible at six weeks, and by eight weeks and beyond, we can do ultrasounds to see the heart. You're well past that, so there's a good strong beat, and when we get the ultrasound you'll see how well developed your baby is getting. I've seen babies sucking their thumb, they get hiccups, we might even be able to tell you if you have a boy or girl." Doc Ridley smiled.

"Can I still work at Neely's?"

"I don't see why not, as long as you don't lift anything too heavy, or wear yourself out. You'll need plenty of rest." He patted Juanita on the shoulder and turned to her aunt.

"She's staying with you, Mary?" he asked. Mary nodded.

"Good. Keep an eye on her, make sure she takes her vitamins, and eats enough for the two of them. She's a little underweight, but it's not serious." Again, he smiled at the girl who sat chewing her thumbnail. "Now, young lady, I want to see you back here in three weeks, unless there's anything on the ultrasound we need to discuss, or you have any problems." With that, he walked out of the room leaving the two women alone.

"Come on, dear. Let's get you home. We'll have some lunch and then you can nap. Carter said Tina will be fine with you taking the afternoon off. If you feel up to it, you can work the evening shift." She hugged the silent teenager holding her hand as she climbed down from the examining table. Leaving the office with a package of vitamins, the two walked arm-in-arm back to Mary's, soaking up the morning sun. Neither one saw the man watching them from behind the cascading fountain in the town square.

TWENTY

July wilted into August. The first few days sizzled, bringing thunderstorms and heat lightning. Dan wiped the sweat from his face, refolded his handkerchief and pushed it into his back pocket. He finished fueling his pickup and walked into the convenience store relishing the cool blast of air that washed over him. Moving to the candy counter, he found what he was looking for and walked up to the cashier.

Dan smiled at the young man. "Hey Glen, thought you'd be out gallivanting around town in that Mustang you restored. A '65, isn't it? Nice job, by the way."

The young man behind the counter nodded and grinned.

"Cassie off tonight?" Dan asked.

Turning sober Glen said, "She's off every night for the next two weeks. No notice, and man-oh-man is the boss ticked off! Went on some vacation, or something, Sheriff. I got to work her shift and mine, until they find someone to fill in.

Hope it's soon 'cause it's killing my night life, know what I mean?"

The kid laughed, his voice sliding up an octave, then dropping back down. He looked embarrassed. Shrugging, he rang up Dan's fuel and candy bar. Putting the money in the till, he counted out the change, handed Dan his receipt and added, "Hope she didn't take off with that creep who's been hanging around her all the time. That guy is one scary dude. Shoot, she wouldn't give me the time of day, but was all over him like honey on hot toast." Shaking his head in disgust, he stared at the sheriff.

Alarm bells rang in Dan's head. Thanking Glen, he pocketed his change and headed out the door. At Cassie Calloway's mobile home, her car sat alone in the driveway. Parking next to the Focus, he climbed out of his pickup and looked Cassie's car over. Nothing unusual caught his eye. He climbed the rickety steps and knocked on the metal door. No answer. Dan knocked harder.

"If you're looking for Cassie, she ain't there. Left with that little greaser that was living with her. They took off in his station wagon, Tuesday night," a smoke-roughened voice called to him from the mobile home across the narrow street. "Weasel Face had his car packed by the time she got home from work, and it wasn't long 'fore the two of them took off. Looked like he had to half carry her to the car. Might of been drunk, might not. Might be a vacation, might not."

"Silas Dean, isn't it?" Dan smiled as he walked across the street to the old man standing on his tiny deck leaning against the wooden railing. Silas grinned at the sheriff and nodded, shifting his cigarette to the corner of his mouth. Reaching across the railing he offered his hand.

"Good memory, Sheriff. Worked with your daddy for a short spell back when he tried working for Buck Anders. Not many folk could work for ol' Buck, him always complaining, telling a body one thing one minute, something else the next. Liked to keep folks on their tippy-toes. What a corker!" His laugh turned into a fit of coughing.

"That's right. I'd forgotten about my father working for Buck. It didn't last long, did it? The two butted heads right off, if I remember correctly." Dan pushed the thoughts of his angry father away. Thinking of the beatings he and his mother endured brought on tension headaches, and in an hour, he would be meeting the men at Neely's for their Thursday night out. He'd laid that burden down a couple of years ago, and refused to pick it back up.

"You say Cassie and that fellow living with her took off Tuesday night? I don't suppose you know where they were going?" When he shook his head, Dan felt a chill run through him. Nearly two days gone. They could be anywhere by now. "Thanks, Mr. Dean. If you remember anything else, let me know, okay? Call the department. They'll get hold of me, and I'll get back to you, quick as I can. Sure appreciate your help." He nodded, tapping the brim of his Stetson, and walked back to his pickup.

Before he headed to Neely's, he needed to go over to the office. Gina would put a description of Felton's car out to the highway patrol, the Boone and Cole County sheriffs' departments, and near-by city police stations to see if anyone could get an eyeball on it. The knot in his stomach told him he was probably too late—for what, he wasn't sure. Would Felton kill Cassie?

Back at his office, Dan wrote out a description of Cassie Calloway, included the photo he had of Eddie Felton along with a description of Felton's car, and handed the papers to his night receptionist. At this point, he had no reason to arrest Felton, but he could have him stopped to see if Cassie Calloway was with him, and if so, ask her if she was a willing companion. He decided to walk over to Neely's Cafe and see if Juanita was still working before meeting his friends. The girl needed to answer a few questions; Cassie's life could depend on her answers.

Five minutes later, Dan wove his way through the tables to where Juanita stacked dirty dishes on a tray. When he asked to talk to her, the girl noted his serious expression and froze.

"I can't talk here," Juanita said, panic flooding her eyes, turning them to dark honey. She looked around the dining room. "Meet me out back in the alley, please?" Her hands fluttered, nervously stacking the rest of the dishes from the table. Dan lifted the tray and followed her to the kitchen.

"Hey, Dan, what's up?" Carter called from the grill where he flipped two sizzling hamburgers, laid a slice of cheese on top of one patty, and stood back, looking at the sheriff.

"Need a few minutes with Juanita, Carter. Do you mind if we step out back?"

"As long as you don't arrest her. She's my right arm in the kitchen." Carter's words were light, but worry creased his forehead. He went back to his grill, laying buns face down next to the hamburger patties.

Dan and Juanita stepped out the back door into the alley. Evening hung heavy with heat, and the bricks of the building radiated the day's warmth around them, bringing instant sweat to their faces. Dusk crept across the sky bringing little relief from the heat while a few crickets warmed up for their nightly concert. The odor of rotting food seeped from the dumpster, thick and cloying in the heat. Dan moved a little further out from the building, hoping to catch a breeze.

"Juanita, I don't have time to beat around the bush. I need to ask you what you know about Eddie Felton. I know he and your mom lived together, and he was there the night she died. He's been living in Hilldale for about a month, maybe more, with a girl named Cassie Calloway. I've just found out that both have disappeared. Did he hurt your mother? Did he hurt you?"

He watched the girl's expressions as they flickered across her face: fear, horror, shame, back to fear. She looked up at him, her face pale, even in the heat.

"He's been here in Hilldale? A month or more? How can that be? I never saw him, not even once. He could have..." Her hands went to her rounded abdomen. She looked around her and drew closer to the building. Terror sparked from her eyes as she struggled to answer Dan's questions.

"I think he gave Mom an overdose of heroin, or maybe cocaine, Sheriff Dan. She kept begging him for more and drinking an awful lot. I couldn't hear everything, but right after I heard her crying and begging him for more drugs, he said something to her. Then Mom got quiet. I went to sleep hoping he'd leave."

Dan studied her face hating to ask the next question. "Did he leave, Juanita?"

She stared at the concrete, then the trash bin, then the concrete again. A small breeze lifted a flaming curl from her damp cheek. Slowly, she shook her head. Not looking up, she said, "No. No, he didn't—at least not right away. He came after me, like he'd been doing for most of a month. Guess he figured whenever Mom passed out, it was okay. He left before I got up for school."

"Is he the father of your child?" His voice gentle, his eyes soft with compassion, his heart ached for the child-woman in front of him. Dan lifted her chin so that she had to look at him.

Tears rolled down her face as she pulled her chin from his hand. Nodding, she wiped her eyes and nose on the bottom of her tee shirt. Bitterness put an edge on her voice. "I guess everyone knows about the baby? So much for keeping secrets in a small town." Her laughter sounded bitter, defeated.

"About a month before Mom died, he started up with me. I tried to fight him the first few times, but he just hurt me that much more. Besides, I've known the routine since I was nine." Shrugging, she looked away, staring down the alley. "I quit fighting. I always quit fighting them. Her boyfriends. They always won anyway." Her shoulders slumped and Dan handed her his handkerchief. She blew her nose, wiped the flood of tears, and stood holding the soiled cloth.

"Keep it. I can get it back later." He paused, then said, "It's not your fault, you know that, right?" She studied his dark face and kind eyes. No condemnation, no disgust for her showed there. Only kind compassion. She trembled beneath his gaze. Her voice became harsh with the terrible hurt she carried inside her.

"So, why do I feel like it is? Like I should have fought harder, screamed louder, let them kill me. Anything. Nope, I just gave up and went away to this place in my head where no one hurts me."

She folded her arms across her abdomen and looked longingly behind her at the kitchen door.

"This place, it's the first time I ever remember feeling safe. I let Mr. Neely lock me in the first week, and you know what? That was the first time I can remember sleeping without wondering who was going to come after me. He's the one that talked Aunt Mary into letting me stay with her. I thought I was safe here. Now, I suppose I'll have to leave. I'll never meet my grandma." Defeat colored her expression, wearied her eyes.

"You don't have to go anywhere, young lady. You are safe here. There's a lot of folks who've taken a shine to you, and they're all looking out for you. No more running, hear me?"

"I can't let him find me. He'll kill this baby—maybe even kill me when he's done with me. He wants me to be with him, but I won't. Not ever again. I'd rather die before I let him, or anyone, at me like that again." Fierceness sharpened her voice. "This girl, this Cassie, do you think he took her, or do you think she went with him because she wanted to?"

"I don't know. That's what I'm asking you. You know him better than I do." Dan said, then cringed at the way it sounded. Juanita answered as if she didn't notice.

"He's mean. He's really mean, but he knows how to be charming, too. He charmed my mom all the time. Tried to sweet-talk me, but I didn't want any part of him, or what he was offering. Maybe he started out nice with this girl. Won't be long though, if she ever disagrees with him, she's toast." A dreadful assurance tightened her face, and her small hands clenched into fists. "I hope you find her, Sheriff. Can I go back to work, please? I don't want

91

to lose my job, and working here keeps me from thinking too much." Her voice dropped to a whisper. "Please?"

Patting her shoulder, Dan nodded. "Go on in, Juanita. If you see or hear from Eddie, you let me know pronto, understand? No waiting around, no running away. You've come home, girl. Hilldale is your home, and we're glad you're here. Let us protect you—and your little one. And your grandmother? I'm thinking it's Wanda Harmon, right?" When she nodded, he continued, a smile lighting his face, "Oh, you'll be a welcome sight to her, I guarantee. Now, go on in and someone will be by later to take you to Miss Mary's. I don't want you going anywhere by yourself for a while."

Juanita nodded, looked up at Dan and started to speak. Shaking her head, she pushed through the back door into the building, leaving the sheriff to watch after the small figure. *Lord, keep her safe,* he prayed, wishing he had Eddie Felton behind the bars of one of his jail cells.

TWENTY-ONE

Gordie sat at the lunch counter waiting for Juanita and Tina to finish wiping down the last of the tables. Tina tossed her cloth into the pail of water, wiped her hands on her apron, then removed it, tossing it behind the counter.

"Good night, you all. I'm bushed. Got to get off these feet!" Tina called over her shoulder as she headed out the front door locking it behind her. Carter pushed through the kitchen door removing his apron, and wadding it into a soiled ball, he tossed it into the tub of used towels and aprons hidden behind the counter.

"Time to go, Juanita. It's nearly eleven. You've done enough, young lady. Tomorrow morning is another day. Long as I've been in this business, none of the chores have run away, or magically disappeared—at least not until you started working here. Go on, now. Don't keep this young man waiting." He grinned at Gordie.

"I'm just going to finish putting the clean dishes away. . ." she started, but Carter held up his hand stopping her words.

"They'll keep. You've had a long day, Juanita. Get on home—or wherever." Again, he grinned.

Blushing, Gordie felt his heart hammering in his chest. Sheriff Dan had asked him if he'd mind waiting for Juanita; he wanted to make sure she got home safely. Though the sheriff explained very little, Gordie knew it had something to do with the man from Juanita's past. He told Sheriff Dan he would be happy to look out for her, and laughing, his friend replied that he thought Gordie wouldn't mind.

Walking out the back door, Juanita glanced over at the young man by her side. "Sorry you have to do this. I'm—" she cleared her throat and looked him in the eye, "I'm grateful."

"I'm happy to do it, Wanda," he replied, leading her around to the front parking lot where he had his car parked.

Juanita stopped in mid-stride, grabbing Gordie's arm. "Wanda? Why do you call me that? You know my name."

Gordie stood still, enjoying the pressure of her hand on his arm. "I don't know. I guess because when I first met you, I thought of a story my ma told me about her ma's best friend. She had bright red

93

hair, and her name was Wanda. It just come to me that first day when I saw your hair sparking like fire." Suddenly embarrassed, he stammered, "I'm sorry if I made you mad." He chuckled, "You called me retard, and that ain't—isn't my name—and it isn't very nice! At least my name for you is nice."

It was Juanita's turn to blush. She felt grateful the evening covered her burning face. "I've been meaning to talk to you about that. I really do owe you an apology, Gordie. I've been teased enough in my lifetime to know how hurtful it is. It's not a good excuse, but I was scared and hungry. Seemed like you and that sheriff friend of yours were intent on taking my food away. Then, when you paid for it after I was so mean—I don't know—it just made me mad all over again! Doesn't make any sense, does it?" She laughed softly. Her hand still held his arm, though not as tightly.

"Did you know my Grandma Wanda?" she asked.

"I didn't really know anyone, excepting the folks Ma told me about. Sheriff Dan is the first outsider I ever met, after Ma died." He grew still, memories flooding his mind. Shaking loose of the past was constant work.

They arrived at the '57 Buick Special that had once belonged to Muley's wife, Emily. Gordie opened the door for Juanita and waited for her to get into the front seat. Closing the door and walking to the driver's side, he felt the empty place on his arm where her hand had been.

"Gordie," Juanita said, when he closed his door, "will you wait at Aunt Mary's while I let her know we're going to take a ride?"

The street light cast a pale purple hue over her face. Gordie tried not to grin. "A ride? We're taking a ride? Sure, that's great." He started the car and pulled out of the parking lot, aiming toward town and Mary Harmon's house. "Where are we going on this here ride?" he asked, watching the road, afraid for her to see the delight on his face.

"I want—I was hoping you would take me by Grandma's place—if it isn't too far. It's late, but I'm not really tired, and I don't want to go in or anything—I just want to see the house my mom grew up in. I'm not ready to meet my grandma just yet." She looked over at the young man next to her. "I guess you know about the baby, too, don't you?" Shame thickened her voice.

Gordie drove in silence as he pulled up to the curb in front of Mary's house. Parking the car, but leaving it running, he turned to face her. "I do. I got an angel tap and I saw you with a little baby girl." He didn't tell her the rest of his vision. "She's gonna be as pretty as her mama, and I reckon she's going to have your temper, too!" he said, laughing. As he spoke, Juanita heard the awe beneath the laughter and realized he wasn't making fun of her.

Shaking her head, she reached for the door handle, "Angel tap? You are one different dude, Gordie. You're not like any of the guys in school, or really, like anybody I've ever met. I don't think you've had an easy life—you have to tell me your story one of these days—but you don't seem angry about stuff. I mean, when I was so hateful to you, you seemed to just let it roll off you and here you are being nice to me."

Sighing, she said, "Me? I'm mad. I'm so angry about all the stuff that's happened to me, everything that's been unfair. I just don't know who to be mad at! My mom? Her folks? The creeps that took advantage of my mom's weakness, her addictions? I want to punch someone, you know?" Her eyes bored into Gordie's. "I just don't know who to punch," she laughed at herself, sadness etching lines in her face. Before Gordie could respond, she pushed open the door, climbed out, and leaned down. "Wait for me?" she asked.

"I ain't going nowhere, Wanda. We're going for a ride, remember?" His voice husky with emotion, he turned away.

She reached back inside and patted his arm. "Double negative, Gordie. Better get it straight, or that sheriff will be after you!" With that she backed out of the car and ran up the sidewalk. Gordie watched her until she disappeared inside Mary's house. He felt his arm where her hand touched him. He didn't understand it, but he knew he loved that girl more than he loved his own life.

Before long, Juanita climbed back into the car and they headed out of town. At the gravel road that led to her grandmother's, he drove slowly past the farm letting Juanita look through the darkness at the old two-story clapboard house lit by a sulfur-yellow security light, and pale moonlight. Silence lay between them, but it was a peaceful silence, and he waited for her to speak first.

"The house is all dark. I guess she's asleep," Juanita said wistfully. "I don't know why I'm so scared to meet her."

"Maybe you're afraid she won't want you. Sometimes I forget about how I look, then when I meet someone, or get on stage to sing, I get scared, thinking them folks will reject me." Gordie turned the corner at the end of the gravel road and asked, "Want to drive by it again?"

Shaking her head, Juanita leaned back against the seat and looked at him. "No, let's go back to town." Wiping the back of her hand across her eyes and nose, he realized she was crying. "I guess you're right. She'll see I'm going to have a baby, I'm not married, I couldn't save Mom—her daughter. There's so much wrong with me," she sighed. Holding out her arms, she studied the tattoos in the dim light cast from the dash board. "I've got scars, too, Gordie."

"I figure we all do, one way or another. Some folks are just better at hiding them," he replied, daring to take her hand. "Ma used to tell me, stuff that happens to us can make us tender-hearted, or make us hard and bitter. She always said, 'Gordie, don't you get hard and bitter. That's the worst kind of scars, because those kind will keep you from loving. Your life will be worthless, if you can't give or receive love.' I reckon that's what happened to my grampa. He had them kind of scars that kept him from loving anyone—even himself—and there was love all around him, just waiting for him."

Juanita stared at him, her hand curled beneath his. "Aren't you angry for him hurting you? He's the one who did that to your face and hands, isn't he?"

Gordie started to pull his crooked fingers from her hand, but she stopped him. He glanced at her and saw the look on her face. Longing. Deep, needful longing.

"When Sheriff Dan first took me to a foster home and I got a look at my face, I reckon I was pretty upset. And at first, when Grampa whipped Ma or Dancer—that's my dog—and his Coonhound, Beauty, I'd get awful angry and want to hurt him like he was hurting us. But being alone so much, I had lots of time to think.

"Being angry wasted too much time. I found out, when I was angry I missed seeing the beauty around me, missed the good things that come my way every single day. When I was angry, I forgot to watch the sun rise, or the colors that shot across the sky before the sun set behind the bluffs.

"I forgot to notice the smell of Ma's lilacs, the smell of the fresh-turned dirt in my little garden behind my shed. I missed hearing the peeper frogs singing with the bull frogs and crickets. I couldn't feel the happiness from singing. When I was angry even hugs felt different. I couldn't feel the love I had for Ma, for Dancer, Beauty, and my old milk cow, Kissy—and even for Grampa."

Looking at Juanita, seeing her eyes drinking in his words, he said, "One day I realized, I didn't have time to stay angry. I was missing out on too many good things in my life." The car grew silent except for the crunch of gravel beneath the slow-moving tires and the night sounds drifting in through the open windows.

Moonlight glistened off the runnels of tears slipping down Juanita's face. Gordie pulled the car over to the edge of the gravel road and stopped, shifting into park. His hand moved back to Juanita's as he stared out the windshield to the moon-lit corn fields that fanned out before them, only stopping when they got to the banks of the Missouri River rolling south.

After a few minutes of silence, Juanita whispered, "Do you want to kiss me, Gordie?"

Pulling in his breath, he turned to look her full in the face, his longing stark in his eyes. "I want to, just don't know how to. I ain't never kissed a girl except Ma's cheek." He didn't pull his eyes away.

Juanita slid across the seat, and still holding his hand, her other hand came up to his face, gently touching his scarred cheek. Slowly, she leaned forward and up until her lips touched his. Her golden eyes closed, and for a moment, fear grasped his heart in a cold grip. Then the warmth of her hands, her lips, melted the fear away and he closed his eyes, savoring the gentleness of their kiss. When she pulled back, she traced the scars one-by-one with her finger.

"You're really something, Gordie. Your scars, I don't know, they make you beautiful somehow. Thank you for not hating me, for caring about me—and—and my baby." Scooting back to her side of the seat, she continued to look at him. Filled with emotion, he dropped the transmission into drive and continued down the road to Hilldale.

He felt like singing.

TWENTY-TWO

Cassie woke up. Her head hurt and her mouth felt as though she'd tried to chew the foam rubber in her pillow. Turning her head brought on pain and nausea, and as she looked around, confusion filled her mind. Where was she?

"Hello?" she called, her voice croaking, barely audible. She tried again. "Hello! Anyone here?" Fear crept up her spine, making her shiver. Breathing deeply, she tried to move her legs to stand, but found she couldn't. Her fear escalated. She lifted her hands and found them tied to the sides of the old wrought-iron bed she lay on. Struggling to sit up as far as she could, she looked down the length of her body and found her feet bound together at the ankles, the rope tethered to the end of the bed. Terror blocked her vision for an instant, roaring through her brain like a tornado, sucking up her thoughts and spinning them away.

"Jeremy? Someone! Where am I? Why am I tied up? HELP! Someone help me, please." Her cries thudded heavily in the dank room. Cassie's senses began to go into overdrive.

The odor of mold and rotting wood overwhelmed her. The air in the room pressed down, still, hot, and muggy, bringing to memory sitting in a sweat lodge with her grandmother, only then the smell was of clean burning wood, fresh air, and the women's sweat beading and running from their skin. This air smelled foul and felt oppressive. Shame flooded her when she realized the foul smell came from her. Whoever had tied her up, had put an adult diaper on her, and she had soiled herself. Panic thundered through her.

"Calm down, Cassie," she scolded herself, talking out loud. "What's the last thing you remember?" Inhaling, exhaling, slowly she brought her mind down from terror level to gut-sickening fear.

"Where are you? Why are you doing this? I need to go to the bathroom. Jeremy Blade!" she screamed as loud as her fear-strangled lungs would allow, because, now she remembered. Jeremy was the last person she'd been with.

Slowly, memories labored up through the swamp of fear and drug-hangover shrouding her brain. She remembered coming home from work and seeing Jeremy packing his car. The porch light cast a faint glow as he pushed the last of some clothes—her clothes—into the back of his station wagon. Curiosity grew into annoyance.

"What? You stealing my clothes? What else of mine you got in there?" she remembered challenging him, feeling anger rising in her.

"If I wanted to steal your pathetic junk, I'd be long gone before you ever got home, now wouldn't I, smart girl?" He'd sneered, and had slammed the rear door closed. Changing his tone, he'd walked over to her. "I took the liberty of packing for you so we could get on the road tonight. We have a long drive ahead of us. Don't look like that!" She remembered how he laughed at her frowning face. "I also took the liberty of calling your boss to let him in on the secret," his voice had turned to sugar.

Hot needles of panic pierced her, as she remembered. Cassie forced herself to lay still on the damp, moldy-smelling mattress. He'd given her a joint to smoke—lit it himself—and then handed it to her, as he led her into the mobile home. Closing her eyes, tears slipped down the sides of her face trickling past her ears. His words rolled across her mind.

"I wanted to surprise you with a trip to Vegas. We have reservations in two days, so we've got to hustle, girl." Laughing, he'd lifted her and twirled her around, kissing her soundly.

"Vegas?" She'd taken a second, then a third deep drag, filling her lungs, letting it out slowly. A strange weakness came over her and she'd dropped the smoldering weed into the sink, running water over it. "Geez, what's in that thing? My head feels fuzzy, and my legs feel like they're going to collapse." Then she remembered looking at him, asking again, "Vegas?"

"Hey, that's some really good stuff you're wasting!" he'd scolded, then smiled. "Yes, ma'am.

We're booked for two weeks of fun and games—casino games. One of my clients came through with a big chunk of dough he owed me. I want to celebrate, and who better to celebrate with, my darling! So, come on, get moving. Grab anything else you think you need and let's hit the road."

Shrugging her shoulders, she remembered telling him she just needed her make-up case. He'd gotten it for her, and had helped her out to the car, chatting along the way. She'd found she couldn't answer him. Wooziness had swept over her. Her limbs had grown weaker, and then she'd lost control of them. Soon, it had been too much effort to keep her eyes open and she remembered how everything had faded away.

Cassie groaned, pulling at the ropes that held her. Kidnapped! The dirty jerk had drugged her and kidnapped her. What for? She gave him everything. Bought the food and his beer, cleaned up after him, did his laundry, slept with him, what more did he want from her? Her fear escalated again. "HELP!" she screamed, feeling like she needed to throw up.

Outside the farmhouse, Eddie Felton listened to Cassie's frantic cries for help. He stepped away from the front door onto a dilapidated porch, closing the door behind him. Listening, he could faintly hear her panicked voice, but a person would have to be right up on the porch to hear her. He smiled. Moving down the steps, he wandered slowly around the house, listening. Pleased with the crude soundproofing he'd done to the room, he headed for the barn and the car parked inside, hidden behind lopsided doors that clung to the barn on rusty broken hinges.

Rifling through the back of his station wagon, Eddie found the last box of food he'd purchased the day before. He carried it back to the house to prepare lunch for them. Walking through the kitchen, he tripped over the large eyebolt screwed into the floor. *Stupid place for an eyebolt,* he cursed. Opening a can of beans, he dumped some in a Styrofoam bowl, found a plastic spoon, and headed toward the locked bedroom. Cassie had slept through nearly two days, so she was probably hungry and thirsty. Thinking of her, having to care for her, clean up her messes, irritated him.

Having to change his plans annoyed him, but after recognizing the bulge at Juanita's waistline, he knew she was carrying his child. He'd seen her and the old lady coming out of the doctor's office and he knew. His child! Pride swelled up within him. He couldn't afford to kill Cassie with drugs—he'd be the first one they suspected—especially after Sarah Elaine's death by an overdose. He had no illusions. That nosy sheriff knew all about Minnesota; he was sure of it, and cops weren't too keen on coincidences. So, change of plans.

No one would be looking for Cassie back from their trip for at least two weeks, and when they started looking for her, they'd start in Vegas—the last place they thought she'd been. He had time. Time to get a room ready for Juanita. Time to nab her. Time to plan a way to get her somewhere far from here to have their baby, to learn to be a family. And if Juanita didn't want to be a family—well, too bad for her. He and his child would be fine on their own. In fact, that might even be better. Time. He just needed some time and he'd have it all figured out.

TWENTY-THREE

"Two nights in a row, eating in town. What's going on, Daniel?" Billy Sumday asked.

"Thanks for coming in. You should let me give you a ride, though. Long walk for you." Dan said.

"Rode my horse in. Getting lazy in my old age," Billy laughed. "What's going on?" He asked, again.

Dan told him of Cassie Calloway's disappearance. "Her boss confirmed what Glen told me about her leaving for a vacation. According to them, the boyfriend Jeremy Blade—I'm guessing that's Felton—said he was taking her to Las Vegas for a couple of weeks, and they would be leaving as soon as she got off work Tuesday evening. Three days gone, Billy." Dan still had no word, and no sightings of the couple or Felton's station wagon. Worry chewed at him. Billy studied his face.

"You think there's foul play, don't you Daniel?" the Kickapoo spoke softly, close to the sheriff's ear. The noisy teenagers were celebrating someone's birthday, and their raucous rendition of *Happy Birthday* vibrated through the cafe.

Dan nodded. "Why would he use a false name unless he was up to no good? I think Cassie was just a convenience for him, a place to hide out in the open until he could get his hands on Juanita. The way the folks Cassie works with tell it, he leached off her, and they said she came to work a few times with a black eye, bruises on her arms. She always had a story about what happened, but her co-workers weren't buying it." Dan sighed.

"Should I call her mother?" Billy asked. "Cassie's a Red Feather. Her grandmother and my wife were best friends, grew up on the reservation

together. Ellen helped Oscar with the ceremony for
the dead, when his mother died. My wife's people
live very close to the Red Feather family, so my son
spent a lot of time with them." He sipped from his
cola.

"Let them know we're looking for her, but
keep it low key until we know more. Maybe she
took him home to meet her family?" Dan suggested.

"No, Cassie blamed her mother and
grandmother for breaking up her marriage. Her
husband dealt in drugs, and they turned him in to the
authorities. The kids hadn't even been married a
month. Far as I know, he's still in prison and will be
for a very long time. Her mother had the marriage
annulled not long after he was sent to Stillwater.
Cassie won't take her man home, especially if he's
questionable." Looking at Dan, he stated, "We know
he's that and probably more, don't we, Daniel." The
sheriff nodded.

"What worries me, Billy, is how Sarah
Elaine died. Cassie's been known to do a little weed,
maybe a few pills, but I've never heard of her using
any hard stuff. But this guy, I think he knows his
way around drugs. He appears to have resources, and
he has reason to get rid of Cassie—she knows him
under a false name, and surely the guy is smart
enough to know that has to come out one day. If he
gets his hands on Juanita, she'll be in the way. What
else can he do but get rid of Cassie?" Shaking his
head, Dan took a long drink of his Coke.

"Changing the subject, for a moment," Billy
smiled, "I hear my granddaughter is in St. Louis.
She's taking PA training?"

Dan nodded. "She's just getting started.
Looks like weekends will be the only time we can
get together for a while." He paused, a shadow

flitting across his face. "She said Doc approached her about taking over his office once her training is complete, should she decide to go for it. I think he wants to retire." He looked over at his elderly friend. "Trouble with all this, Billy, is it reminds me of Lynette leaving me for a bigger, better job. I know Molly is different, and I believe she loves me—I know she loves me," Dan amended. "We've been married over a year. It's just these nagging little doubts that insinuate themselves in my brain..." He tried to laugh and failed.

"Daniel, Molly will be back. If she gets her PA training she can work in Hilldale, close to home. No doubt in my feeble old mind, my granddaughter loves you, son." He placed his hand on Dan's arm. "No doubt at all."

"What you two mumbling about?" Obed Martin sat down across from Billy and Dan. "Look thick as thieves, you do," he frowned.

Tina, busy with a table of teens motioned to Juanita stacking mugs behind the lunch counter. The girl grabbed her order pad and walked over to their table, a smile lighting her face. When she asked Obed what he wanted to drink, he ignored her. Blushing, the girl asked again. Billy and Dan looked at him. Still, the old man refused to answer or even look up at her.

"Bring him a cream soda, though the old coot doesn't deserve it," Dan said, smiling apologetically. Juanita nodded and walked back to the soda cooler behind the lunch counter.

"Got a burr under your saddle, Obed?" Dan asked. "You were pretty rude to that young lady. What's going on?"

Harrumphing and scooting around in his chair, Obed slapped his hand on the table. "What's going on?" he grumped. "I'll tell you what's going on. You see her at church last week? That piece of no-good trash waltzed into our church with Miss Mary, just like she owned the place. Ain't she got no shame? Folks like her are ruining our town. Ought to be run off, you was any kind of sheriff," he sniffed, staring Dan in the eye. "What's worse is our preacher and them folks at church, why they're treating her like she ain't done nothing wrong!" Indignation oozed from him.

The cafe door opened, ushering Muley and Gordie into the air-conditioned dining room. They headed over to the table, weaving their way through the full room. Seating themselves, they greeted the others. Muley looked at the two men across from him.

"Looks like a funeral. What's wrong?" Muley asked. Just as Dan was about to answer, Juanita returned with Obed's cream soda, setting it on the table before him. Smiling at Gordie, she laid her hand on his shoulder for a moment, then held up her order pad. Gordie smiled back. Obed's cheeks flamed, and he looked up at the girl getting ready to take the new-comers' orders.

"You take that there bottle out of here. Find Tina and send her to wait on us, and you get your tainted self right on out of here. Don't think I don't see you sashaying yourself around this here boy what don't know no better the kind of woman you are. You think you waltzing in to us decent folks' church is gonna change what you are?" His voice grew loud while those around them stilled. Heads turned their way.

Obed's eyes shot fire at the stunned girl, venom spewed from his mouth. "Git, I said. You ain't waiting on us. You ain't touching nothing of mine with your filthy self." With that, he crossed his arms over his chest and turned his face from her.

Juanita's cheeks paled, leaving her freckles stark against her skin. "Yes sir," she managed to whisper as she picked up Obed's bottle of soda and headed back toward the kitchen. Dan pushed back his chair, his face stiff with anger.

"Let's go, Obed," he said, his eyes opaque, his jaw working.

"Go where?" The old man looked up at the young sheriff, the boy he'd rescued from sure death when he was nine-years-old; the boy he'd gotten Muley and his wife, Emily, to look out for when the law didn't stop the boy's daddy from whipping his Ma and him. "You ain't standing up for that no-account trollop, are you, Danny? You can see what kind of loose woman she is," his voice whined.

"Come on," Dan ordered quietly, ignoring the stares of the customers surrounding them. Billy and Muley stood, moving to Gordie's side. The boy sat shocked at the words he'd just heard hurled at the woman he loved. His scars stood livid against deathly pale cheeks. Quickly, the two old men took him by the arms and led him back toward the kitchen in search of Juanita.

Dan took Obed by the arm and forced him to stand. "Follow me out of here, or I swear I'll arrest you for—for indecent exposure!" he growled.

"What!" Obed exclaimed, anger beginning to replace the triumph in his eyes. "I ain't exposed nothing!" he replied, belligerence sharpening his voice.

"You sure did, Obed Martin. In all my days, I'm not sure I've ever seen such ignorance and hatefulness exposed. You coming?" he said quietly, removing his handcuffs from their place on his belt.

Obed scowled, shook off Dan's hand and moved toward the door. Eyes followed the two men out. Whispers turned to a buzz of voices, as they began to rehash what they'd just witnessed.

Once outside, Dan walked the angry old man around the corner of the building away from curious eyes. Standing in the deepening shade of an ancient pin oak that overshadowed the rear parking lot, the sheriff stopped and faced Obed.

"That girl in there, the one you've been treating like a worthless piece of trash—that girl had no say in anything that happened to her. You hear me, Obed? She had no say. Just like I had no say in what my father did to my mother and me, way back when. Just like Gordie had no say in the whippings he and his mother got with that bull whip Bobby Lee used on them.

"That girl's our family. Juanita is Sarah Elaine's child. She's Wanda and Willie Harmon's granddaughter. You humiliated her in front of her customers, folks who could be her friends and neighbors, and worse, in front of the young man who loves her—loves her more than he loves his own life. What's happened to you, Obed?" Dan's sadness made his voice dull, his shoulders sag.

"What you mean, she didn't have any choice?" Obed retaliated. "Them doo-dads on her arms, her belly full of a bas...." Dan halted him with a raised hand.

"Don't!" He ground out. "Don't you dare say what I think you're about to say, or I swear I will arrest you. I'll lock you up and think of some way to keep you locked up until you come to your senses, old man!" Fury darkened his face.

"Danny!" Obed yelped, fearful the sheriff was going to strike him. "She coulda fought off the man—or men—what made advances. She was probably asking for it, the way she looks." His tone grew unsure as he felt the full measure of the sheriff's furious glare. "Well, couldn't she?" he asked, his chin thrust out, his eyes narrowed.

"Could I fight my father, Obed? A scrawny, nine-year-old kid. My mother, how could she fight back? Juanita is a kid. Small as she is, you see her fighting off a grown man? What those men did to her wasn't her choice. She didn't ask for *it*. She was forced. Do you understand? Those men didn't ask her permission—they took what they wanted, marked her as if she was nothing more than a trophy, and left her suffering hurts like we'll never know." Dan took a deep breath and blew it out.

"And, as far as coming to church? You should be rejoicing that she has the courage to come, knowing there are folks like you ready to judge her, to shun her. Jesus didn't turn folks away who came to him for help, now did he? What makes you better than our Savior? What gives you the right to say who can and can't be redeemed? I'm disappointed in you, Obed Martin, and more than that, I love you, but right now, I don't like you very much."

With that, Dan turned and walked away, leaving the stunned man staring after him, mouth open, shaking his head. In spite of the heat radiating from the building and the parking lot, Obed Martin shivered.

*****

"I can't go back to Neely's. Everyone heard what that old man said about me!" Juanita sobbed as Mary held her trembling body, trying to comfort her.

"Someone's at the door, dear. Sit here on the couch and I'll see who it is, then I'll be right back with a nice glass of ice water, and we'll talk. Sit, dear," she gently commanded, settling the distraught girl on the sofa with a box of tissues.

Gordie stood at the front door, his anxious expression cueing Mary on his feelings for her great-niece. "Oh my," she sighed, as she opened the door for him to enter. This must be Neva Sue Bently's boy, the one she'd heard so much about. Smiling, she shook his hand.

"I'm Mary Harmon, though I expect you already know that, young man. And I believe you must be Neva Sue Bently's boy? Your mother was in my eighth and ninth grade literature and composition classes. Now, if I remember correctly, she wrote beautiful poetry. Yes, I do believe I'm correct about that. As a matter of fact, I may still have a few of her poems around here somewhere. I kept copies of many of my students' best work." She stopped.

"Goodness, here I am prattling like the old lady I am, and you must be worried sick about Juanita. Come in." She led him to the living room where Juanita sat, still weeping. Mary left the two alone and headed to the kitchen.

Gordie sat down next to Juanita and took her hand. She leaned against him and he put his arm around her shoulders while she wept, silently praying for the girl he loved. He longed to take her sorrow, but knew he could only help her carry her burden. He wished he could tell her how much he loved her.

"I can't go back there, Gordie. I just can't face those people, face Mr. Neely—not after what they heard. And it's true, too. I am no good. I'm used trash, and I'll never amount to anything good. What's going to happen to my baby? I'll have to give it up, because I'll never be good enough to raise it."

111

Juanita blew her nose and pulled another tissue from the box on her lap.

"Ain't true, Wanda. You know it ain't true, too. What Mr. Martin said is his opinion, and he don't have all the information. Lots of folks say things, make judgments before they know the true story. He's wrong. He's made a judgment call that ain't his to make, because he don't know your heart, and he don't know your thoughts. Shoot, he don't know you!" Gordie tightened his arm around her slender shoulders, and she nestled her head against his chest, hearing the thumping of his heart. She felt comfort radiating from him.

"Look at me," he continued. "You don't know most of my story, but a lot of folks in this town—well shoot—in near all of Mid-Missouri, know it. The murder of my ma and grandpa was in all the newspapers, on the TV, on the radio. There wasn't anywhere I could hide. Even if I wanted to, folks knew me on account of my face being shown everywhere. Some folks are hard put to be around me, what with my scars, my broken fingers, and—well—my birthing." His voice dropped to a near whisper.

"Your birthing?" Juanita asked, sniffling. He pulled another tissue out of the box and wiped her damp cheeks.

"Reckon the way Ma conceived me was about the way this here little girl got conceived," he said, placing his hand on her abdomen. Just then, the baby kicked against the pressure of his hand. Grinning, Gordie looked down into Juanita's tear-reddened eyes.

"Well, look at that, will you!" he exclaimed. "I think she likes me!" The wonder on his face

112

caused the icy fingers gripping her heart to warm and loosen.

"It doesn't gross you out—you know—to feel it move?" she whispered, laying her hand over Gordie's. "I love feeling it, but I wondered what it would be like for someone else."

"First off, you got to stop calling her *it* or she'll think you don't love her. Second of all, she's a miracle. How could she ever be gross? Oh, and third thing?" he grinned down into her upturned face, "She needs a name." He laughed as the baby kicked his hand again. "See, she agrees."

Mary, standing ready to bring in ice water and cookies for the two teenagers, stopped at the partially closed door, and listened. Smiling, she turned and headed back to the kitchen, setting the tray on the countertop. She reached for the telephone and dialed her sister-in-law. When Wanda answered, Mary spoke quietly, "It's time, Wanda. The child needs you. I'm going to have her young man bring her to the farm in the morning. She's scared you're going to reject her, but you won't do that will you?"

Silence met her from the other end of the line. "Wanda?" Mary prompted.

"Reckon I'm a bit scared, myself," Wanda Harmon replied, her voice strained. "What if she don't cotton to me—or takes a look at this old run-down farm and wants to run—like Sarah Elaine? Can't hardly bear the thought of losing another child." Mary heard the tears in her sister-in-law's voice and knew the admission was difficult for the proud old woman. Her heart swelled with love.

"She's going to love you, you silly old thing. And she's going to love that old farm, and everything you have to offer her, dear. Don't you worry yourself any about that. I'll let Carter know she won't be at work for a few days. We'll need to let the foolishness of the day run its course and then she can come back here, if she wants to. I suppose we ought to leave a few decisions to her," Mary said, laughing.

"You always were a sentimental fool," Wanda said, abruptly hanging up.

Mary headed back to the living room with the tray. She had some fast talking to do, but she believed she could count on Neva Sue's nice young son to help her out. Sighing, she thought back over fifty years ago. If only there'd been a way for her—but then—times were different, and her beloved Ronald never made it back from the war. Shrugging off the sad memories, she pushed the sliding pocket door open and walked into the living room. Looking at the two seated on the couch, Mary could see the love that surrounded them, like a light straight from heaven.

"Well!" she smiled at them. "I have some good news for you."

TWENTY-FOUR

Early the next morning, Juanita showered and dressed, her nerves making it difficult for her to button the maternity blouse Aunt Mary had given her. The girl looked into the mirror. Her red curls tangled around her head, freckles stood out against her pale skin, looking as though they'd been dotted on her face and neck with a magic marker. Sighing, she pulled her damp hair back, corralling it with a ruffled elastic tie. Since she didn't wear makeup, there was nothing for her to do about her freckles but live with them. Another sigh escaped her. Grandma Wanda—what if she didn't want her? Tears threatened, but Juanita scolded herself, straightening her thin shoulders, forcing herself to calm down.

Voices from the hallway told her Gordie had arrived. Butterflies whirled in her stomach, and her baby decided she needed to do a somersault. Putting her hand over her abdomen, Juanita smiled. "It doesn't matter how you got there, little one, I love you!" she whispered. Opening her bedroom door, she walked into the beginning of the rest of her life. She'd always longed for family and now she had Aunt Mary, and soon, she'd be meeting her grandmother. "Please, God," the girl prayed not really knowing much about God. "Please, please let her like me—even if it's just a little."

Gordie's eyes lit up when she walked into the hallway. He shoved his hands inside his pockets and shuffled his feet. "You eat breakfast?" he asked. When she shook her head, he frowned, "You got to eat, Wanda. You're feeding your daughter, too, you know." She looked shocked at his scolding, then grinned.

"Yah? Who made you the food police, Mr. Gordie Adam Bently?" Gordie looked relieved at the lighthearted banter.

"Ain't—shoot—We aren't going nowhere until you eat a bite," he replied, looking to Mary for support.

"Double negative, Gordie," Juanita poked his arm. Gordie scratched his head.

"I still don't know what that means," he said.

Mary laughed at the two young people. "Breakfast is ready. You two stop your fussing and follow me." With that, she led them to the kitchen and seated them at the table. Juanita surprised herself and the others by eating a large helping of scrambled eggs, two slices of bacon, and a piece of toast smothered in Aunt Mary's blackberry jam. She washed it down with two glasses of cold milk, then sat back in her chair.

"Sure glad you aren't hungry," Gordie teased, cleaning up the rest of the eggs from the bowl, and the last three slices of bacon Miss Mary slid on his plate.

Laughing, Juanita looked at the two people sitting across from her. "Thank you for helping me—both of you." Blushing, she looked away, then forced herself to face them. "No one has ever treated me like this—not ever. I'll never forget what you've given me." A solitary tear rolled from her lashes, down her cheek, dropping from her chin. She wiped it away.

"We're proud of you, Juanita, aren't we, Gordie? And, my dear, we love you." Gordie's face reddened, but he didn't look away. Nodding agreement, he reached across the table and took Juanita's hand.

"Reckon we best get going." His voice, soft and low, sent shivers through Juanita. Pushing back from the table, she went to her aunt and gave her a hug.

"Thank you for everything, Aunt Mary. I'll be back in a few days, if you and Carter will still have me."

Mary patted the girl's shoulder, "We'll talk, dear. You stay at your grandmother's for as long as you want to. Carter will understand." She watched as Gordie and Juanita walked out of the kitchen, and listened as the front door closed behind them. "God go with you, child," she whispered.

Gordie drove slowly through town. Once they reached the county road headed west, the old

Buick picked up speed. Juanita sat silent, staring out the window.

"It'll be fine, you'll see," Gordie said. "Your gramma's been waiting for you for a long time, she isn't going to turn you away, I promise."

"You promise?" Juanita looked over at him. "What? Is that an angel tap thing telling you that?" She smiled and lightly punched his arm before turning back to the window. "I've never been out here except for that one night, but it feels like I've always known this place. Strange, isn't it?"

"Home is in your heart, and you've been waiting a long time to come home. Sometimes, I wonder if it ain't born in us—like something our parents pass on to us? Like maybe how heaven will seem when we get there." Gordie fumbled for the words he wanted.

"Built into our genes, is that what you're saying? Like home is written in our genes?" She smiled. "I think you're right, Gordie. I've dreamed of this day for so long and now that it's here, I'm scared to death, but I'm excited, too." She wiped her palms on her cotton slacks. "I just want her to like me—she doesn't have to love me, you know? I just want her to like me."

Gordie reached out and took her hand, glancing over at her. "She isn't going to like you, Wanda, she's going to love you—both of you." He squeezed her hand, "You figure out a name for her yet?"

"You sure are pushy, mister." she said, squeezing his hand back. "And did you know you only say *ain't* when you're upset or excited? Something I just noticed." She blushed. "Never mind. Just drive, okay?" Grinning, Gordie withdrew his hand and saluted, "Yes, ma'am."

And then they were there. He pulled into the long driveway and parked in front of the porch steps. "Want me to come in with you?" he asked.

Juanita shook her head, setting her pony tail in a wild dance. "Just hand me my bag of clothes and go on. If she throws me out, I'll walk back." She tried to smile through her trembling lips. "It's only a ten- or twelve-mile hike, right?"

Gordie reached into his pocket and pulled out a cell phone, handing it over to her. "Closer to fifteen miles. Here, take this phone. I don't know how to use it very well," he laughed, "but if you dial Miss Mary's number, push the green button, it's supposed to work—according to Sheriff Dan. You call, I'll come. I promise, Juanita IraLilly Edmonds." He reached out and touched her cheek. She covered his hand with hers and stared into his eyes.

"You know so much about me, how can you still care? And, I like it when you call me *Wanda*—like I'm special to you," her cheeks grew pink.

"Oh, you're special to me, all right," he said, trying to get his breath. Looking at her made his heart thump and his stomach feel queasy. "You're real special to me." Shaking himself, he pulled his hand back. "Call me when you want to come back home to Hilldale, okay?" She nodded.

He opened his door, pulled her bag from the backseat, and walked around to open her door. When she climbed out, she quickly kissed his cheek, then told him to leave. He did, but he stopped at the end of the driveway and looked back. She stood at the top of the steps and Gordie could see she hadn't knocked yet. Uncertain whether to leave or to wait, he finally decided to head back to Hilldale; she would call if she needed him, and Gordie knew this was something she had to do on her own. Knowing that didn't make him feel any better leaving her behind.

*****

Juanita heard the crunch of gravel beneath the tires as Gordie drove away. Panic stole her breath. She stood on the front porch, staring at the rusty screen doing its best to pull free of the old wooden door.

"Knock," she scolded herself, but paralyzed with fear, she couldn't bring her small fist up to rap her knuckles on the old wood.

Beyond the door, the girl could see the back of a tall woman dressed in a faded cotton print shirtwaist dress worn thin with too many years of use. The woman's hair was wound up in a large untidy bun at the nape of her neck, and she appeared to be washing dishes. If she heard the teenager on the porch, she never indicated it—just kept washing dishes, Juanita waiting fearfully on the other side.

Her chin thrust forward, Juanita rapped on the door, holding her breath, waiting for the woman to turn and look at her. Waiting for her first glimpse of her Grandma Wanda.

"Door's open," a husky voice said. Deep and melodic, like her mom's. Juanita's stomach did a little flip as she reached for the big wooden spool that served as a door handle. Pulling the screen door open, she stepped into a large farm kitchen, and stood uncertainly on a faded, hand-braided rag rug. The woman turned from the sink, took a step forward then stopped, thick white clouds of soap suds falling unnoticed from her large hands to the worn linoleum.

"It took you long enough," the old woman said, her voice not really angry, more tired than anything. "Could have been dead by now."

Juanita stared across the kitchen at her grandmother's wrinkled, freckled face, an older version of herself, the red hair faded to a rusty gray, the mouth, a bit soft with age, was her own wide, full-lipped mouth. And her chin! That's where she got her chin! *Ha*! she shouted triumphantly in silence.

"So, what do you see, girl?" Her grandmother stood before her, letting her get her fill of looking without scolding her, or turning away.

"Grandma," the teenager smiled with shy certainty. "I see my Grandma Wanda."

And then the tears came. First in droplets that rolled over her eyelashes and trickled down her cheeks, then in torrents, washing past her chin, a chin just like her grandmother's.

Only then did Wanda Harmon move from her place by the sink. Wiping her hands on her apron, she crossed the kitchen and enfolded her granddaughter against her soft, ample bosom. Juanita was home. She felt the welcome resonate deep within her loneliness. She felt the belonging. She recognized the thread that bound them with their ancestors further back than either of them could remember.

There were stories. Late into the evening, they talked over sweet tea and biscuits slathered with honey. When the two women grew too tired for talking, Juanita took fresh sheets upstairs and slept in her mother's bed.

Early morning brought the sun spilling across breakfast laid out on the old wooden table covered in a red-checkered oilcloth, warming the words that tumbled from her grandmother's memory. Stories that had waited so long to be told tripped over one another to get out into the light and leap joyfully into the waiting need of the young girl.

Juanita sat at her grandmother's table, delighting in the stories and the new experience of fresh-fried sausage stirred into milk gravy, poured generously over homemade biscuits. Never had she eaten such food! She devoured the stories along with the eggs she helped gather, whisked into a fluffy scrambled pile; a mountain of sunshine surrounded by the white-and-dark speckled milk-and-sausage gravy. She couldn't get enough—of the stories or the food.

It was as though she'd been starving all her life, and in truth, she had been. *I belong here. I belong to this woman I've never met, but I've always known. This is my home—our home,* Juanita's mind whispered to her heart, and to the tiny heart beating beneath hers.

Even through the smiles and laughter, the tears rolled down, wearing away the rough edges of the scars of abandonment, neglect, of living so long unwanted, unloved. She'd finally made it home and she could hardly bear it for the fear of losing it.

The third evening there, both women in tears, Wanda Harmon took her granddaughter in her arms, holding her, rocking her.

"Hush," she whispered into Juanita's mess of red curls, wiping the tears from her granddaughter's face with her work-worn hand. "You ain't going nowhere ever again, child. This is all yours. You're home, now. This old farm's been waiting for you all these years. Me too."

Juanita smiled up into her grandmother's wonderful, homey face. "Double negative, Grandma.

121

That means I am going somewhere. Say it right so I can stay, please."

Confused, the old woman gazed into her granddaughter's golden eyes, dark with yearning.

"This place is yours, child. I'm yours. Can't shake us loose, now. That plain enough?" And then she laughed, a deep satisfying laugh, as she held the child-woman close.

TWENTY-FIVE

Cassie stared at the man in front of her. "You're who?" she whispered, her heart drumming staccato, her stomach churning.

"Are you deaf as well as stupid?" Eddie Felton growled. The girl tethered to the iron bed cringed. He liked that. Smiling, he softened his voice, just to keep her guessing. "You know what small towns are like. I wanted to surprise an old friend, and you can't surprise someone if they know you're there, right? So, that's why I told you my name's Jeremy Blade."

Fear and anger warred for dominance in her. She held up her hands, tied to the sides of the bed, "Why do you think you have to tie me up? And this doesn't look like Las Vegas to me, Jeremy," she fumed.

"Eddie," he corrected her. "Hey, you were out of your head with that dope you were smoking..."

"You gave it to me!" she interrupted, her anger mixed with fear. "That wasn't just a plain joint, Jer—Eddie, you laced it with something else. Why? What's going on?"

"Like I said, I need your help surprising an old friend. I can't have you ruining my surprise, can

I? Now, I can take the ropes off you while I'm here, if you promise to be a good girl, or I can leave you tied up. It makes no difference to me. When I have to go for supplies, well, I'll have to tie you up again. Sure don't want you getting lost in these woods. Anyway, you'll feel better when my friend gets here, you'll see." He studied her expression, watching her weigh her options. "Don't even think of running. I'll catch you and you won't like what happens then." She nodded, and he leaned close to her face.

"Okay. I'm going to take off the ropes, Cassie," he eyed her, a dark warning flashing from his eyes. "I don't want you trying anything, understand? You do, and I'll leave you tied up—tight—diaper and all, tight—got it?" His stare sent ice through her veins. Nodding, she promised, hating herself for her fear.

Eddie untied her, then helped her stand up. He touched the bruise on her face. She winced and pulled away from his hand. "Sorry about that," he smiled, not looking the least bit sorry, "but you had it coming, screaming and cursing like a crazy woman. Come on, let's get something to eat. You can use the restroom on your own—get cleaned up, then help me in the kitchen."

As he led her from the bedroom, she saw the locks on the doors, the Styrofoam insulation and plywood nailed across the bathroom and kitchen windows, just like the bedroom windows. With fear racing through her, Cassie Red Feather Calloway realized she wasn't the crazy one here. Trembling with that knowledge, she quickly used the restroom, then followed the man she thought was her ticket out of Hilldale, into the rundown kitchen.

"I'll cook," he said, looking at her, "and you clean up the dishes and counter tops. Wipe that table off, too. We can eat out here, because, " he glared at her, "I'm sick of waiting on you and cleaning up after you." Shocked by the vehemence behind his orders and the look he gave her, without a word, she obeyed.

TWENTY-SIX

"I haven't heard from Wanda," Gordie said, sipping a glass of ice water. "She's got my cell phone and she's supposed to call me when she wants to come back to Hilldale," he sighed, looking at Dan. "I thought she'd call, just to—you know—maybe tell me she's okay." His voice drifted into silence.

"I haven't heard anything about Cassie Calloway and it's been over a week. An army buddy of mine, who works security in Vegas, said he's checked all the hotels and motels in the area and there's no one registered under Felton, Blade, Calloway—he didn't take her to Vegas. My gut says she's still around here, and I need to be finding her." Dan sighed, sipped his cola and looked at the young man across from him.

"Aren't we the pathetic duo?" He tried to laugh, but didn't quite make it. "Here we are sitting in Neely's Cafe worrying about women." He sighed again. "At least my wife and your girl are safe. It's Cassie I'm worried about. Who knows what's happened to her? That Felton scares me silly. I don't think he'd blink an eye getting rid of her, if he thought she was in his way. All I can hope for is that he needs her for whatever he's got planned." Looking at Gordie, he continued, "Why not take a drive out to Wanda Harmon's farm and check on Juanita. Or, I could ask Mary Harmon to call and check on her?" Dan grinned. "Of course, it'd be more fun for you to go to the farm, see for yourself that she's all right."

Not appearing to realize the sheriff was teasing him, Gordie nodded, a serious expression wrinkling his face. "Good idea, Sheriff Dan. If she gets mad at me, I can always tell her you sent me to check on her." He grinned back at Dan.

Shaking his head, the sheriff laughed. "Son, you catch on quick! Here I was, taking you seriously and you're making jokes."

"It's only partly a joke," Gordie smiled. "I've been looking for a good reason to head to the Harmon place, and seems to me this is as good a reason as any."

"My shoulders are broad," Dan said. "If you need to use me for an excuse to visit your girl, well, guess that's the way it is." He looked up as he felt a hand on his arm.

"Hello Tina," he smiled at the waitress. "What's going on?"

"Carter's worried about Juanita—and truth be known—I am, too," she replied. "She's been here such a short time, but it appears we've both gotten spoiled by that girl. She's a good worker, and honest as can be. Any word on how she's doing, Danny?" She sat in the chair next to Dan, absently wiping at a spot on the table.

"Nothing yet," he said. "Gordie's thinking of going out to Wanda Harmon's and checking on how they're getting along. Would have been fun being a mouse in the corner when those two gals met."

"Well, let us know if you hear anything, will you?" She looked at the sheriff and then at the young man sitting across the table. With that, she pushed up from her chair, and headed back to the kitchen.

Gordie smiled. "Now I have two good reasons to check on her!"

*****

He wasted no time heading out to the Harmon place. Nerves caused him to feel a little nauseated and Gordie laughed at himself. "Being in love feels a little like having the flu!" He turned off the blacktop and headed down the gravel road, noting the huge clouds of white dust whirling up around him, drifting on the wind to the side of the road, leaving the weeds and trees looking like a winter painting.

Pulling up to the farmhouse, he took a deep breath and reached for the door handle. Just as he started to push the car door open, Juanita came bounding out of the screen door, swiftly moving down the porch steps, grabbing the door handle, opening it for him. She threw her arms around his neck and gave him a quick hug.

Breathless, Gordie laughed. "Okay, I'm leaving you at your Gramma Wanda's more often." Straightening up, he hugged her again, amazed at how natural it felt to have her in his arms. Her eyes lit with joy. He smiled down at her, blushing when she stretched on her tippy-toes and gave him a kiss on the cheek. "I don't need to ask how it's going. You look great," he said. Stepping back, she took his hand and led him inside the house.

"Grandma, this is Gordie. Gordie Adam Bently."

Gordie moved to take the older woman's hand, but she pulled him into her arms, and her tears fell on his shoulder. "You look so like your ma, young man." She smiled, pushing him back so she could study his face. "And I can see your Gramma Sarah in you. You've got her eyes, your ma got

126

them, too. My, and you sure enough got your gramma's smile."

Startled, Gordie looked at Wanda Harmon. "You're my Gramma Sarah's best friend! Ma used to tell me about your red hair and how the sun lit it up like fire." He smiled, shyness lowering his eyes to the worn linoleum.

Wanda's voice softened. "That we were. Best of friends until she took up with Bently. He didn't cotton to Sarah or Neva Sue having any friends. Then after Sarah died, why Sarah Elaine never hardly saw your ma, and them two friends since they were babies. Didn't even know about you until a few years back, Gordie. Sorry about your ma, son. I'm right proud to meet you." She patted his hands still cradled in hers.

"Reckon you can stay and share our noon meal? I'm trying to teach this young 'un to cook something besides food out of a can. She's doing just fine, if I do say so myself." Laughing, she let go of Gordie's hands and pulled her granddaughter into a hug. "Well, we'd best get to fixing more potatoes now we got company." She turned back to the sink full of garden vegetables.

The three settled into a comfortable pace of scrubbing potatoes, slicing carrots, onions, and celery, which went into the pot of simmering broth. Gordie's mouth watered, and the women laughed when they heard his stomach growl.

"I was in such a hurry to get here and check on you, I forgot to eat breakfast—and I was right there at Neely's, too. Tina said to tell you they miss you. She said you spoiled them, you're such a good worker."

Juanita grinned, blushing with happiness. "See," she chortled, "I told you I was doing a good job at the cafe. I really like working there, too. You should come have lunch with us one of these days, Grandma." She leaned her head against her grandmother's shoulder for a quick moment, then resumed scrubbing and chunking carrots.

Gordie finished chopping up the celery and onions slipping the pieces in the simmering stew pot. Juanita followed with the carrots, and Grandma Wanda added the scrubbed and quartered potatoes. Replacing the lid on the large pan, she turned, "Why don't you two get yourselves a glass of iced tea and go out on the porch swing? Enjoy the sun. I do believe I'll catch a cat nap. This pot will cook better without us watching it."

Out on the porch, Gordie and Juanita sipped their cold drinks while they visited, a light breeze keeping the heat from becoming oppressive. Grandma Wanda dozed in her recliner, soft snores drifting through the open window. The day lay peaceful, and contentment filled the two young people side-by-side on the swing.

"I'll come back to Hilldale with you, Gordie," Juanita said. "Doc Ridley wants me to come see him about the baby. I had another ultrasound and he's going to show me a picture of her." She smiled up at the young man swinging next to her.

"Want to come see little Wanda Marie?" she laughed. "Hey! That rhymed." She looked up at Gordie, "You can meet me at Doc's and see what she looks like. I can show you the pictures later, if you're busy."

"I'd love to come see her! You gave her a beautiful name, Wanda—uh—Juanita. Guess I'd best start calling you by your rightful name, now we'll have two Wanda's." He pushed a curly strand of hair from her cheek. "It's great, you letting me come to Doc's with you. I want to be part of her life—yours, too, if that's okay with you."

Juanita stared across the farm yard at the dusty trees swaying and tossing their branches in the breeze. Turning back to him, she said, "I do want you to be involved, as much as you want to be, Gordie. Actually, I wondered if you would attend birth classes with me, and be there when Little Wanda is born. Maybe you would drive me to class instead of asking Aunt Mary?" She hesitated, then grinned ruefully, "I'm pretty scared. I've been doing some reading, and they say it hurts a lot, but I figure if you're there, I've got someone to punch when I need to."

Gordie couldn't believe what he'd just heard. "Of course I'll take the classes with you! You can punch me as much as you want, but I get to hold Little Wanda all I want. Deal?"

She raised her hand, and he took it in his. "Deal," she said, grinning from ear-to-ear.

Wanda listened to her granddaughter and Sarah Bently's grandson. The girl was going to do all right with that young man. He had a gentleness about him, like his mother and grandmother, and Juanita having a baby didn't seem to put him off. She could see how he loved Juanita, and it appeared to her, her granddaughter loved him—she just hadn't figured it out yet.

Wanda. She smiled to herself. That little baby was going to be named after her. She drifted off to sleep again, the young folks' hushed conversation like music to her heart. It had been a long time since she'd heard that here at the farm.

After they'd eaten and cleaned up the dishes, the two young people took their leave and headed back to Hilldale, promising to return often for visits. When Gordie parked in front of Miss Mary's house, he turned to Juanita. "I want you to think about something. Don't answer me right away—think on what I'm going to say. I've given it a lot of thought and I've talked some to Sheriff Dan and Papa Muley, so this ain't just off the top of my head, okay?" He watched her face letting her see his love for her radiating from his eyes. She nodded. He swallowed and took her hand, holding it gently.

"I've been studying on what happens when you have Little Wanda. I have enough money to help you, and you don't have to live with me, or anything, but if we got married before she was born, she could have my name, and you two would have enough to live on without you having to work, at least for a while. I mean, she's going to need her ma for a while, right? And, well, I never knew my Pa—well, the way a kid should know his Pa—and I'd be right proud to marry you and give that little girl my name." He gulped, shivered, and squeezed her hand. "Besides, I love you, Juanita. Have since I first laid eyes on you and all that hair sparking fire in the store. I ain't never felt nothing like this and I don't reckon I ever will again. At least think about it, will you?"

His summer-sky eyes warmed her heart. "I'll think about it, Gordie, but I'm sure leaning toward saying *yes*. I just can't imagine why or how you can love me, but I see it—I feel it when I'm around you, and I think I love you, too. That kind of love isn't something I've ever known, and it scares me about as much as having this baby. You don't have to pay for us, I'll work and pay my way. But giving Little Wanda a daddy—someone I can trust and know will protect her and love her like a daddy's supposed to—you'd be my first choice."

She slid across the seat into his arms and the two sat silently soaking in each other's emotions. Finally, Juanita pulled away and reached for the door handle. "You think about your offer, and I will, too. When you're ready to talk about it again, you let me know. Oh, and classes start next week. I can let you know the time when I see you again, okay?" She took the cell phone from her pocket, handed it to him, and pushed the door open. Gordie handed her the bag of clothing from the back seat.

"I won't change my mind," he said, a grin plastered across his face. "Way I got it figured, you got less than two months before Little Wanda's born, so reckon that's long enough for you to study on it. I'll see you at Neely's tomorrow."

"Doc says nearly three more months, and yes, I'll see you at Neely's tomorrow." She grinned back at him and headed up the sidewalk to the front door. Before she went inside, she turned and waved to the young man who would be her little girl's father. Juanita knew in her heart he would love and care for her child as though she were his own. Watching him pull away from the curb, she noticed the old man who lived across the street spying on them, a scowl on his face. Quickly turning, she went inside and closed the door.

TWENTY-SEVEN

"Three weeks," Cassie muttered, despair bringing tears to her eyes. She took the long nail she'd found under the bed and scratched another notch on the scarred wooden molding behind the door. "Give or take a couple of days I don't remember, it must be about the middle, or end of August." She rubbed her head, trying to focus. Tears fell in earnest.

Eddie had established a routine with her and everything she did, everything she ate, even when she ate, he controlled. Her stomach felt queasy. Having refused breakfast that morning, there would be no food until he returned to the farm house—and she never knew when that would be.

He'd said he was going to Columbia to get supplies, and sickened, she'd realized her birth control pills were nearly finished. She had to ask him to get her prescription for her, and to get her personal items, as well. Humiliation had washed over her leaving her weak. He'd acted disgusted, told her to forget her pills and he'd have to see about the other items. No birth control—what would she do if she got pregnant by him?

The way she had it figured, her chances of getting out alive appeared to be zero. He couldn't afford to let her go—she'd tell the police what he'd done. Why had he kept her alive this long? The friend he'd been talking about since he'd brought her here had never materialized. When he left her alone, he no longer tied her to the bed, he just locked her in the bedroom. Though there was no running water, she was grateful that there was a bathroom connecting the bedroom, and a five-gallon pail with a lid for a toilet, and another filled with clean water for washing up.

Finishing ten sit-ups, Cassie shifted on the dusty braided area rug. She had tried picking the lock to the bedroom door, then the connecting door from the bathroom into the kitchen, but what looked so easy on television didn't work so well in real life. She rolled over and did a few girlie pushups. Then she did ten more sit-ups. Standing up, she stretched her leg muscles, touching her toes, then reached high for the cracked-plaster ceiling before she began to jog in place, breathing deeply. If only she could get some fresh air in here, feel the sun and the wind on her face. Exhaustion seeped through her. She'd started talking aloud to herself when Eddie left her locked in the bedroom. The sound of her voice soothed her, as though someone else shared captivity with her.

"Mom, Grandma," she panted, still running in place, "I'm sorry. I wish I could tell you in person, even if you yelled at me, I wish I was there with you." Her tears slid freely down her face, as her breath came in short gasps. She slowed her pace. "Out of shape," she wheezed, before crumbling back down on the rug, sobs wracking her body.

"No one will ever find me," she wept to the empty room. "My family will never know what happened to me." Curling into a ball, Cassie cried herself to sleep. A slender ray of sunshine found its way through a crack in the insulated plywood boards, and crept slowly across her thinning body, as though it wished to comfort her for as long as possible.

*****

The toe of a boot in her ribs woke her. Sitting up, she saw Eddie standing over her, holding a book in his hand. "I got you a book on how babies are born. It explains how to deliver a baby in an emergency, and it has great pictures." Excitement lit his eyes as he squatted down beside her. Handing her the book, he said, "Read it. Study it, so you know what to do."

Confusion wrinkled her forehead. "There's no way I'm going to have a baby here. And there's

133

absolutely no way I'm delivering one for someone else! I'd pass out, I'd throw up...." Before she could continue, a sharp slap struck her cheek sending her over sideways on the rug.

"Shut up!" Eddie yelled, his face turning red. "Just shut up. You'll do what I say, or you'll wish you had." He dropped the book in front of her along with a small spiral notebook and an ink pen. "I figure you have a month or two to learn everything that's in that book. When my friend gets here, she may need your help." His voice faltered for a moment before he continued, "I don't know much about the birth process, but you will learn. You're a woman, and you're supposed to know this stuff. Read it, get it in your head. You may need to use it." He stood and stared down at her, disgust twisting his mouth.

"Get yourself cleaned up. I'm going to take you outside and show you where to dump your slop, where to get clean water. It's time you started doing some of the work around here. You get your chores done, I brought some Chinese food for us." His voice slipped into his smooth, easy-going tone.

"Keeping busy will be the best thing for you, Cassie. It's tough for you to be alone so much, but there are folks who've got it a lot worse than you. At least you've got a roof over your head, food, and me. Now get up and get going."

As though they were sitting at the kitchen table having a normal conversation instead of captor to prisoner, he continued, "I bought the parts to get the generator fixed, and who knows, maybe in a few days, we'll have running water and lights! How about that?" He smiled, expecting her to show him gratitude. When she nodded without enthusiasm, he swore at her and stomped out of the room, ordering her to haul her slop and water pail out to the kitchen.

Still on the floor, Cassie picked up the notebook and pen. Eddie might want her to take notes on birthing babies, but she had another idea. She would find a good place to hide notes, somewhere he wouldn't find them.

Trembling, she looked around the room. Someday, maybe someone would find them and contact her mom and Grandma Ellen. Cassie took small comfort in the thought, but felt a bit better having a plan. A plan Eddie Felton knew nothing about.

TWENTY-EIGHT

The last week of August simmered with heat and humidity, and feeling nearly as big as a house, Juanita found as many reasons as possible to stay inside in the air conditioning. Aunt Mary refused to let her mow the yard, or pull weeds, hiring the neighbor kids to do those jobs, finding easy indoor chores for the very pregnant young woman.

Sitting in Doc Ridley's office, Juanita listened as he explained what he'd found in her latest exam.

"You need to let Carter know you can't haul heavy trays, scrub the floors, or do any reaching over your head for—well, for whatever you reach over your head for," he finished lamely. "Far as I can tell, you're most likely to deliver early October. Looks like your little gal is growing at a normal pace and you seem like you're doing pretty well. You've put on a little weight, but I'd sure like to see a few more pounds before next month. Most of my mother's-to-be get the opposite instructions." He smiled, his bushy mustache covering the bottom of his nose.

Smiling back at him, she climbed down from the table and buttoned her sleeveless shirt arranging it over her cotton shorts. "Yah, okay, thanks Doc," she said. "I try to eat more, but I think Little Wanda is taking up any extra room I have." They laughed and he patted her shoulder.

"Well, Juanita, keep up the good work. You're healthy, and I really don't anticipate any delivery problems. Are you attending Lamaze classes?"

"I am," she answered, blushing. "Gordie Bently takes me. He's the man I brought with me to see Little Wanda's picture. He'll be my coach and he's agreed to be in the labor room with me. We're not sure about the delivery room, yet."

Surprised, Doc scratched his chin, smoothed his mustache, and said, "Yes, I know Gordie Bently. He's a fine young man and I imagine he'll be a great . coach, if he can stand seeing you through your contractions. Are you two an item, as we used to say in my day?"

Still blushing, Juanita looked up into the doctor's eyes, noting the kindness there. Nodding, she answered, "He's asked me to marry him before the baby's born, you know, give her his name and everything."

Doc said, "You two are young, but it has to be your choice. At least now, one of my questions is answered," He made a note on her chart, closed the file and opened the door for her. "He's been paying your account. In fact, he's recently paid a substantial credit for further appointments, and said he would be responsible for your hospital bill. Like I said, he's a fine young man."

Juanita looked embarrassed, nodding as the doctor followed her from the room. "Thanks, Doc Ridley," she murmured. "I've tried to tell him I can pay for myself."

Doc smiled, patting her shoulder. "Never mind, young lady. The boy has been through a lot, and yet, he's kind and compassionate. Probably because he's never played those cursed video games we hear so much about." He laughed. "They get blamed for everything from muggings to murder, and I suppose they can be an influence, but I think all the ingredients need to be there, before the cake is baked."

Juanita looked confused and shook her head, "The cake is baked...?"

"Never mind," he said, rubbing the back of his head. "I get detoured way too easily these days. I suppose it's my age." Looking at Juanita, he said, "Make an appointment for early September and we'll see where you're at. My money is still on around October 9th." He walked over to the only other closed examine room door and pulled a file from its holder on the wall. Tapping lightly, he entered the room, closing the door behind him.

Juanita left the office with her appointment slip and a new bottle of prenatal vitamins. She'd grown considerably in the past few weeks, and though Doc said she needed to gain weight, she felt huge. As she walked slowly down the sidewalk toward Miss Mary's, her mind went over and over Gordie's proposal. Did he really love her or just feel sorry for her? She didn't want to marry him because he pitied her or her unborn child. She'd always dreamed of loving someone who would love her back. Never having seen or felt that kind of love, she doubted her ability to choose wisely, for herself, and for her baby.

Trying to fathom just what she did want, Juanita tried to see herself as Gordie and others saw her. A mouthy red-head, a used up woman—no scratch that—she wasn't even a woman yet, was she? She was seventeen. What man in his right mind would want her—used, damaged goods, all that baggage, and a baby, too? How would she ever trust a man with her daughter? Questions whirled around in her head.

Could Gordie be for real? He seemed to care about her baby and she wasn't even born. She wanted to believe he was what he appeared to be. Could he see past her tarnished surface to the person she longed to be, the one she worked so hard to become? Did she even dare to hope again? She'd been that route before and knew how often hope was lost to the cruel life she'd been forced to live. She sighed. Trust was not her strong suit.

Aunt Mary had talked to her about God and his son, Jesus. How much he loved her, right where she was, just as she was. She'd urged Juanita to let God work out the problems in her life, to let Him put all the broken pieces of her life back together, bring her healing from the past, but Juanita wasn't sure. If God was so good, why would He want to hang around her? Heck! Why did He let that stuff happen to her in the first place? A tiny voice whispered in her heart, "What about Gordie? You know he's a good young man who's suffered as you have, and he wants to hang around you."

Arriving at the house, she pushed open the front door and went inside. Aunt Mary stood in the kitchen arranging freshly washed grapes, ripe purple plums, and fuzzy kiwi fruit in a large red bowl that caught the sunlight streaming in from the kitchen window, splashing it out over the counter in brilliant red splinters.

"Aunt Mary?" Mary Harmon looked up from her task and smiled at the slightly flushed young woman in front of her. Taking a deep breath, Juanita's words tumbled out, "I want what you said. I want Jesus to come into my heart, to help me sort out my life. I want Him to love me and forgive me, like you said," she finished lamely.

Joy lit Mary's face. "Of course, my dear. He's been waiting for you, and all of heaven is rejoicing right now." She moved around the table, took Juanita into her arms and held the trembling child-woman close to her heart. There in her Aunt Mary's kitchen, Juanita surrendered to the Savior who thought she was worth dying for.

Like the story of Lazarus, pastor had read them, she felt the stone from her tomb removed. She felt, rather than heard, the deep rumbling, gentle thunder that called her forth. In her heart's eye, she saw herself rise from the dark grave of her past and move into the light, and as she did, Juanita IraLilly Edmonds felt the filthy, stinking rags of her sorrows, betrayals, and abandonment fall away from her, and a sweet perfume filled her nostrils. Her tears mingled with her Aunt Mary's, and Juanita knew beyond the shadow of a doubt, she had come home.

TWENTY-NINE

Eddie looked in the rear-view mirror of the beat-up, faded green Ford 150 he'd just purchased. "Good!" he congratulated himself, noting the full beard, mustache, and almost shoulder-length hair. Flush with cash from a few backroom, high stakes poker games, and two ATM rip offs he'd pulled down at the Lake of the Ozarks, he'd dumped the Escort station wagon and bought the older pickup. "Fits right in with those small town hayseeds," he gloated at the unfamiliar image in the mirror. "In fact, seems like I saw one just like this with some old man hauling watermelons. Nobody will pay any attention to me." Laughing at his brilliance, he entered the highway. "Now, the lumber yard."

It was after one when he returned to the abandoned farm. He backed inside the barn and unloaded his building supplies. He might have to hide out longer than he planned, and he wanted the house secure for Juanita and their child, and for Cassie, at least until she helped deliver his son—for he was certain, with his luck, the child would be a boy. He would be named after him, and Eddie hoped the kid would have his smarts. The world held enough stupid humans and he wanted his kid to be like him—clever, an achiever.

He'd been gone over night, so he'd locked Cassie in her bedroom with a fresh bucket of water, a clean slop pail, and a couple of peanut butter sandwiches. With the bottles of drinking water, he'd left a treat for her—a can of Mountain Dew. It'd be warm, but still, she should appreciate his thoughtfulness.

Unloading the last sheet of plywood, he added it to the pile of two-by-fours, dusted his jeans off, and headed to the house. Satisfaction filled him. He figured he'd have the generator running by the next evening. The pump had been cleaned and put in working order, and he'd bought all new fuses for the old fuse box in the pantry. With the windows shuttered over with plywood and insulated Styrofoam sheets, they would be able to have lights in the evening, run the small space heaters he'd purchased for the cool evenings that would soon arrive, and best of all, he would order Cassie to use the electric cook stove.

He unlocked the new screen door, then the heavily reinforced wooden front door. Entering the dusky stillness, he stopped for a moment, listening. Scowling, he headed for the bedroom. The crazy woman was crying and talking to herself again! She'd better straighten up before Juanita arrived. He wouldn't tolerate her ungrateful behavior around his soon-to-be-bride, and mother of his son. Turning the key in the lock, he kicked the bedroom door open and pushed into the dim room. Cowering on the floor, the emaciated Cassie Calloway threw her arms over her head, knowing what was coming. Mercifully, with the first blow she faded into darkness.

THIRTY

Dan hung up the telephone and re-read the notes he'd scrawled on the paper in front of him. A Ford Escort wagon matching the description of Eddie Felton's car had been found near Camdenton, abandoned in the thick undergrowth of a wooded area not far from the highway. A worker from MODOT spotted it when he was picking up trash from the ditches along the road. The sun glinting off the windshield had caught his attention, and after examining the car, decided it was recently abandoned, and it looked like it'd been deliberately covered with brush. He'd called the highway patrol, and once they'd investigated the car, they'd called Dan.

The officer explained to him the vehicle appeared to be stripped clean of papers, license, personal items, and dusting for fingerprints offered nothing. The Escort had been towed to the impound yard in Jefferson City, and after running the VIN number and ascertaining the registration belonged to an address in Zumbrota, Minnesota, the highway patrol contacted the owner who told them they'd sold it in a cash deal to one John Brown Smith. HP informed Dan the car most likely belonged to Eddie Felton, and it now awaited the sheriff's inspection.

Dan and his deputy, Randy Carter, went through the Escort a second time. Nothing had been found that could tell them where Felton had taken Cassie Calloway, but one thing was for sure, it wasn't Las Vegas.

Randy, meticulously working through the front of the car, returned his attention to the empty glove compartment. He'd already removed the front seat, checked the creases and cracks along the dashboard, and now he had his flashlight trained at the back of the box. Slowly, he swept the light across the recessed area, inch-by-inch.

"Dan," he called to the back of the Escort, where the sheriff had removed the rear floor that covered the storage compartment. Dan looked up at his deputy.

"Find something?" he asked.

Randy held up a short sales slip, squinting at the typed information. "Missed this the first time through. It was stuck down in the seam at the back of the glove box. Says it's from a bookstore in Camdenton. Land sakes, Dan, it's a book on delivering babies!" The deputy's eyes went wide with surprise, then his mouth tightened. Staring at his friend and employer, Randy said, "He's planning on delivering Juanita's baby. We've got to stop him."

142

Dan crawled from the rear of the Escort and walked up to the front of the station wagon. Taking the sales slip, he held it up to read for himself. Frowning, he took a zip lock bag from his pocket and slipped the piece of paper inside, sealing it.

"Doesn't look good, does it?" he said. Handing the bag to Randy to add to the tiny bits of evidence they'd collected, he rubbed his chin. "I'm going to call Gordie and the station, get someone to pick up Juanita and stay with her at Mary Harmon's. This Felton guy is crazy on top of dangerous, thinking he can deliver that baby using a book. Wonder where Cassie fits in all of this?"

Taking his cell phone from his pocket, he called the station and asked Vicki to send Jeff Springer after Juanita, informing his receptionist that the girl was most likely at Neely's. Then he dialed Gordie's cell phone number and waited for the young man to answer.

"Hello?" Gordie said, his breath coming in short huffs.

"Gordie? You okay? This is Dan."

"Kissie's calf took out a section of pasture fence and I just finished fixing it. That little stinker sure likes to jump. Reckon he thinks he can jump higher than he really can. Got his back legs hung up."

"Everything under control?" the sheriff asked, in a hurry to get to his reason for calling.

"Yep," replied the young man, his breathing settling down. "What's up?"

"Listen, Gordie, I need you to get over to Mary Harmon's place and stay with Juanita. We found Felton's station wagon and there's a sales slip showing he bought a book on delivering babies. Date on it says he bought it two days ago. We're not

143

taking any chances with him getting hold of her. Jeff Springer is picking her up at work and bringing her home. He'll stay until you show up." Dan's voice carried a note of anxiety that transferred itself to Gordie.

"Soon as I let Papa Muley know where I'm going, I'm on my way." The phone went dead.

Hanging up, Dan asked Randy to stay with the car and continue searching it, while he headed back to his office. Midway to Hilldale, his cell phone rang. He pulled to the side of the road and answered it.

"Dan?" Jeff Springer asked.

"Go ahead, Jeff," the sheriff replied, a feeling of dread lacing his words.

"She's not at Neely's. I'm headed to Mary Harmon's right now. You reckon she's out walking, or with Gordie?" Jeff sounded nervous.

"She's not with Gordie, I just talked with him a minute ago. Has Carter seen her at all today?"

"I asked him, and he said she never showed up for work. He didn't think anything about it because Doc wanted her to take it a bit easier. He did say she usually calls in, but didn't this morning."

Dan's heart sank. "If she's not at Miss˙ Mary's, call Doc Ridley, I think she had an appointment sometime today—no, better yet, drive over there. See if she's out walking. See if she's at Doc's. If she's not there, then make sure Gordie's at Miss Mary's. Call me right back. Thanks, Jeff."

Dan closed his phone returning it to its holder on the dash. His mouth was dry and fear prickled his scalp. Eddie Felton had Juanita. He'd stake his badge on it. They were too late, and now that creep had both girls and a book on how to deliver a baby. Dan's throat constricted and he sat silent, parked at the side of the highway, praying and not even remembering the words that flowed from his heart to the Father.

And then he called Gordie back.

THIRTY-ONE

Juanita forced her breathing to calm. The bearded man driving the truck looked pleased with himself, glancing over at her as she huddled as close to the passenger door as possible.

"Hey, don't let the beard and long hair fool you, kid, it's me. You knew I'd come back for you." Eddie Felton gave her a hard look. "You can't run far enough, Juanita. I'll always find you. But hey, you won't be running anymore will you? Now that you're carrying my son, you really have to let me take good care of you, and that means we stick together. A family, that's what we are." He smiled, his teeth glinting through his dark beard.

Swallowing her fear, Juanita glared at her abductor. "You have to let me go, Eddie. The sheriff and my friends will be looking for me, and when they find you've kidnapped me, you'll be in big trouble." Her voice wobbled.

"That hayseed sheriff couldn't find his ridiculous hat sitting on top of his head. Friends? You think someone like you has friends? Wait and see, kid. They'll forget you ever existed. I'm your ticket, baby. I'm your man, the father of your kid—our kid. We're going to be a family. You'll get used to it, wait and see."

Juanita refused to look at him, not responding to his claim on her and the baby harbored inside her. A picture flashed through her terrified mind: Aunt Mary standing with her arms wrapped lovingly around her, praying the salvation prayer, sunbeams lighting the pleasant kitchen. Peace flowed from the memory into her thoughts. radiating warmth throughout her body. Little Wanda did a flip and kicked her soundly. Juanita almost laughed out loud. Placing her hand over her bulging abdomen, she prayed.

Please let Aunt Mary be okay. I don't know how to pray like her, Lord, but I'm asking You to keep Little Wanda and me safe from this man. I don't know why all this is happening to me, but please don't let me find my grandma, my Aunt Mary, Gordie, and all the people who've become my friends just to let me lose them all again. Please. Thanks. That's all, Lord.

Little Wanda dug her toes into Juanita's ribs as though letting her mother know she was in agreement with her prayer, and the young woman felt a sense of peace settle over her. Turning to her abductor she stated, "This is not your baby, Eddie, and it's not a boy. It's a girl and I've named her Wanda after my grandma. I found her and she's never stopped looking for me, never stopped waiting for me to come home. She won't stop now, and when she finds me, you will be in big trouble. My Grandma Wanda isn't anyone to mess with. And Sheriff Dan, Gordie, Aunt Mary, and Mr. Neely . . ." Her voice faded into joyful realization. She was loved. Someone would come for her, would search until they found her and her baby. For the first time in her life, Juanita felt she was not alone. Fear fled as that knowledge took hold and blossomed within her.

She was loved.

Eddie drove in angry silence. How dare the girl defy him. He'd have to be careful until his son was born, then he'd teach her who was in charge. She'd learn. Just like before, he would teach her obedience, respect. As her husband, he would have the right to all this and more. As far as he was concerned, that baby couldn't come fast enough. His hands clenched the steering wheel as he turned from the blacktop onto the gravel road that would take them to the old farmhouse.

Eddie looked over at the girl. "I have a present for you, babe. Someone to help you deliver our son, take care of you until he's born, even take care of you after our baby is born—for a little while anyway. We won't need her for long, though, will we." His smile sent shivers through Juanita, and fear tried to reclaim her heart and mind.

THIRTY-TWO

Obed Martin watched the bearded man pull the girl out of Miss Mary's house, watched the girl struggle as the man strong-armed her down the sidewalk, forcing her into an old Ford pickup idling at the curb.

"'Bout time someone got that trollop out of Miss Mary's," the old man grumbled, watching the truck drive away. Then Dan's words echoed in his head. Another thought brought him to his kitchen door and outside, pushing him quickly toward Mary Harmon's house. *Had that bearded fella hurt Miss Mary?* he wondered, fear stinging his conscience. When he reached the front door he found it ajar. Stepping into the hallway, Obed called out to his old friend and neighbor.

"Help!" A weak cry came from the living room. He hurried toward the plea for help and found

Mary Harmon lying on the carpet, her left leg twisted beneath her.

"Oh, Obed! Thank the Lord you came so quickly. You've got to call Dan. Tell him that awful man took Juanita. Oh, that poor child." Groaning with pain, Mary tried to push herself up. She fell back to the floor. "My leg is broken, Obed. Hurry. Call Dan and then call Doc Ridley." With that, Mary Harmon slipped into unconsciousness.

Obed raced to the kitchen where he dialed 911 asking the dispatcher to send the sheriff and an ambulance. Then he dialed Doc Ridley's number demanding to speak to his old friend. Satisfied that Doc was on his way, Obed went back to Miss Mary's side, covering her limp body with a crocheted cover he pulled from the back of the couch.

As he sat and waited for help to arrive, Obed thought of the girl and a spark of fear mixed with shame ignited in his heart. Maybe he was wrong about that wee bit of trouble. Seemed most folks had taken to her, even with all her flaws. Worry creased his forehead. *Don't reckon he'll kill her, what with her being with child and all,* he thought. But Obed remembered the times he'd seen the man watching the house, watching the girl. He'd have to find her, save her from that man, redeem himself with Danny—*and with you too, Lord*, he thought, remembering his own need for forgiveness, and how his estranged son had freely given it to him two summers ago. Someone was knocking at Miss Mary's door and hollering for her. Looking up, Obed groaned with relief as Deputy Jeff Springer hurried toward them.

THIRTY-THREE
Gordie fell to his knees the phone dropping from his hand. He'd just finished informing Muley about Juanita's disappearance when he'd answered Dan's second call.

"Lad!" cried Muley as he watched Gordie's face twist in anguish, tears running down his scarred cheeks. "Gordie, lad, what's wrong? What happened?" Muley's voice trembled with fear.

"Wanda," the young man groaned, "Someone took Wanda and hurt Miss Mary. His voice grew to a cry of agony as his body shuddered. "That awful man took Wanda."

Confusion rattled Muley for a moment. Wanda? Why would anyone want to kidnap that ornery old woman? And what did Mary Harmon have to do with it? And then his brain kicked in and he realized the boy was talking about Juanita. "Lord have mercy, we gotta help Danny find her. Get yourself up and stop that there noise. We got work to do. You get the car, I'll meet you out front. Get on with you, lad. We'll find her."

The old man steadied the younger one as he stood up and gently pushed him toward the door. Gordie ran for the barn where his car was parked. Never before had he felt the need to mortally hurt someone. Even when his grandfather had whipped his Ma, himself, the dogs, he'd felt sadness, even anger, but he'd never wanted to physically retaliate to the point of his grandfather's destruction. But now, fear mingled with rage and grew like a storm whirling within him. *I will kill him*, he whispered—then shouted the words to the clouds that scuttled by.

THIRTY-FOUR

Eddie unlocked the heavy wooden door and pushed it open. Inside, a dim light cast a gloomy pall over a meagerly furnished large room. Faded wallpaper, water-stained and torn in places added to the gloominess of the room. Boards over the windows blocked all but tiny shafts of sunlight forcing their way through the cracks, and dust fairies danced their welcome as Juanita stepped inside.

"Welcome home, kid." Felton looked around the room. "I know it isn't much but once our son is born, we'll move north. I got connections that'll help us get on our feet. For now, you got the run of the kitchen, this room, and you share a bathroom with Cassie." He looked at Juanita, measuring her response. "She's the surprise. She's going to help you have the baby, take good care of you, you'll see. If she doesn't," his voice turned soft with cruelty, "she'll wish she had."

Juanita turned and faced her abductor. "You can't keep me here. And that girl, Cassie? You got to let her go, too. You're going to get caught. Just leave and let us go, Eddie. We won't tell. Just leave and by the time we're found, you can be long gone, across the Canadian border, wherever you want to go. I promise," her voice faded knowing he wasn't listening to her.

Grabbing her arm, Eddie pulled her toward another door leading into a bathroom, then through another door that led into a room nearly identical to the one she'd just been in. In the dank dusty dimness, Juanita saw a figure curled into the fetal position on a rug. Eddie walked over to the figure and toed it into life. A pale haunted face lifted, cheeks gaunt, dark eyes dull, listless. Juanita gasped. This was the girl from the convenience store! The one who always seemed so sure of herself, sassy, bored, and angry with life. Fear crept like ice through her veins. What had Eddie done to her?

"Get up, you lazy slut," their captor growled. "Show some respect for my soon-to-be wife. I brought groceries. You're cooking," he ordered. With that, he kicked her harder causing the woman to cry out in pain as she struggled to stand unsteadily on her feet. Juanita moved quickly to help her.

"If she's supposed to help me have this baby, she'll have to have better care. Look at her! She's sick and needs a good bath. I'm going to help her so she can do a better job taking care of us." Juanita looked defiantly at Eddie.

A flame of rage instantly lit Felton's eyes, then just as quickly faded into humor. Sucking in his breath, he nodded. "Go ahead, kid. Knock yourself out. She isn't worth your time, but maybe you're right. She does stink, and she's gotten kind of skinny, haven't you, Cassie?" He lightly poked her in the ribs causing her to flinch and shrink away from him.

Juanita felt cold horror at the drastic change in Cassie Calloway's personality, fighting the fear that continuously insinuated itself in her mind: a dark worm eating away at her new-found faith, and the knowledge of the love she'd given and received since she'd arrived in Hilldale. Determination to stop Eddie from destroying them rose up like flood waters, saturating her heart and her thoughts. Together, they would defeat him.

Shrugging at Juanita's decision, Eddie pointed to her swollen abdomen. "Do what you want as long as you don't put my son in harm's way. Got it?" His voice took on a threatening tone Juanita knew well.

151

"I would never do anything to harm my—our child," she looked him in the eye. "How do we get bath water? You said there's food to prepare?" Juanita's hand held Cassie's as she tried to encourage the demoralized woman.

"There's a generator to run the pump. In about half-an-hour I'll have the pressure tank filled and you can use the tub in your bathroom. Meantime, there's food in the cooler and canned goods in the cabinets. Maybe between the two of you I can get a decent meal?" He tried to smile but it came across as a nasty sneer.

Cassie's head hung and she didn't respond, but Juanita nodded, and still holding the older girl's hand, she pulled her toward the bathroom. "We'll wash up a little with the water in the pail. It is clean, right?" Juanita said, keeping her voice light, hiding the fury that flared through her.

"If that lazy cow hasn't fouled it up," Eddie laughed. He turned and walked from the room leaving the door open.

Cassie's dark eyes traveled to Juanita's golden ones and settled. "He didn't lock us in. I'm too weak to run far, but you have to get away. He's dangerous and he's going to kill me anyway." Tears leaked from her eyes rolling past her lashes and down her hollowed cheeks. "He can't let me live after this." Her body sagged and Juanita slipped her arm around Cassie to help her stay upright.

"He's not going to kill you, Cassie. We're going to get out of here, but right now, our first job is to wash up and get lunch. I'm starving." Juanita laid her hand on her bulging belly and laughed. "This little baby takes up everything I eat, and I'm always hungry. Come on, forget about Eddie for a little while and let's see what we can fix to eat." The two walked arm-in-arm to the bathroom where they washed their hands and faces, Juanita taking a minute to comb out Cassie's tangled black hair. "There, you're going to be okay, Cassie, I promise. God has a plan." Juanita sighed heavily, "I sure don't know what it is, but He's got one—that I do know."

THIRTY-FIVE

Dan sent Gordie and Muley back to the farm, explaining that as soon as he had news, they would be the first to know. Despondent, the men drove back home in silence. They found Billy in the kitchen placing glasses of iced sweet tea on the table with thick slices of his cinnamon sugared fry bread stacked on a platter. Gordie sat in silent misery with Billy Sumday on one side, and Muley Burger on the other. They watched the young man as he wrestled his emotions into control. Billy laid his hand over Gordie's and began to pray.

"Father God, we thank You for all You've done for us and are doing for us. Things we can't see, don't know, may never know until we're face-to-face with You and Your Son. These are trying times, Lord, and we're asking You to see us through them, to keep Cassie, and Juanita, and her baby safe. We're grateful for their presence in our lives, Lord, and we thank You that even now You are watching over them, showering them with Your almighty love and mercy and peace. Keep us from anger, and hate, Lord, and cover us with Your love and forgiveness. For this, we give You honor and glory, for You alone are worthy of our praise."

Tears rolled down Gordie's face and Muley moved to the boy's side and put his arm around his shoulder, holding him to his chest. The old men's tears mingled with the young man's as they shared their sorrow. Gordie looked into each man's face and confessed.

"I surely wanted that Eddie Felton dead, and I believe I could have struck the first blow." Looking at Billy, Gordie wiped his eyes and gave the Native American a weak smile. "Thank you for your prayer, Uncle Billy. I needed reminding that revenge ain't mine, it's God's. Now if you all don't mind, I reckon I'm going to the barn and milk Kissie, and do me some more praying. God's got an answer for this situation and I hear Him best when I'm alone, or with my critters. I don't mean any disrespect to you all, but I got to get quiet before Him."

Muley gave his shoulder a squeeze and Billy patted Gordie's hand. "Go on, we understand. You're doing just right, young man," Billy said.

Gordie headed to the barn and let his mind settle on God's word, on God's promises to His children, reminding himself that he, Gordie Adam Bently, was one of the Father's beloved sons, and he should be waiting on the Lord to guide him in what he should do. Gordie longed to leap into action and go looking for Juanita on his own, but where? *Show me, Lord*, he prayed. *Please, show me where Juanita is.*

THIRTY-SIX

Cassie woke up to someone in her bed. Stifling a scream, she lay still listening to the soft snoring of the person next to her. It didn't sound like *him*. For a moment she felt confused. And then she remembered. The teenager, Juanita, Eddie's other captive lay asleep curled up next to her. She released her breath with relief. The girl seemed to hate Eddie as much as Cassie did, but she was pregnant with his baby, and by the looks of her, it wouldn't be long before she went into labor. Fear gripped her stomach. She would be expected to deliver the kid. That idea scared her nearly as much as knowing Eddie wasn't about to let her go—ever.

She watched in the dim light as Juanita turned over and stretched, groaning at the stiffness that had settled into her muscles. When she opened her eyes, Cassie whispered a soft greeting and saw reality hit Juanita. They were prisoners of a crazy man. A man who wouldn't think twice about killing anyone who got in the way of what he wanted, what he thought was rightfully his. Despair threatened to overwhelm her. Cassie heard Juanita breathe a prayer for strength and courage to stand up to their captor. When the teen finished her prayer, she stared into Cassie's eyes.

"Good morning," Juanita whispered. "I couldn't stand the thought of sleeping alone in the other bedroom. Hope you don't mind? Did you get any sleep, or did my snoring keep you awake all night?" She tried to smile.

"I just woke up and I'm really glad you're here," Cassie replied. "You don't snore very loud, nothing like...." she stopped.

"It's okay," Juanita said. "I know what and who you mean. We're both in the same boat." Little Wanda took that moment to stretch and kick her tiny heels. Juanita grinned ruefully, "Well, sort of."

"You sounded like my grandma, praying that way. You okay?" Cassie asked, worry making her voice louder than she wanted. Quickly hushing herself, she continued, "How close are you to going into labor? Jere—I mean, Eddie, expects me to deliver your kid and says he'll make me pay if anything goes wrong. The way I figure it, he's going to kill me no matter what." Her voice choked and she took a deep breath before continuing. "Regardless of what I do, I'm not getting out of here alive. You, on the other hand, you've got his baby for collateral. It is his, right?" Biting her bottom lip, Juanita nodded.

"So, you still have a chance," Cassie said, tears starting to roll across her cheeks, soaking into her pillow. "We'll have to work out the delivery process together. I'm pretty weak though I've been trying to exercise, and I'm trying to eat as much as I can. He doesn't leave a lot of food—one of his ways of training me. Got any ideas? I've got the book he gave me, we can go over that together. Think anyone's looking for you? I really doubt anyone will be looking for me. He told everyone we were going to Vegas for two weeks. I don't even know how long I've been here, but it's got to be at least a month. What day is this?"

"It's the end of August. I'm not due until October 9th, according to Doc Ridley. And yes, there're people looking for me. They're looking for you, too, Cassie. Sheriff Dan asked me about you a few days after you disappeared. We stay calm until they find us—and they will find us. We're going to be okay," Juanita sighed, trying to convince herself as much as the older girl.

Cassie reached out and took Juanita's hand. "Thanks, Juanita. Maybe the two of us can get the jump on him, find a weapon of some kind? I feel better knowing the sheriff is looking for me, too. At least we have a chance. I'm going to get up and exercise, and since the water's fixed, I'm going to take a quick bath. Maybe Mr. Creepy will let us have breakfast seeing he'll want to keep you healthy. I'm sorry you're here—but glad, too. I know you have your own bed, but I'm really grateful you slept in here. I feel safer, the two of us together." Cassie looked ashamed. "Being alone with him, I was losing my mind, losing myself. With you here, I feel—" she laughed bitterly, "I feel really really angry."

"I understand," said Juanita, giving Cassie's hand a squeeze. "Oof!" she grunted grabbing her bulging middle. "This little girl kicked me right in the bladder!" Carefully, Cassie reached out and touched Juanita's unborn baby. Little Wanda shifted and pushed against the light pressure of Cassie's hand, making her smile in wonder. In her mind she saw a tiny flickering flame. Hope. Juanita scooted to the side of the bed and ran to the bathroom. Cassie's genuine laughter followed her.

THIRTY-SEVEN

Molly Halloran lay in her husband's arms listening to his soft snoring. Her heart ached for the two missing women, for Gordie, and for Dan. He felt responsible for Juanita's abduction, felt like he should have seen it coming earlier, and found a reason to arrest the man he believed committed the kidnappings. Molly sighed. She loved Dan and couldn't imagine not being his wife. Touching her sleeping husband's face, she prayed for the women, Gordie, and for her man.

Married for a little over a year, she marveled at the relationship they'd developed: gentle, kind, supportive, and oh, so loving. They'd had their differences, every marriage did, but they'd worked them out with loving respect, without fear of punishment, and that drew them even closer together. Molly finished her prayer and snuggled against Dan's chest, inhaling his scent. Placing a soft kiss on his shoulder, she felt herself drifting into slumber, smiling.

*****

Gordie lay awake, tossing and turning, twisting himself up in his covers. Kicking them off, he got up and walked to the window, staring into the night. The moon glowed huge and bright through his open window, drawing him out onto the porch swing. His Doberman joined him, laying down at the young man's feet, knowing his master's mood, comforting him with his presence. Gordie reached down and patted Dancer's head, scratched behind his ears, and sat back putting the swing into motion.

Where is she? he wondered, finding himself continually praying—no—begging God to show him where Juanita was being held. Had Felton left Missouri with her? Was he still around Hilldale somewhere? Gordie's heart ached and he fought the panic rising in his mind. Swinging in the moonlit night, he waited on God.

*****

Jimmy Joe Bledsoe followed his Bluetick hound, Sadie, along with her offspring out of the woods near the old Bently place. The hounds had a coon treed in an old pin oak at the back of the abandoned property. Moonlight lit the house giving it a spookier-than-usual look. Jimmy Joe crossed himself. Boarded up, the windows appeared like dark tunnel openings into old man Bently's torture chambers. All Hilldale had heard about what he'd done to his daughter and grandson, and how he'd got himself murdered two years ago. For good measure, Jimmy Joe crossed himself again.

He walked as quietly as possible through the overgrown yard headed for the gravel road. Tired of coon hunting, more than a little spooked, and gut-growling hungry, he gave a whistle, calling his hounds. As he passed the west-side of the house, he saw a tiny ray of light through a crack in the plywood covering the windows. Surprised, he stopped and studied it, making sure it wasn't moon glow on metal.

Sure enough, it was a pale beam of light coming from inside the house. Someone must be camping out in the old place. Jimmy Joe shivered. Couldn't pay him enough to go in there where poor Neva Sue and her boy once suffered—her spirit probably roaming around in there crying out. Reckon he'd have to ask Muley what he thought about folks camping in the place. The boy, Gordie, still owned it, but never set foot there after his ma was murdered—leastways that was the story going around Neely's. Yep, he'd have to talk to Muley and see what the old man knew.

THIRTY-EIGHT

Dan skimmed the lab report on the findings in Eddie Felton's abandoned Escort. Not much to go on. A lumberyard manager just north of Camdenton thought he recognized the photo as that of a man who'd bought sheets of plywood, lumber, and parts for repairing a generator a few days earlier. He couldn't positively identify him, noting the man he remembered had a full beard and longer hair. But the eyes were the same. Dark broody eyes that kept looking around like he was casing the place. Gave him the creeps, he told the sheriff. Dan nodded. Sounded like Felton, all right. Buying lumber and working on a generator? He had himself a hideout, and the sheriff would bet it was somewhere in Lund

County. *Now all he had to do was find it.* He sighed to himself, worried about the status of the two girls.

Shaking his head, Dan rose from behind his desk and headed out to his receptionist, hoping for some of Vicki's baked goodies. He smelled fresh coffee brewing in the break room and waited patiently as Vicki finished her phone call. Smiling up at the troubled sheriff, she reached in her bottom desk drawer drawing out a cellophane-wrapped package. "For you," she said, her voice soft with sympathy and kindness.

"Thanks, Vicki," Dan returned the smile. "How's things with you and Randy? I could sure use some good news," he said, knowing the two had started dating.

A full-blown grin lighting her face and eyes, she replied, "Great! The boys love him and Randy seems to genuinely care about the boys. He's good to them, but he doesn't let them get away with everything. I like that. He's not trying to be their buddy to get to their mom." Laughing, she continued, "The boys weren't sure about sharing me, but now they can't get enough of him! He likes my cooking, and I believe he really likes me—just like I am," Vicki added, deep scarlet color brightening her cheeks.

"He'd be crazy not to!" Dan eyed his package and held it to his nose. "Pumpkin pecan bread?" he questioned. Nodding, Vicki grabbed up the ringing phone in one hand and a pen in the other. Dan carried his package to the break room, retrieved the pot of coffee and headed back to his office. A cup of coffee, a few slices of Vicki's pumpkin pecan bread, and then he would go back to work.

THIRTY-NINE
Juanita and Cassie sat side-by-side on the dust-laden rug in the center of the room, Cassie cross-legged, Juanita cradling her active unborn baby in her dwindling lap. Cassie pulled back the frayed rug showing the younger girl the hole bored into the old pine floorboard. "I think there was one of those big eyebolt thingies in here—just like the one in the kitchen I keep tripping over. About two years ago this awful guy and his daughter got murdered, and I think this is where they lived. You probably saw this kid around town—all scars and busted up fingers and stuff?" Cassie looked to see if Juanita was following her story. "Well, he and his mother were kept prisoners for years and years while old man Bently tortured them and helped steal her babies, and the boy turned out to be his son—" she hesitated, seeing the look of horror on Juanita's face.

"Bently?" Juanita stuttered, her voice quivering with emotion. Cassie nodded and continued.

"Gordie Bently—that's the guy's name. His mom was Neva Sue and story has it her step-father kept her and her kid prisoner, and the only time the mom got out was when this big-shot lawyer came to get her to—well, you know," she finished lamely. "Anyway, when the sheriff found her in the woods, she had this big chain bolted to her ankles. I heard she was kept chained up at home—so I figure the big bolt things were where the old man chained her up.

"Said he beat them with a bull whip and broke the kid's fingers one-by-one for punishment. The old man wouldn't even let the kid live in the house. Hey, you've probably seen him, he hangs around the sheriff all the time." She looked around the dimly-lit room. "This must have been the mom's room. Creepy, huh?" Cassie shivered.

Juanita sat still, face pale and eyes swimming with tears. *This was the farm Gordie lived on until Sheriff Dan rescued him. Gordie!* She cried from the depths of her heart for the kind young man, for the horrors of the life he endured, and the terrible loss of his mother. And she had been so mean to him, making fun of his scarred face when she first met him. Shame flooded her and her tears fell in earnest.

"Hey," Cassie rushed to hold her. "Hey, I'm sorry I scared you. Don't go having that kid right now, okay? We don't have a plan. Besides, I think that boy, Gordie, is okay. Last I heard he got a boat-load of money from the lawyer's estate, and he gets paid for singing. I heard him once when I got roped into going to church with this old Kickapoo who knows my mom and my grandma up on the rez, and Gordie sang a solo. Raised the hair on the back of my neck. Funny how he doesn't seem angry or bitter, you know?" Shaking her head, she squeezed Juanita's shoulder and said, "You going to be okay? No baby yet, right?" Worry creased her forehead.

Sniffing, Juanita shook her head. "I'm okay. I do know Gordie, and knew he'd had a tough life, but I didn't know any details. He—he just married Little Wanda and me. We went to Jefferson City a few weeks ago, but we haven't told anyone. We were waiting until—well, until I felt ready to be a wife—whatever that means." Blushing, she continued, "He wants to take care of us and he's the kindest person I've ever met."

"Little Wanda?" Cassie wrinkled her nose, perplexed. "He asked two women to marry him? What a—" Juanita hushed her.

Patting her abdomen, she explained, "Little Wanda."

"Oh, the kid. So, you said he's kind, but I didn't hear you say you love him? Me, I'm a dreamer. I always thought I'd marry for love, and look at me. The men I get involved with are losers—big time losers." Sadness dulled her laugh.

"Listen, I don't know your Gordie, but he seems real nice, a little shy, maybe because he's so messed up. Oops, sorry," Cassie blushed. "Sometimes my mouth gets me into trouble. He's not bad looking for a—oh, darn, never mind. I'm just getting myself in deeper," she giggled. "I get this great scoop of gossip and I can't tell anyone! Go figure." Sighing, she took Juanita's hand and patted it. "Listen, I hope your marriage works out and you live happily ever after. But first, we've got to get out of here."

Nodding, Juanita struggled to her feet. Whenever Eddie allowed them outside for the fresh air and exercise she'd insisted they needed to keep her and the baby healthy, she explored the buildings and weed-infested grounds. Must be almost three weeks she'd been gone. Maybe more. She and Cassie tried to keep their days marked, but sometimes days ran into nights, and they would wonder if they'd counted right. Her mind snapped back to her new husband.

Gordie. Her heart thudded in her chest. Love swept through her like a fresh breeze and she felt a deep abiding joy in the midst of her captivity. She did love him. "Thank You, Lord," she whispered. "Thank You for all You've given me, and please help us get rescued."

"Why do you keep doing that praying thing?" Cassie grumbled. "My mom and my grandma always do that. I thought I'd go crazy listening to the two of them." She stopped, a stunned look crossed her dusky features and her dark eyes glittered with unshed tears. "Except now I'd give everything I own to hear them again. For real. I miss them so much. I hope they're still praying for me, 'cause I've sure gotten myself into an awful mess."

Juanita reached her hand down and helped the older girl to her feet. "Never mind about the past. This wonderful old lady I live with told me about this amazing king who loves me so much He died for me." Looking into Cassie's eyes she smiled, "He died for you too, Cassie, and He doesn't care about our past mistakes. He cares about saving us, loving us, helping us find our way out of the dark places we've been, leading us into His light."

She took a deep breath knowing that even being held as Eddie's captive, she was free. She couldn't explain it yet, not with words, but if God rescued her from this place, she would beg Aunt Mary to teach her everything she could about living with this wonderful Savior. In the short time she'd known Him, her life--her very heart--had been turned around. Not only did she know how real love felt, for the first time in her young life, she accepted the love offered her, God's love, and the sweet love of Gordie, Gramma Wanda, Aunt Mary, even Sheriff Dan and his wife. Once again, a peace that didn't make any sense in her circumstances, flooded her being. Gordie would find her. He would rescue Little Wanda and everything would be all right.

FORTY

Obed sat in his recliner, his house dark except for the glow of the street light spreading through the kitchen into the living room. He sipped his sweet tea and pondered just how he could make things right with Danny. He loved that boy almost as much as he loved his sons, and his heart hurt knowing he'd disappointed him. Could he be wrong about that little gal that was the cause of all this trouble? Being wrong wasn't easy for him. Never had been. His Beryl used to scold him when he refused to say he was sorry to their boys. A heavy sigh escaped his lips. *Well, God, reckon you'd best show me the next step in this here mess. I'm listening.* His silent, heart-felt prayer went straight to heaven.

*****

"Ain't too likely anyone from around here would be camping out at the old Bently place," Muley looked at his friend on the swing next to him. "Reckon could be someone from out-of-town, maybe one of them hunters what like to poach off someone else's land. Could be we ought to let Danny know." Muley patted Beauty's head then reached for Cootie II as the young dog struggled to get between his mother and his master's hand.

"That place gives me the creeps," Jimmy Joe grumbled, petting Sadie's head. The Coonhound closed her eyes in pleasure. "Can't imagine anyone in their right mind staying in that there house-- leastways nobody what knows the story about the place. Anyways, just wanted to pick your brain and see what you thought.

"I heard the boy don't go there no more, so hated to see someone ruining what's left of the place. What in the world he'd want with that evil-filled house, I sure don't know. Ought to be burned to the ground and the place sold for hunting grounds, or some such. Ain't none of my never mind, just

165

wondered if you ought to tell the boy." Jimmy Joe stood to go, his hound bounding down the porch steps ahead of him. "Been a spell since you come along with us. Coon hunting soon? " he questioned his old friend.

"Soon," Muley replied, patting Cootie II's head. "This young 'un is about ready to try the woods again. Been working with him two years, and he's been a bit gun-shy. But we're working on it, ain't we, boy?" He rubbed the delighted pup's ears and patted his head.

*****

Gordie sat upstairs in his room, his window open just enough to let in the fresh cool fall air. *Someone's camping at Grampa's?* His scalp prickled and his stomach clenched. *Juanita and Little Wanda? Could that Felton fella be holding the women prisoners at his grampa's place? Coincidence? Evil seemed to return to where it once thrived.*

Sickened by the thought of his beloved Juanita trapped in that house where his mother suffered so much torment at the hands of her step-father, Gordie waited until he knew Jimmy Joe had left and Muley had headed to the kitchen to start supper. Evening was gliding in on golden slippers, lighting the newly turning leaves to brilliant yellows and reds. Grabbing up a flashlight and his pocket knife, Gordie headed down the stairs to the kitchen.

Muley turned from the stove and grinned at the young man. "You fixing to be hungry yet? Got some fried taters, catfish fresh caught in yonder pond, and green beans just picked this morning. Sound good?"

"Yep, it sure does, but I got to go out for a bit, Papa Muley. Hope I won't be too long, but you go on and eat. I'll fetch me something when I get back." Gordie picked up his cell phone from the table.

Worry wrinkled Muley's forehead. "What's wrong, lad?" he asked. "I know that look, and if you're going into some kind of trouble, you let me come along to help you. Leastways, if you can't take me, call Danny."

"No trouble," Gordie tried to smile convincingly. "Just going to check out an idea I have. Got my phone," he held up his cell phone, "so if I need to, I'll call Sheriff Dan, okay? Don't worry, I'll be fine." He walked across the kitchen to the old man and hugged him. "Sure appreciate your caring, Papa Muley," he spoke softly, tears gathering in his eyes.

"Go on with you, then," Muley said, his voice gruff with emotion. "You mind what I said. Call if you need help."

Gordie nodded and headed out the door toward the barn where he'd parked his car. Muley watched through the window as the young man walked away. Love swelled up so hard it hurt, and he heard himself moan. Heading to the living room, he reached for the phone and begin to dial. *Wouldn't hurt to give Danny a heads-up.*

*****

Obed rummaged around in his bedroom closet until he found the shoebox he was looking for. Pulling it from beneath a pile of well-worn long underwear, he opened the lid. Reaching inside, he lifted out the old pistol he'd brought home from WWII. Turning it over in his hands he wondered if he still knew how to use the thing. It'd been packed away since his boy, Tommy, died in Viet Nam.

167

Sighing, he dropped the box on his bed. *Now where had he stashed the bullets?* he wondered.

Fear wrenched his gut. Danny figured they were still around Hilldale somewhere and Obed figured the sheriff was right. He had a hunch where that low-down scoundrel might have taken them girls, and if he was right, it wasn't a place he wanted to go—at least not without his gun.

Climbing into his nearly new pickup, he fumbled with the starter forgetting he had to hold the brake pedal down to get the dadblamed thing to shift. *New fangled contraptions sure give a body trouble.* Obed headed west through Hilldale and out of town. Staring hard at the road ahead of him, trying not to stray across the middle line, he crept down the county road, his gun resting on the seat next to him, his hands clenching the steering wheel to keep them from shaking. Determination tightened his jaw. He had some mending to do, and by golly, if God was with him, he'd have them gals back before morning.

*****

Dan stopped and stared. Obed Martin sat behind the wheel of his new Ford Ranger, creeping through town, looking scared as could be. The sheriff couldn't remember the last time he'd seen the old man driving and a feeling of dread washed through him. Something was up. Heading to his office to check out for the evening, his cell phone rang. Pulling it from his pocket, he saw it was Muley. Swallowing hard, Dan answered his phone. "What's wrong?" he asked.

*****

Eddie's face darkened with rage. Slapping hard, he dropped Cassie to the ground before he turned his fury on Juanita. Fear coursed through her as she struggled to pray, only coming up with *please, God. Please God.* Felton's hand snaked out again and the girl cringed, waiting for the blow. The hand stopped just before striking her face.

"You're lucky you have my son inside you. You'd be dead, just like this tramp will soon be—d.e.a.d—dead." He emphasized the word with a rough kick to Cassie's ribs forcing her to cry out. Snarling, he ordered the girls to head back to the house.

Juanita helped Cassie to her feet trying not to hurt her any further. Desperation widened her eyes. The older girl clung to the teen whispering, "Please, Juanita, don't let him kill me. Please."

Screaming obscenities at them, Eddie Felton ranted and raved about their breaking his trust. He'd been kind to let them go outside and look how they'd repaid him! Trying to escape. Juanita tried to explain they were curious about the outbuildings, just exploring, not trying to escape. In his rage, he refused to listen to her, shoving them in front of him up to the porch, through the door which he locked behind him. Marching them to Cassie's room, he warned them he'd be back, and when he returned, they'd be sorry they'd tried to cross him. Cassie would pay with her life, and Juanita would pay by having his son without the aid of another woman.

"Please, Eddie," Juanita hated the desperation in her voice, "please don't hurt her. I need her to help me have my baby. Our baby."

"Tough!" he shouted at them. "You chose to make me mad, you pay the consequences." He stormed from the room slamming the door and locking it.

The girls clung to each other trembling, whispering, praying. They could smell frying meat and knew he'd cook his meal, leave them hungry, and then come for them. Juanita cried out silently for God's help. She knew she wouldn't die today; she carried Eddie Felton's child. But she knew he would do as he threatened and kill Cassie. Juanita's heart wrenched within her as she prayed for her new-found friend's life.

FORTY-ONE

Gordie parked the old Buick Special down the gravel road out of sight from his farm. Gathering his flashlight from the seat, he checked his pocket assuring himself he had his knife and cell phone. Quietly, he stepped from the gravel into the woods. Knowing a back way to the house where he felt he wouldn't be spotted, he began weaving his way through the brush and trees, praying as he went.

FORTY-TWO

Obed drove his pickup down the gravel road until he reached the long rutted drive of the Bently place. His legs felt weak, his mouth dry. Parking at the end of the lane, he climbed from his truck, quietly closing the door. Didn't want to give that fella warning he was coming. Hefting his gun, he felt awkward holding it, but didn't know what else to do with it. As silently as possible, he shuffled down the rutted road wishing the sun hadn't disappeared behind the bluffs. It left him cold, and the dim light left him vulnerable to the ruts waiting to trip him up.

As he approached the house, he heard yelling and watched from behind a patch of sumac as the man who'd hurt Miss Mary, the devil man, as

170

Obed had come to think of him, pushed and shoved two women up the porch steps and through the door. Obed felt his heart skip a beat, and felt a bitter cold seep through his veins. Forcing himself to move forward, he crept up to the house and hid behind the porch, listening. He could hear that fella yelling he was going to kill them, and he heard the sound of flesh against flesh and one of the girls cried out in pain.

"Oh, Lordy, what am I getting into?" he whispered to the dusky evening enveloping him.

Tiptoeing up the steps he tried the door. Locked. Back to the yard and around to the side of the house. The windows were boarded over and the side door nailed tight. Obed continued around the house until he reached the tiny porch that led to the kitchen door. It stood open, the screen door leaking light and the smell of frying meat. His mouth watered in spite of his fear. *Shoot! He'd forgotten to eat supper and hadn't brought any food with him. Too late now*, he chastised himself. And then he saw him.

Silhouetted in the kitchen light, the devil-man poked at something in a pan on the stove. Obed made his move. As quickly as his trembling old legs would allow, he climbed the steps, yanked the screen door open, and leveled his gun toward the surprised man.

"Git 'em up and keep 'em where I can see 'em," his voice, high-pitched with fear, quavered. The weight of the gun caused his hand to wobble, and he fought to hold it steady.

"Well, what do we have here? The nosy old neighbor has come to rescue the damsels in distress?" Eddie mocked, a sneer twisting his face. His eyes glinted and he took a step forward. "Bet if I yelled BOO! you'd wet yourself, old man. Get out of here and I might let you live." As he spoke, he leapt at Obed, seizing his arm. Obed pulled the trigger. The thunder of the gun and the recoil stunned him, pushing him back toward the screen door. Eddie Felton stopped, surprise, then rage, widening his eyes. Blood began to seep from his side.

"You crazy old fool!" he raged. "You shot me! Give me that gun or I swear I'll kick you to death before I shoot you."

Obed straightened his arms using both hands to steady the gun. His breathing grew ragged and he knew he needed his inhaler, but he couldn't let go of the gun. "Take me to them there girls what you kidnapped. You don't, I'll shoot you again. You gonna let 'em go, you hear me, you devil-man!"

Eddie Felton grabbed his side. A searing pain flared up and spread through his chest. Deadly calm settled over him, as he glared at the old man. "Fine, follow me." He turned and unlocked the padlock on the door behind him. Pulling it open, he disappeared inside a dimly lit room. Carefully, Obed followed, and as he entered the room he saw Juanita and Cassie sitting on an iron bed, eyes wide with terror.

Before he could react, Eddie grasped his arm and tried to wrench the gun from him. Obed held tight, struggling to keep his balance against the younger, stronger man's determination. Eddie pulled Obed toward him, giving the old man's arm a vicious twist. Gasping in pain, Obed tried to pull away. A loud report, and the force of the gunshot thrust him backwards. Eddie Felton stood before him, blood pulsing down his shirt from a new wound. His eyes filled with hate. His mouth spewed filth. Bellowing with fury, the younger man grabbed the old man's

172

trembling hand and forced the gun toward his chest, squeezing the trigger finger until the gun fired a third time.

A hot sting bit through Obed. Weakness tugged at his legs and he knew he'd been shot. Dropping the gun, he wrapped his arms around Eddie Felton and let his heavier weight pull them to the floor with a jarring crash. The girls cried out. He could hear them, but couldn't see them. He couldn't see much through the fog that closed in around him. Determination clamped his arms like a death-grip around the body twisting to be free, just like his Pa's pigs wiggled and bucked when Obed had to wrangle them down and insert a ring in their nose. Just like Pa had taught him, Obed held on.

The younger man fought to free himself, but Obed could tell, he was getting weaker. Gladness lifted him above his heightening pain. If he could just hold onto him, if he could keep him down until the devil-man fainted or died from his wounds, he could save the girl. He had to let her and Danny know he was sorry—so sorry for his unkindness toward her. Land sakes, he was getting tired. Darkness crawled over him and sure enough meant to swallow him.

*****

Juanita struggled to stand. Her back ached and she felt light-headed. Cassie stood next to her, the two watching the men writhing on the floor in front of them. Could they get past them into the kitchen? Out the door to freedom? The girls stared through the door and cried out. Fire engulfed the frying pan, burning a path across the stove top and whisking up the ragged curtains hanging nearby.

Fear fueled Cassie's legs. She leapt over the dying men and raced into the kitchen. Grabbing the dishpan of sudsy water from the sink, she tossed it on the burning grease only to have it explode and splatter in all directions. Screaming as the fire ignited her clothing, she ran back toward Juanita, begging her for help. As she passed the men, now quiet on the floor, Eddie Felton pulled his arm from beneath Obed, and with a feeble curse, grasped the gun and fired.

Cassie Calloway crumpled to the floor, fire crawling up her body toward her hair. Grabbing a blanket from the bed, Juanita threw it over the flames, snuffing them out. She turned and kicked Eddie's hand hard, sending the gun flying across the floor. The man stared at her, his hatred hitting her like a fist. Blood oozed from his mouth and his eyes clouded over. He tried to speak but only strangled gurgling sounds issued from his mouth. Juanita turned away from him to tend to Cassie. Racing to the bathroom as fast as her swollen, aching body would allow, she wet some towels to stop the smoldering fabric that clung to the fallen girl.

Flames engulfed the end of the kitchen creeping toward the bedroom door. Juanita slammed the door against the fiery heat. She had to get Cassie out. Sharp pains stabbed her abdomen, grabbed her low in the back. Crying out, Juanita felt a warm wetness flood around her feet. More pains taking her breath away. Little Wanda! Her baby was coming and there was no one to help her. Smoke whispered beneath the door. Juanita grasped Cassie under the arms and tugged until she got her away from the door and on the rug near the bed. Another contraction ripped through her and she struggled to stay upright. Back in the bathroom she soaked the blanket and took it back, spreading it over Cassie's still and bleeding form.

Catching movement behind her she turned in time to see Obed roll off Eddie, his eyes wide, his voice weak. "Git now," he rasped, staring at her. She moved to his side and knelt down to hear him better. His hand reached up to her face and Juanita covered it with hers. "Forgive me?" he whispered, his voice fading, his eyes growing dim.

Nodding, her tears fell, wetting his face. With a sigh, Obed's hand dropped to the floor and he closed his eyes. "Git," he said, slipping into unconsciousness.

Juanita stood and moved back to Cassie's limp body. Another cramping pain rolled down her back, across her abdomen, doubling her over.

"First-time babies aren't supposed to come this fast, Little Wanda," she panted, sinking to the floor, crawling beneath the smoke that seeped under the door. She reached the bathroom and stood. Flipping on the light switch, relief flooded her when the room lit up. Quickly, Juanita soaked all the towels and the spare blanket and tossed them into the bathtub. Horrified, she noted blood rapidly staining her pants. Stripping them off, she climbed into the tub and squatted over the wet towels. The painful need to push hard made her cry out.

The smoke hadn't reached the bathroom yet, and Juanita prayed she had time. Time to deliver and somehow save her daughter and Cassie. Ripping pains tore at her and grasping the side of the tub, she screamed, forgetting all but the need to push, to be free of the terrible pains that forced her to her knees, panting, weeping, begging God to help her.

*****

Gordie smelled smoke. As he pushed through the last of the brush, he saw flames raging through the kitchen windows, watched in horror as the windows exploded and the insulation and plywood that had covered them, dissolved into embers and ash, sparking toward the sky, dancing wildly in the evening breeze.

"Wanda!" he cried, fear and adrenaline rushing through his bloodstream. He raced to the kitchen porch, through the screen door, and into the smoke and flames. "Juanita!" He heard her scream, a terrible, long, pain-filled wail. And then a smaller, feebler, cry followed. Gordie's legs nearly crumpled beneath him. Little Wanda! He rushed to the padlocked bathroom door ramming himself against it, over-and-over until finally, the hinges gave way, and with a crash, it fell onto the bathroom floor.

*****

Fire raged around her. Juanita felt the heat searing her face. The tub grew warmer, smoke insinuating itself through the air. The bedroom hadn't burst into flames yet, but thick, black smoke roiled and blossomed through the room hiding Cassie from her view. Juanita quickly lifted her daughter from beneath her trembling legs and tried to remember what to do with the cord that bound them together, mother and child. And then the need to push again came upon her. Grunting, she expelled the afterbirth, the cord still attached. The room grew hotter, the smoke thicker. Coughing, she placed the placenta and cord onto her daughter's tiny heaving chest praying nothing awful would happen because she couldn't cut the cord, or tie it off. Juanita wrapped her baby in a wet pillowcase and then a wet towel. Cradling her, she kissed her daughter's damp face, grateful for the cries coming from her.

Frantic, she looked around her. How could she get them though the smoke-filled bedroom, through the raging flames of the kitchen? She turned to the window near her. The boards had to come off, and she'd have to do it in a hurry. Heat licked at her face, her exposed skin. Ignoring the heavy bleeding that pooled beneath her, she laid her child on the wet towels and blanket at the bottom of the tub and stood. Little Wanda continued to cry. Digging her fingernails into the cracks between the sheets of plywood, Juanita began to pull.

A crash shattered the locked door behind her and she whirled to see what new disaster awaited. Gordie pushed through the doorway, over the fallen door and rushed to her. His eyes glowed dark with terrified determination. Relief flooded through the two young people as they spied each other.

Juanita reached for her wailing newborn and held her out to Gordie. "Hurry, take her, keep her safe. Please, Gordie, save our daughter. Please." Anguish at letting her child go twisted her face, but she quickly thrust the baby into Gordie's reaching arms. "I'm right behind you," Juanita cried.

She wrapped a wet towel around her waist, turned from them, and climbing from the bathtub, she headed into the bedroom just as the door across the room erupted into flames. Dropping to the floor to avoid the heavy smoke, she crawled to where she believed Cassie lay. Finding her, Juanita grabbed the unconscious girl beneath her arms and pulled.

Cassie's body shifted slightly, then settled back in place. Juanita knew she'd have to stand to gain purchase to drag her friend out. Bleeding heavily, beginning to feel faint and growing weak, she shifted her hold and pulled again. The rug beneath Cassie grudgingly slid across the floor and Juanita struggled to drag the unconscious woman into the bathroom, smoke choking her lungs, stinging her eyes.

Soon she was across the threshold gasping for air. Dark billows rolled into the room and the heat from the roaring flames behind and in front of her blistered her skin, and smoldered in her hair. Reaching down, she grasped Cassie once more, and pulled until her legs trembled and nearly gave way. Her breath labored hot and painful in her chest. She fought the darkness that tried to pull her in. Still she pulled. Just as she reached the fallen door so close to freedom, her strength gave out and she felt herself fading.

"Oh Lord, please not now. Help Cassie. Help me." Her words faded into the darkness that rolled over her, claiming her even as the fire licked up the far bathroom door and slowly engulfed the wall around it.

*****

Obed struggled to move away from the body next to him. He'd killed a man. Even in the war he'd never killed anyone. He knew this was a bad man, a devil-man, but still the knowledge that he'd taken a life weighed heavy on his heart, his mind. "Forgive me, Lord," he prayed. "Didn't see no other way 'cept to take his life so's them girls could live. Still, I'm sorry for it."

He saw that little gal, Juanita. She bent over him, held his hand, accepted his forgiveness. Relief helped ease the terrible pain that gripped him. He closed his eyes and waited for help to come.

Even with his eyes closed, Obed saw a light coming toward him. At last. They were finally coming to get him. He sighed. The awful heat seared his chest, his lungs. "Hard to breathe," he whispered, his breath stolen by the flames. Just when he thought he couldn't stand the burning pain any longer, a coolness washed over his body, fresh air filled his ruined lungs, and a blessed sense of peace filled him.

The light was right over him now, and he felt as right as he'd ever felt in his life. He'd saved them girls and that baby, and he'd been forgiven. He couldn't rightly explain how he knew this, but a smile etched across his blistering, blackening face as he absorbed the truth of it. A great sigh left his body as the light surrounded him, lifting him from the husk of what was once his earthly home, lifting him above the pain and sorrows of a lifetime. Obed Martin rose with the Light.

*****

When Juanita awoke she lay on the cool ground, her daughter cradled in the crook of her arm. A warm blanket covered their nakedness. Trying to sit, her body refused to obey. Shouts, cries and wailing sirens accompanied the sound of hungry flames devouring the Bently farm house. Juanita IraLilly Bently sank back into unconsciousness.

FORTY-THREE

Gordie sat next to Juanita's hospital bed gently brushing out what was left of her scorched red curls, smoothing them against her pillow. When he finished, he took up the jar of burn cream the nurse left for him, and slipping on sterile gloves, he began to gently work the soothing cream into the raw skin where the fire's heat had reddened and blistered it, his love for her radiating from his fingertips into her pain. And he prayed.

Floating in and out of consciousness for two weeks, Juanita lay silent, unmoving except now and then, to cry out in fear or pain. Gordie refused to leave her side except to shower, change his clothes,

and bring Little Wanda in to nestle with her sleeping
mother. He read to his "two ladies", as he thought of
them. He sang. He prayed. And Gordie poured out
his dreams for their little family to the unconscious
woman, even as he stroked her hair, gently massaged
her legs and arms to keep them vital, helped turn her,
and always he assured her of his love for her and for
Little Wanda.

*****

Molly Halloran entered the private hospital
room followed closely by Dan. They found Wanda
and Mary Harmon watching Gordie sleeping in the
rocking chair, Little Wanda tucked safely in his
arms. Molly gently lifted the baby from him cradling
her close, nuzzling her sweet-smelling neck.

Startled, Gordie opened his eyes, saw his
friends and drifted back into exhausted slumber. The
two older ladies smiled up at the young couple.
Wanda stood, giving her stiffened legs a moment to
hold her up. Mary looked up from her wheelchair,
her leg encased in plaster. "Now that you're here, we
need to go home and clean up, maybe catch a cat
nap. That young man refused to let go of Little
Wanda for longer than a few minutes. I'm glad
you're here to take over," Mary whispered,
admiration for Gordie filling her eyes.

Dan pulled up a chair and motioned for
Molly to sit. She shook her head setting her dark
curls into a lively dance. "You sit," she smiled at her
husband. "It's about time you held our god-
daughter." He looked panicked for a moment, then,
at Molly's urging, he sat. She lay the baby in his
arms and smiled at the wonder that lit his face.

"Good," Molly patted her husband's cheek,
smoothed his curls. "You're going to need the

180

practice one of these days." Dan shook his head, doubt clouding his face.

Molly laughed. "We'll be having a baby when I finish my PA training," she assured him with a kiss. Little Wanda began to fuss and Gordie woke with a start. He reached for the baby bottle Sue Miles, the night duty nurse, had placed in the bottle warmer. Looking at Dan, he handed him the bottle. Turning toward the bed, he caught his breath. Watching them, a peaceful smile on her face, Juanita whispered, her voice husky with smoke damage, "Family." Her eyes closed and she sank into a deep healing sleep.

FORTY-FOUR

Cassie moaned. Her chest hurt, and when she tried to take a deep breath her damaged lungs rebelled, even with the cool, moistened oxygen helping her breathe. Forcing her eyes open, she explored what she could from the limited radius of her hospital bed. The room lay in heavy shadow, lighted machines beeped and blinked at her—her only company. A single tear slipped down her cheek soaking into the painful blisters that covered her face. Loneliness washed over her and she felt it sucking her down into darkness. A gentle hand wiped her tear away.

"You're awake, Cassie Red Feather," said a voice with relief and deep affection. She turned her head to see the face of the man at her side. Kickapoo Billy Sumday smiled.

"You've been wandering through some strange lands, Miss Red Feather. We've been waiting for you to come back home."

"We?" her raw voice croaked. She tried to reach out her hand but felt a sharp pain.

"Whoa, now. You took a bullet in your wing, young lady. Won't be flying for a wee bit, so relax and let us do the work." His smile calmed Cassie's fear and she turned her head as the door opened, letting in the bright hallway light. Two women entered the room carrying steaming cups of coffee, their faces puffy from the many tears shed over the past weeks. Cassie's heart leapt with joy mixed with a touch of trepidation. Her mother and grandmother had come to her.

"Nimaamaa! Nookomis!" she managed before sobs robbed her of her words. She wanted to beg their forgiveness, pour out her love for them, but she could only weep.

Billy stood and moved from the side of her bed making room for her family. As he left the room, he watched the women's loving hands gently caress Cassie's damaged head and arms, careful of her burned skin, leaning into her and holding her as best they could through the wires and tubing that ran to the various machines monitoring her life.

Through the injured woman's tears, she spoke. "I'm so sorry Mama, Gramma. Please forgive me. I love you so much. Please tell me you forgive me."

The two women shushed her, nodding through their own tears. "Already done," they whispered in unison. Her mother continued, "We love you, Cassie. We've been waiting for you. Will you come home with us? When you are well, we won't hold you to the reservation. You choose how and where you'll live your life. We only pray that you'll let God be part of that decision."

Cassie nodded. Her eyelids began to droop and she said, "We'll talk, Nimaamaa. But one thing's for sure—wherever I go, whatever I do, I want to learn more about God and His Son, Jesus. I gave Him my life and thought I wasn't going to live. He gave me back my life, and I want to know more." A weak smile painfully stretched her burned lips. "That teaching me, it might take you awhile. Seems I'm a slow learner."

The two women laughed and kissed her even as Cassie fell into a peaceful sleep. Love lit the room as her mother and grandmother settled beside her holding her hands, sipping their coffee, and watching as their child slept, no longer wandering the hot, dry, empty desert of her nightmares.

FORTY-FIVE

The small church was packed with Hilldale's folks squeezed together in the pews, filling the folding chairs, standing wherever there was a place big enough to hold another human. Obed Martin's casket rested on the platform where the podium usually stood. Nearby, his son, Timmy, and his family sat tearfully waiting. Pastor Hughes rose and moved to the rear of the casket laying his hands on the polished wood, as though in benediction. The sanctuary lay silent except for the soft weeping.

"We are gathered here this morning to say farewell to a father, brother, and an old and dear friend. Though it's taken a few weeks to receive his earthly body, we are grateful that now, we can all come together as a family, to say our good-byes. Obed Martin lived amongst us all of his life and he'll be sadly missed. But in the midst of our sorrow, we can rejoice, because Brother Obed knew his Redeemer lived.

"Not long ago, Obed came to me, his heart broken, his spirit weary from wrestling with his humanness." Pastor Hughes smiled. "Our brother had his convictions, but he loved the Lord and that love won out. He came to me to ask how to make restitution for what he felt were his sins. 'Simple,' I told him as I've told this congregation many times. 'Confess your sins to your Savior, let Him free your heart and mind, and then seek how God would have you right any wrongs you've done.'"

A few *amen's* echoed through the church, and the pastor continued. "As we gather here today, we all know Obed did just that. We know the repentant heart he had, and we all know how he saved the life of the one he felt he'd wronged.

"This morning, let us celebrate our brother's going home. Let us rejoice through our sorrow at the joy he must now know, kneeling in the presence of his Savior, who is saying, 'Well done, good and faithful servant.' So come, beloved people, rejoice for one who's sin-scars once crippled him, but now he runs free. Give thanks to the Father, and to the Son, and to the Holy Spirit, for they alone are worthy. Amen."

Gordie Bently stepped forward to stand beside the old upright piano where Terrance Sampler sat. As his friend began to play, the shifting bodies and weeping sounds settled into stillness, and Gordie looked from face to grieving face.

"My Ma wrote poetry. I never knew that until Miss Mary Harmon showed me some of the poems she wrote in high school. Thank you, Miss Mary for saving them. They're precious as gold to me." He looked to the people waiting, listening. "This song is one of Ma's poems she wrote before I was born. My friend, Terrance, put it to music. I like to think Ma must have known that one day her son would cherish these words." Tears gathered in his sky-blue eyes that seemed to see beyond this life, eyes so like his mother's. Gordie began to sing.

> *I've found there's joy in the storms*
> *That rumble through my life,*
> *Bringing cleansing, building strength*
> *Pruning, sometimes painful*
> *Like a surgeon's healing knife.*
> *When thunder sounds,*
> *When lightning strikes,*
> *I begin to sing,*
> *Praises for His mercy,*
> *Jesus Christ, Almighty King.*
>
> *When I'm weary of the battle*
> *Life's wounds have brought me low,*
> *Alone, frightened, confused I come,*
> *Seeking peace and refuge*
> *From the one hope that I know.*
> *Sorrows forgotten,*
> *Joy uplifts,*
> *As I begin to sing,*
> *Praises for His mercy,*
> *Jesus Christ, Almighty King.*
>
> *There's beauty in your scars, He said,*
> *I have them, too, you see.*
> *Forgiving scars inflicted,*
> *Love conquers hatred,*
> *This truly sets us free.*
> *When forgiveness reigns,*
> *Evil flees,*
> *Love rises and I sing*
> *Praising God's sweet mercy,*
> *Jesus Christ, Almighty King.*

The music faded and silence filled the sanctuary. Gordie opened his eyes and looked into the congregation. Sitting near the rear of the room, her wheelchair surrounded by Gramma Wanda, Miss Mary, Sheriff Dan, and Molly, Juanita IraLilly Bently met her husband's eyes with all the love that welled up in her heart.

Gordie believed the hard shell of hurt that had held her heart captive for most of her life had cracked, broken, and had been washed away by the love of those around her. He hoped what he saw in her eyes was love for him. And then, Juanita blew her husband a kiss. Gordie reached out his hand and captured it, bringing it to his mouth. As he stepped from the platform and walked back to his wife, Terrance began to play through the list of Obed Martin's favorite hymns.

FORTY-SIX

Gordie pushed Juanita's wheelchair close to the hospital bed and locked the wheels. He helped her out of her shoes and settled her on the bed. "Blanket?" he asked. Juanita shook her head glancing at the open door. She scooted back against the stack of pillows and again, she looked at the door. The young man smiled. "You're waiting for Little Wanda. Me, too. Paper, scissors, rock for who gets to hold her first!" Juanita laughed.

"You hold her first while I get her bottle warmed up. I get to feed her. You have her all night until you bring her to me in the mornings, so learn to share," she declared, her eyes showing the gratitude and love she felt for how her young husband surrounded them with his kindness and love.

As soon as Little Wanda had been released from the hospital, Gordie had taken her home, hired a woman to come teach him how to care for the tiny infant, and insisted she wasn't any problem. When Juanita feared the care-giving would be too much for him and Muley, he laughed.

"Ain't—shoot—isn't any worse than Beauty's pups and Kissy's calf. Little Wanda don't give us near the trouble we get from them little stinkers."

"Wait until she's walking, then come tell me that," said a pleasant voice from the doorway. Nurse Sue Miles grinned as she carried the sleeping subject of their conversation into the room. "She's slept most of the morning while I cleaned house, but I think this wee one's about ready for her folks and her bottle. Who's doing the honors this time? You kids fight over her like she was special or something." Laughing, she placed Little Wanda in Gordie's outstretched arms.

"This here little girl is special, just like her ma. Thanks for taking care of her while we paid our last respects, Mrs. Miles. We appreciate everything you've done for us since we first got here. It seems like years ago, but it's only been a few weeks. Sure thank you for your kindness." Gordie blushed, but held the nurse's gaze.

"Looks like Wanda—uh, that Wanda—" he said, tipping his head toward Juanita, is going to get to go home soon. We're looking at maybe next week. Doc Ridley said her surgeon thinks she'll be good to go as soon as she's walking and her plumbing starts working the way it's supposed to." Again his cheeks stained with embarrassment. "I'm talking too much, and that's way too much information." Looking down into the face of the little girl in his arms, he whispered, "Can't wait, can we, Little Wanda?" Nurse Miles laughed and patted the young man's shoulder, then turned to her patient.

"Juanita, you look like you're walking just fine, and we'll discuss the rest of the requirements . when we have some privacy." Juanita nodded, grinning, but her eyes were on Gordie and Little Wanda. The moment of tenderness dissolved when a tall, lanky, blond-haired woman strode into the room, her face unsmiling, her disapproval clear in her eyes, as she took in the man holding the newborn baby.

"Mary Johannsen, Boone County Child Protective Services." The woman pulled her identification from her large purse giving Gordie a quick look at it. Replacing it, she withdrew a folded piece of paper. Reaching for the child, she held the paper out to Gordie insisting he give up the baby and take it from her hand. Instead of giving Little Wanda to her, he turned and handed the baby to her mother. Juanita snuggled the child close, fear widening her eyes.

Gordie unfolded the single page and read it, his face paling, his eyes searching Mary Johannsen's unsmiling face. He looked to the concerned nurse, handing her the paper, then moved to stand between the social worker, Juanita, and the baby. Sue Miles read the paper, folded it and handed it back to Gordie. "It appears legal. You and Juanita will have to comply. We'll get someone to help sort this out, but for now, you'll have to do as the paper says. Little Wanda will have to go with Ms. Johannsen." The kind nurse turned to Juanita. "Go on and feed your daughter, hon, this lady can wait that long before taking her." She looked back at the social .

worker defying her to stop the young mother from feeding her baby.

"Fifteen minutes," Mary Johannsen stated, her voice firm. "I'll be right outside this door. Don't do anything foolish," she directed her gaze and words to Gordie. Juanita swallowed, her voice cracking as she tried to speak.

"What? What are you talking about? You're not taking my baby—our baby? You can't take her!" She clutched Little Wanda so tightly the baby began to fuss. Juanita took the bottle from the warmer and comforted her daughter, tears spilling over her cheeks and slipping down her chin. "You can't," Juanita repeated, rocking her newborn.

"Fifteen minutes," the social worker said, then turned and left the three adults in various states of stunned disbelief.

Gordie pulled his cell phone from his pocket and pushed in some numbers. When his call was answered, his voice was unsteady, tears threatening to undo the young man. "Sheriff Dan? We got trouble here. Some woman from social services says she's got to take Little Wanda away. She gave me a paper that says I'm unfit to care for her while Juanita's in the hospital, and they're going to put her in protective custody until I get checked out for—what's that word?" he asked Sue Miles.

"Competency," she whispered. Gordie handed her the phone, unable to finish. In misery, he sat next to his wife and wrapped his arms around the two women he loved most. Juanita laid her head against his shoulder, her tears wetting his shirt.

Nurse Miles closed Gordie's cell phone and handed it to him. "He's calling Shannon Eckerly to see if she can help clear this up. It'll be okay, wait and see, kids. You're wonderful parents to that little girl, and there's no one around that can say or prove differently."

True to her word, Mary Johannsen pushed her way through the door fifteen minutes later. Picking up the baby quilt lying at the end of the bed, she reached down and took Little Wanda from her mother's arms. Sobs echoed through the hospital room and the baby woke up, staring solemnly into the social worker's determined face. Little Wanda didn't cry. Reaching her tiny hand out, the baby touched the woman's face and stared up into her eyes.

"Precocious little thing," she said, trying to sound detached. She pressed the baby's arm gently into the folds of the quilt and looked at the two young people, tears streaming down their faces, eyes dark with shared misery. "You'll get a notice from the office regarding your hearing and rights while your child is in custody. I warn you, it'll make it more difficult for you to get her back if you make trouble, or try to see her without permission. She'll be in a good home until this can be sorted out. We only want what's best for this little girl."

Looking at Gordie her mouth twisted in distaste. "I rather doubt that the way you were raised will help you in caring for this child. We'll see what the court thinks. Again, she'll be in good hands, so don't worry about her."

A deep, firm voice interrupted. "You've got that straight, lady. 'Cording to Judge Sapp—just got off the phone with her Honorable self—this here babe is not going anywhere with you. We're going to comply with everything you're demanding except, we have the temporary home all set up for this child."

Shannon Eckerly engulfed Gordie in a bone-crushing hug, gently hugged Juanita, then straightened to her full height, thrusting her large body in front of Mary Johannsen. Her round face held thunder clouds that threatened to erupt on the woman holding Little Wanda. "I am struggling to keep myself in check, here, Ms. Johannsen, for you are messin' with my babies, and nobody—nobody messes with my babies. Now, the couple that will be taking temporary custody of Little Wanda will be here shortly, and you will turn that darlin' little child back over to her grieving mama until they arrive."

The social worker started to speak. "Nope," a finger with a very long, bright purple fingernail wagged itself in the startled woman's face. "Don't want to hear anything you got to say just yet. Give that baby back to her mama." Shannon snorted, "Makin' me come out in public in my jogging clothes, no make-up, not to mention I had me a nice pork roast dinner with all the fixin's just about ready to eat." As she scolded the stunned woman, the door opened admitting Dan and Molly.

Smiling, Shannon opened her arms and the two walked into them for their hug. "See, I told you they'd be here shortly. Dan, Molly, this here is Mary Johannsen who thinks she's doing her job. We're going to give her a hand and help her out here so she don't end up looking too much the fool when this is over and done. Hear what I'm saying?

"She has taken the notion that Gordie is not fit to care for Little Wanda while her mama is here in the hospital. Don't know where she got such an idea, but we are going to find out, aren't we." Shannon made this statement to Mary who stood furious, her jaw clenching against words that she

191

longed to fire back at the woman in front of her, usurping her authority.

"Now, Gordie, please let me see that paper this well-meaning woman handed you." Shannon took the paper, read it, then handed it to Dan. "The murky waters are clearing a bit," she said as she narrowed her glittering black eyes at the social worker. "Looks like you been doing some background reading on this young man. I'm wondering what got you stirred up about him? Newspaper articles from the fire? From the way his mama died? Why you going after my baby here? He's a fine young man and I should know—I'm the one got him emancipated. Kept close tabs on him the past two years. Close tabs. I know him like I know my own kin and you're meddling where you oughtn't to meddle.

"Now, I'm not going to lose my temper, 'cause I do believe you're trying to do your job, but I'm thinking you reading them articles and old office files isn't the same thing as knowing this boy. Have you interviewed him? The folks who know him? Have you read any *recent* articles on what this young man is doing with his life?" Shannon's hands rested on her ample hips, her bright purple nail polish a stark contrast against the lime green sweatpants.

"You'll get your hearing, and you'll learn a thing or two about your job when this is finished, so there's good gonna come from this." She aimed this remark to Juanita and Gordie. Looking back at Mary, she arched a black eyebrow, dug a finger into her huge Afro giving her scalp a quick scratch, patted her 'fro back in place and said, "You may speak."

Mary Johannsen's mouth worked for a moment, her face flushed and her eyes sparked fire. "How dare you interfere. This is my case, my jurisdiction, and I have every right to do what I think is best, if I believe this child is in danger from this—this young man."

"Enough!" Shannon said, her face going still, her voice dropping lower. "Need I remind you I'm supervisor over Lund and Boone County? Before you say anything you'll wish you could eat later, we'll stop right here. Judge Ariel Sapp's our authority. The Hallorans' have Judge Sapp's permission for temporary custody, visitation rights will be at their discretion, and we will see you in court, Ms. Johannsen. For now, we're finished."

"I'll be there," Mary Johannsen ground out. Head high, shoulders stiff, furious at being dismissed, she strode from the hospital room and never looked back.

FORTY-SEVEN

Mary Harmon watched her sister-in-law. "Do stop fussing, Wanda," she said. "I'm fine. My leg aches a bit, but that's only natural, don't you think? After all, it's broken, dear."

"You don't have the brains God gave a gnat, Mary Ethel Harmon. What were you thinking, trying to knock that man out with a frying pan? A frying pan! He could have broken more than your leg, you silly old thing." Wanda shook her head and grumbled, "You watch too many movies." With uncharacteristic gentleness, she smoothed an afghan over Mary's lap and tucked it beneath her cast. "Good thing I sold the cows last year. Why, who would take care of you, the shape you're in?" She dropped to the couch next to her sister-in-law, reached for her hand and squeezed it. Mary smiled.

"You, dear. Under all those porcupine quills, you are a sweet lady. I love you, Sis. Don't you wish our Willie was alive? He'd have made short work of that horrible man, coming after his granddaughter like that." A shudder ran through her. "That child is a gift to us, Wanda. You know that, don't you? Her and that sweet baby are a gift to us foolish old women, and we need to take care not to hold on to her too tightly. She's married, you know."

Wanda Harmon sighed. "Too young. They're too young for all this responsibility. What you reckon we can do to help them? You got all the bright ideas," she said, patting the hand that held hers. "That boy sure loves them girls, don't he? Sarah and Neva Sue would be proud of him, don't you reckon? What can we do to help them, Mary?" she repeated.

"First off, Sis, we let them find their way on their own. They're going to need a place to live and I'm happy to have them here, but I'm an old lady with a broken leg. Juanita's going to have enough to do to take care of herself, her husband, and Little Wanda. She doesn't need another job heaped on her."

"Reckon they could stay out at the farm. I'm staying here with you so's I can keep you out of trouble. If they've a mind to, the kids can live at the farm."

"That's sweet, Wanda, but Gordie has his animals to care for, and I think Muley Burger has come to rely on him a good deal. We'll make our offers and let the children sort it out." A tear escaped and rolled down her wrinkled cheek. She swiped at it, wiping her hand on her afghan. "That baby is so blessed to have both of them, don't you think, Sis?" Wistful and sad, Mary's voice broke as another tear escaped.

Wanda looked at her sister-in-law. "You're thinking of Ronald and your daughter, aren't you?" she asked, her voice gentle.

Nodding, Mary sighed. "There's not a day goes by that I don't think about that little girl I gave up for adoption. I wonder how she is. Is she happy? Is her life good? Does she have a kind husband, children, grandchildren? Sometimes I think it would have been worth going far from Hilldale and raising her on my own. When news of Ronald's death came from overseas, I just couldn't think. Why, Mama and Papa would have died of shame, though I do think Mama suspected." She shrugged, weariness lining her face.

"That's water over the dam, as Papa used to say. But I do wonder. . ." Mary looked up at her dearest friend. "You're a wonderful blessing for being such a crotchety old woman, Wanda IraLilly Harmon. My brother knew what he was doing when he married you."

Wanda gently elbowed her, "You always were a sentimental old fool. Now, it's time I get supper cooking. Enough of this foolishness. We'll let the young'uns figure out where they want to live. Then we'll claim our rights to spoil that wee babe of theirs, and remind each other how blessed we are."

"Why Wanda Harmon, I do believe you're going soft in your old age," Mary chuckled. "I think I'll nap a bit while you stir up something to eat. Thank you for being here, Sis."

Wanda pushed herself up from the couch. "Go to sleep, old woman," her voice gruff, her cheeks pink. "Only thing soft around here is your head!"

FORTY-EIGHT

Dan sat listening to his wife explain the competency exam to Gordie. The teen looked frightened, but paid close attention to everything she told him. "Reckon I'll pass the tests they give me, Miss Molly?" he asked.

"Oh, you'll pass them just fine, Gordie," she replied, giving him a hug. "I believe I know the doctor who'll be administering them, and she's fair as well as intuitive. Dr. Lehman seems to have a sixth sense when it comes to evaluating people. She still goes by the book, but she doesn't negate her intuition, and I like that about her. Don't worry, we'll be right there with you. My next Physician's Assistant classes won't start for a few days, and I'd be there with you even if they had. You won't go through this alone. You're family." Molly smiled and hugged him again.

"Okay, I can do this. Besides, I got to get this over with. Wanda—my Wanda—comes home at the end of the week and I've about got our rooms ready, just in case," he blushed, "you know." His voice trailed off.

Dan nodded and patted Gordie's knee. "Listen, son, Juanita plans to stay in town with Miss Mary and her grandma. That way, she can have custody of Little Wanda. She just can't live with you until we have the results of the hearing. You understand it's not you she's avoiding, don't you? She wants her baby with her. Can't say as I blame her," he finished, sadness for the young man next to him lowering his voice.

"Oh, it's okay, Sheriff Dan, I know about all that. Besides, I told Wanda that we could be married in name only. She don't have to live with me. I just want Little Wanda to have a daddy, give her my name, and be responsible for their bills and stuff. It costs a lot to have a baby, you know." His gaze took in his two friends. "You best be saving up, you two."

Surprised, Dan looked at Gordie. "We have a long time before we have to worry about that, right?" He looked from Gordie to Molly, then back to Gordie. "Well?" Dan said. His wife shook her head. "School, remember?" The young man just shrugged then grinned at them before turning serious.

"All I want to do is love them girls and help take care of them. They're my life." Gordie looked embarrassed, then shrugged. "Miss Molly, maybe I ought to get them operations going before Little Wanda gets big enough to be scared of me. Wanda don't seem to mind my scars and such, but I don't want to scare that little baby."

Molly's heart ached. "Oh Gordie, honey, don't you worry about that. Little Wanda won't notice those scars. They'll be invisible with her love for you. But, if you're really wanting to start the operations, I'll contact the doctor's and get some appointments set up for you. Have you talked to Juanita about this? She is your wife, and she really should be part of this decision."

"She's been going through enough, what with the kidnapping, having her baby alone in that awful fire. She could have died," he whispered, his voice breaking. "I don't want to bother her with this business. She just needs to get well and be a good mom to Little Wanda. Speaking of that little girl, I think she's ready for a clean diaper and her bottle. Mind if I take care of her?"

Dan and Molly looked at each other, then at the young man. "That would be wonderful, Gordie. But she's not awa—" Dan laughed as he heard a cry from the spare room. "Guess I should know by now you're tuned into that daughter of yours. Uncanny how you know when she's going to wake up. There's a bottle ready to warm, and diapers at the end of her crib. I'll warm the bottle; you get the diaper." Dan grinned as Molly swatted his shoulder.

"You're going to have to practice one of these days, Sheriff Daniel Halloran," Molly scolded.

"Well, I still have time to learn, right Gordie?" Dan looked to the retreating teen for support. "Coward!" he called after the silent young man headed down the hallway.

FORTY-NINE

Randy Carter sat next to Vicki, their hands entwined. The boys were sleeping, the supper dishes were drying under a clean towel in the dish drainer, and the two adults were listening to Michael Bolton singing softly to them from Vicki's stereo, filling the small, dimly-lit living room with peace.

Looking at the woman next to him, Randy released her hand and cleared his throat. "Vicki?" he said, his voice a soft whisper.

"Hmmmm?" Her eyes closed, her head on his shoulder. When he didn't answer Vicki shifted slightly, opened her eyes and sat up. "You okay?" she asked. "You look—well, you look—I don't know. Did the lasagna make you sick? Too spicy?" Worry creased her forehead.

"Oh shoot, no!" Randy exclaimed, then hushed himself, afraid of waking the boys. "No, it was delicious. You've got to be the best cook I've ever met, bar none, honey. I'm just a little nervous. I have something I need to say." He gazed down into her brown eyes.

"I know I'm not much to look at. All knobby, nothing but skin and bones. Folks make jokes about me looking like that scarecrow in the Wizard of Oz. You know about my divorce, how it left me pretty messed up. I don't make much money as a deputy, enough, but not a lot for extras. I still struggle with wanting to smoke, and well, I'm trying to tell you, I'm no bargain." He sighed again, "Darn, I'm rambling. Wish I could say this better."

Vicki's eyes widened. "Randall Paul Carter! You are a good looking, honest, hard-working man. You didn't go after a divorce, your wife—ex-wife—did. Of course that's got to be painful." Her eyes went dark, and she paled. "What's wrong?"

She drew her bottom lip between her teeth and blushed. "Oh, this is it, then. I think I know where you're going with this. You want out, right? I'm overweight, I have two kids, and memories of a dead husband chasing after me. Look, we're just friends, if you want it that way, Randy. I know I'm nobody's prize. I hear the comments about my size. Just the other day at the mall, right in front of the boys, these teenage girls walked by and *mooed* and *oinked* at me, giggling their heads off. Made Benny so mad I thought he was going to punch one of them. It's okay. Just please don't stop being our—the boys' friend." Vicki put some space between them.

"What are you talking about?" Randy yelped, forgetting about the sleeping boys. Digging into his jeans' pocket he pulled out a small box.

"Here I'm scared you'll want out of this relationship and you're just as scared as I am! Good grief, we're worse than teenagers." He laughed. Hope filled his eyes as he reached for her hand and scooted back beside her. Pressing the box in her other hand, he said, "I got this for you. It isn't much, but maybe later, if I can save up a little, I can do better. I just want," he gulped, "well, Vicki, I want you to marry me—you and the boys." His face reddened and he stared at her, waiting.

Mouth open, eyes wide with surprise, Vicki handed the box back to him. Randy's face fell. She laid her palm against his lean cheek as she held up her left hand. "You put it on me, my love. Yes! Yes! Yes! We'll marry you. All three of us! Are you sure?"

A grin lit his face. "Never more sure of anything in my life. I've felt like I've been in this cold dark place for a very long time, and then one day, I dared to step out toward the light, and there you were, waiting for me. Sweet, kind, generous, loving. A wonderful mom, a beautiful woman inside and out. I didn't think I'd have a chance, but I had to try. Seeing you, your sweet spirit, how you treated me like I was something special. This is the first time I've ever really fought for something I wanted. I love you and the boys so much. I had to try."

He took the ring from the box and slipped it on her finger. "This much I know. I love you. I'm never going back into that dark place again. I want to spend the rest of my life with you, Vicki. With you and your boys. Our boys. I'm not trying to take their dad's place, and I'll help you help the boys remember him, but I want to take up where he left off." He leaned into her and took her face into his hands and kissed her ever so softly. Her arms drew him closer and she returned his kiss, her tears of joy wetting his cheek.

"As long as we live, we'll be a family. I promise," she whispered. And then their kiss deepened as Michael Bolton crooned his love songs, just for them.

FIFTY

Gordie walked alongside Juanita as she climbed Miss Mary's steps. When they entered the house, they found Dan and Molly, and Gramma Wanda holding Little Wanda, all sitting with Mary at the kitchen table. Juanita lifted her daughter from her grandmother's lap into her arms and hugged her. She kissed the baby's cheeks, murmuring in her ear. Eyes shining, she sank into the chair Gordie pushed behind her.

"Thank you for being here. I've got a lot of making up to do." She looked at her great-aunt. "You sure it's okay if we stay here until after the court hearing?" she asked. "Gordie said Little Wanda doesn't cry a lot, and she can stay in my room so you won't hear her," she looked worried, "at least not much."

"My land, child, of course it's all right. Why, I've listened to your grandmother's snoring for three weeks now, and if I can sleep through that, I can sleep through anything!"

Wanda snorted, glared at Mary, then poured herself some hot tea from the cozy-covered pot. Mary smiled at her sister-in-law and continued, "Since you've been gone, the cats have taken to sleeping with me again. It might be better if they don't sleep where the baby is."

Sipping her tea and eyeing the family around the table, Wanda winked at Juanita then looked at her sister-in-law. "I'm not the one who snores around here, and it sure isn't me who does all that talking in her sleep," she grumped, a hint of amusement lighting her eyes. "Reckon I could do a little blackmailing, if I'd a mind to." She turned her gaze back toward her granddaughter, and great-granddaughter. "That wee one won't bother us old women. Reckon we'll be the bother, wanting to hold that sweet baby." Patting Juanita's hand, she glanced over at Gordie. "There's a couch sleeps okay, if you take a notion to stay?"

"I wish I could, Miss Wanda, but I reckon Kissy needs milking, and no telling what amount of trouble her calf's gotten into. I'd best be getting on." He touched the baby's head, gently stroked her cheek. Juanita took his hand in hers.

"Be here tomorrow?" she asked, her voice soft. "Little Wanda will miss you if you don't come." Her cheeks colored and she lowered her eyes. The other adults grew still and looked away from the two young people. Gordie bent down, kissed the downy head cradled in the crook of his wife's arm, then he kissed Juanita's cheek and put his lips close to her ear.

"Wild critters couldn't keep me away," he whispered gazing into her golden eyes, his smile just for her. "I really do have to milk Kissy. Her calf will have her drained dry if I don't get there first." He held her eyes for a moment longer, letting his love show, then stood and said his good-byes.

Molly busied herself pouring tea and reaching for a warm cranberry-walnut muffin from the basket Wanda placed on the table. Dan jumped up to help Juanita as she struggled to her feet and excused herself, tears of weariness and sadness shimmering across her freckles. She wiped her cheeks against her shoulders and tried to smile. Her grandmother patted her arm. "Go on child, you must be dog-tired. You nap for a while. Won't be long and that wee one will be hungry." They watched the young mother as she walked from the kitchen, her baby snuggled close to her chest.

FIFTY-ONE

Gordie stood before the judge. "Do you have representation, young man?" she asked.

"No, sir—er—ma'am. Ms. Johannsen has my paperwork, and I asked that a copy be given to Miss Shannon. I reckon the rest is up to you, Judge—ma'am."

"Judge Sapp will do, Gordie. We're here to see if your wife's infant daughter will be safe in your presence? Is this your concern, Ms. Johannsen?" Judge Ariel Sapp directed her question and gaze at the social worker standing next to Gordie.

"That is correct, Your Honor. This young man's history does not speak well for him to be in a responsible position around this defenseless infant girl. Having reviewed said history, I ask the court to bar him from being near this child. He married the mother to gain access!" Disgust dripped from her voice. Head erect, she drew herself to her full height and refused to look at the miserable young man next to her.

Judge Sapp turned her attention to the woman sitting next to Shannon Eckerly. "Sue Miles?" When the nurse nodded, the judge continued. "It states in this affidavit that you have observed Mr. Bently attending the infant and you are willing to vouch for his capable, compassionate care. Your sworn statement says that he shows 'great love and gentleness for both baby and mother,' and I'm quoting you. Do you wish to add anything to your statement?"

"Your Honor, being new to Columbia, I just want to say that, though I don't know much about this young man's history, I have observed Mr. Bently for weeks, caring for his wife while she lay in a coma, and then when she woke up, and I couldn't have done a better job of personal care for Mrs. Bently. There was never a time that he showed signs of anything but patience, love, and prayerful concern for both his wife and his daughter. That's all, Your Honor." Sue Miles smiled at the young man, and sat down. Judge Sapp thanked the nurse and shifted her attention back to Gordie.

"We have a little history, ourselves, don't we Mr. Bently? And I did read in the file where you got married. Congratulations." She smiled. "I remember you quite well from two years ago. I must say, you've certainly come a long way from the situation you were in. Actually," the judge's smile broadened, "I've been following your progress these past two years, and even without Dr. Lehman's report, I'm impressed. By the way, your solo at last year's Christmas concert at Jesse Auditorium was stunning." Looking at Miss Johannsen, she frowned, "You did catch that concert?" When the social worker shook her head, her eyes sparking anger, Judge Sapp nodded. "Too bad. You really missed an opportunity to see this young man in action.

"Well, Gordie, what do you say we hear what you have to say for yourself? Please address the court regarding your qualifications for parenting…" she checked the paperwork in front of her, "Wanda Marie Bently?" Looking at Gordie, she raised her eyebrow. "The child has your last name. Am I to understand you are her father?"

Taking a deep breath and clasping his hands in front of him to stop their trembling, Gordie looked at the judge. "Yes ma'am, and no ma'am. Is it okay if I explain?" The judge gave her consent. With that, he told how he met Juanita. His eyes glowing, he explained how he fell in love with her the first time he saw her in the convenience store. He spoke about how he knew she was going to have a baby and that she needed help, and how he believed God brought them together and filled him with love for Juanita just for that very reason.

"Little Wanda is getting a rough start in this world, Judge Ma'am," he said, sorrow turning his eyes to midnight blue. "That little girl needs her mama, but she needs me, too. I know it here." He touched his hand to his heart. "Wanda—my Wanda—needs help, too. She needs money to pay the doctor and hospital bills, money to take care of herself and our daughter, and I got money. Plenty of money, and I'm making more every time I sing.

"But Ma'am," he continued, his eyes alight, "more than money, them girls need love. Wanda married me, maybe just to give Little Wanda a daddy's name, but I believe she loves me. I know I love her. I ain't pushing her to live with me. She ain't never had the freedom to choose her life until she come home to Hilldale. She's got the right to choose to stay with me, or not. Don't matter. I'm choosing to be responsible for them two girls the rest of my life." Gordie stopped and looked at his twisted fingers before he pushed them deep into his pockets.

"I ain't much, Ma'am." He looked straight into Judge Sapp's eyes. "You asked me if I'm Little

205

Wanda's pa. Yes, in my heart, my mind, and my soul, I'm that baby's daddy. Did I do the planting? No, I did not. Ain't never—" His voice cracked and horror washed over his face. "That's too much information, ain't it?" A dark flush colored his neck and spread across his face.

Crossing her arms over her chest, Mary Johannsen smirked, giving the judge a knowing look.

Judge Sapp tapped her fingernails on the hardwood in front of her, her gaze traveling from the social worker back to Gordie. She studied him for a long moment, his head hung in embarrassment. "Gordie Adam Bently, look up here at me," she ordered, her voice gentle.

"Yes, Ma'am," he replied, lifting his head, his scarred face paling under her gaze, their eyes locked.

"Gordie, I've made my decision. I will first address Ms. Johannsen and her petition to have you barred from being around your daughter," she gave him a tiny smile before looking at the woman next to him.

"Ms. Johannsen, I appreciate the dedication to your job, and this court wishes to thank you for your concern regarding the safety and care of our at-risk children. Having said that, I would also like to see you in my chambers after court is dismissed. We have a few issues to discuss regarding research and such." Judge Sapp turned her attention back to Gordie.

"Young man, it is the opinion of this court that you are indeed the rightful father of Wanda Marie Bently. I would suggest you and your wife," she smiled at him, "look into you legally adopting Wanda Marie in the very near future." Judge Sapp glanced at the grinning face of Shannon Eckerly. "I'm sure Ms. Eckerly will be more than happy to walk you through this process, am I correct?" Nodding happily, her huge Afro dancing around her joyful round cheeks, Shannon promised to help her babies get legal.

"I believe we've got this settled, then, have we not?" Judge Sapp looked at the fuming social worker standing before her.

"Your Honor, I must protest. Look at this boy. Do you know who his father was? How this boy was raised?" Her blustering voice echoed in the near-empty courtroom.

"How he was fathered and raised is not the issue here, Ms. Johannsen. How he will raise his daughter, and how he will treat his wife are the court's concerns. I've watched this young man rise above more adversity than you and I could ever hope to imagine.

"Unlike you, I've researched and interviewed those who've been closest to him these past two years, read Dr. Lehman's glowing report, the results of the competency tests administered at your request, and I've looked into this young man's heart.

"I've been on this bench far more years than I'd care to admit to, and this young man is one of the systems' successes." She lifted her gavel and smacked it firmly down on solid wood. "Judgment in favor of Gordie Adam Bently." Looking at Mary Johannsen, she finished, "My chambers—now." Judge Ariel Sapp stood, and with a soft swish of robes, she walked from the courtroom.

FIFTY-TWO

Gordie held the door open while Wanda walked with her sister-in-law out of the cold December morning, into the welcome warmth of Neely's Cafe. Juanita carried Little Wanda, and with her husband at her side, the five joined the group of people gathered at several tables that had been pushed together making enough seating for everyone. Muley, Kickapoo Billy, Dan and Molly quietly visited with Carter Neely and Tina Sapp. The sign in the window showed Neely's closed for the day, but each person sitting around the tables had received a personal invitation from Carter. Now, all were curious to see what this meeting was about.

Tina held out her arms and Juanita grinned, handing over her child. "Goodness how she's grown!" Tina crowed, kissing Little Wanda's cheeks. When the baby smiled up at her, the waitress punched Carter's arm to get his attention. "Look, honey, she likes me. She's smiling at me." Looking back at Juanita she asked, "She's about three months old now, isn't she?"

"Tomorrow," Gordie answered, leaning around Juanita. "She's smart. Been smiling since she was just a couple of weeks old. Smart and pretty, like her ma. Now if she would just sleep through the night so these ladies could sleep. . ." Everyone laughed while the older women insisted they didn't even hear the baby crying to be fed through the night. Gordie poured Juanita and himself some tea from a pitcher close by, then helped himself to the buttered-hot pepper pretzels from the basket nearest him, offering them to his wife.

Carter interrupted the noisy group, loudly clearing his throat. "Okay, quiet down. I have an announcement. Well, a couple of announcements,

208

and I want you all to be the first to know." He looked around the tables at his dearest friends. "I'm closing Neely's next month."

Silence greeted his announcement and all eyes focused on him. Flushing to the roots of his thinning hair, he put his arm around Tina, kissed her cheek and grinned. "This here very patient lady has agreed to marry me, and we are going to spend a month traveling to places we've wanted to see but were always too busy to get it done. Hopefully, warm places!" He grinned.

The people around the table erupted in congratulations, clapping and laughing. Little Wanda joined in, patting Tina's face with her tiny hand and cooing softly. Carter continued, "After all that's happened, we decided not to keep putting off getting married, being a family, visiting the places we've always wanted to visit. Life's too short," his voice broke and he wiped tears from his eyes. Leaning across Tina he looked at Juanita. "We're so grateful you and Little Wanda are okay. We love you, young lady. You're family to us. You and your little one have brought us a lot of joy and, speaking for myself, you've shown me just how important family is."

Looking around the table he smiled. "Neely's will be closed until we get back. Hope I still have a business then, but if folks take a notion to quit me, well, that's okay. This lovely lady and her son are more important than this place."

Dan shook his head. "Won't anyone be quitting you, Carter. We'll be waiting for your return. Congratulations, you two!"

Juanita looked into Gordie's eyes, silently asking him a question. Understanding lit his face and he nodded, kissing her flushed cheek. She turned to

Carter and Tina. "Why not let me try to run Neely's while you're honeymooning?" When she emphasized *honeymooning*, everyone laughed. Glancing across the table she noticed Billy Sumday grinning at her.

"Need a cook?" he asked. Hoots of joy echoed around the room as Carter and Tina thanked Juanita and Billy.

"I never expected this," Carter said, his voice filled with emotion. "That would be great, if you two could just do breakfast and lunch. And honey," he continued as he patted the baby in Tina's arms, "this little gal can hang out here anytime you want. Put a crib or whatever new-fangled thing they got for babies now by the back booth so you'll be able to keep an eye on her. She'll be good for. business!"

"Well, now, I reckon I could help out some, too," Gordie said, his arm around his wife.

"Now that my cast is off, Wanda and I can work some in the kitchen, and help keep an eye on Little Wanda." Mary Harmon smiled at the couple across from her. "There, we have it all figured out for you two. We are invited to the wedding, aren't we? Once that's over, why, you two are free to *fly the coop*, as my mother used to say."

"Of course you're all invited. Pastor Hughes will marry us next week and then we'll get everything arranged to leave a few weeks later, end of January, if all goes well. Tina's son will be staying with a friend, so it's all set. Looking around the table, he said, "You all are the best friends—no—the best family a guy could ever have. Thank you." Everyone clapped, assuring the couple of their support.

As Gordie looked around the table at the faces of his adopted family, his heart filled with joy and just a touch of sadness. *Ma, I hope you can see me, 'cause I know it'd make you right happy.* He reached across Juanita and held his hands out for his baby girl. Little Wanda gurgled with joy when she looked into her papa's face.

FIFTY-THREE

"Are you sure, Sis?" asked Mary. The two women sat across the table from each other, Wanda eating a bowl of steaming oatmeal laced with ground flax seed, and Mary finishing the last of her toast and grapefruit.

"Got too good an offer to pass it up. I'll look for a place here in town, and soon as I find it, the farm is sold. Obed's place is for sale. I could live across from you. Don't look at me like that! I'm ready to let go of the farm. Living here the past few months spoiled me. I've gone plum soft, just like you said," Wanda chuckled. Her sister-in-law could see it was true. Wanda didn't seem to be agonizing over her decision to sell her farm.

"What about passing it on to Juanita?"

"The kids are fixing to stay on at Muley Burger's place. Heard them talking—oh, don't give me your evil eye, Mary Harmon! I wasn't eavesdropping. Them young'uns were right here at your table while I was fixing tea. Neva Sue's boy said he'd buy the farm from the old man and leave everything the way it is until Muley's ready to move, or dies. Well, Gordie didn't say it quite like that," she laughed. "The kids can use the money from my place, what I don't spend living high on the hog here in town."

211

Mary smiled at Wanda. "Why not move in here? Save you some money and we've gotten along all right, haven't we?"

"Thought you'd never ask," Wanda said, thumping the table, a grin lighting her face. Turning serious, she said, "Reckon we can look out for each other, and seeing as how we volunteered our services at Neely's, it'd be a whole lot easier to be living in town. And, it would save a good deal, not having to buy a place. I'll pay rent, or some such. We can work out the details later."

Looking across the table she said, "Thanks for asking me. I'm not much good at saying it, but I love you, even if you are a foolish old woman, whacking that killer with a frying pan! Ought to put that in some kind of record book." The two women grinned, then lifting their mugs of coffee, they saluted one another.

"To our new adventure!" Mary said.

"To that and to the young 'uns!" Wanda added. "That granddaughter of mine, she sure got life stirred up for us. Like a breath of fresh air in a stuffy outhouse!"

"Good land!" exclaimed Mary, pretending to be shocked. "Don't you be teaching Little Wanda that kind of talk, Sis."

Laughter rang through the kitchen as sunlight bathed the two elderly women in its wintery glow.

FIFTY-FOUR

Juanita, carrying the baby, walked down the hallway peeking into the various upstairs rooms at her grandmother's farm. She assessed the three bedrooms and bathroom, estimating the boxes she'd need Gordie to bring her. Sorting and packing her

212

mother's room was her job, according to Gramma, and she and Gordie had offered to help with the other rooms. But Gramma Wanda had told her that her mother's bedroom was up to her; she couldn't do it. Gordie came up behind her. "Want me to take Little Wanda and get her fed and down for her nap? I got us some lunch ready for the table, whenever you're ready."

Nodding, Juanita turned into her husband's arms. "This is going to be a bigger job than I thought."

He held his two girls gently but firmly, relishing the feel of them, the sweet smell of Juanita's hair. Speaking into her curls, he said, "We'll get it done. Your gramma's settled in town, so all we got to do is try to keep the place from being robbed. Papa Muley, Uncle Billy, we're taking turns staying nights, so reckon it'll be okay."

"When is Mr. Burger staying here?" Juanita asked, her face buried in Gordie's chest.

"Tomorrow night it's his turn. Uncle Billy is camping out here tonight. He cooked up food for all of us."

"Can Little Wanda and I stay with you tomorrow night?" Juanita asked, her voice muffled. Gordie felt her trembling in his arms. His heart leapt in his chest and he swallowed hard.

"Good land, yes!" he whispered, tightening his hug. Little Wanda squirmed and reached her arms up to Gordie. He released Juanita, took his daughter up and kissed her cheeks.

"Ready for lunch and a nap, sweet baby?" he tickled her and grinned at her delighted laughter. Little Wanda patted his face cooing, her golden eyes alight as she gazed into his. Gordie put his arm around his wife's shoulders. "Reckon that means

213

yes," he laughed. "Let's eat. I'm starving and that stew Uncle Billy left us is good and hot. Sure wish I knew how to make biscuits." The three of them headed downstairs, Gordie replaying Juanita's question over in his mind as he wondered, would she be staying with him, or in the room he'd fixed up for Little Wanda?

Fear and joy fought for dominance as he settled the baby in her seat and headed to the stove to retrieve their lunch.

Was he ready to be a husband if Juanita was ready to be a wife? Pushing the thought from his mind, he set the pan of stew on the potholder nearest him and looked up to see his wife smiling, shyness and love shone in her eyes as a blush swept across her cheeks. As if knowing what he was thinking, she spoke, her voice soft.

"I'm ready to be your wife, Gordie. I'm not sure if I'll be a good one, there's so much I've got to work through, but I want us to be married for real. To be a family for real. Gramma's moving into Aunt Mary's and it's time we get on with our lives together, with our daughter." Her voice faltered and she looked up at his face. She felt so full of love and joy, it hurt. "I love you," she whispered.

Gordie let out the breath he hadn't known he'd been holding. "You're already a wonderful wife, Wanda. You're a great mother and I love you more than I know how to say." He stopped.

"I know you love me," she answered, joy lighting her face. "I really do know, and for me, that's a gift. Until you, and Gramma, and Aunt Mary, I didn't know how to accept love, and what being loved—the good kind of love—meant. I believe my mom loved me, but she was so lost she couldn't show me that love." Tears seeped from her eyes.

214

"Gordie, I want to be your wife. I won't lie, I'm scared. So much is in my past, what if I can't love you the way you need or want to be loved?" Her tears fell in earnest.

His arms gathered her to him and he felt his own trembling. "We're both new at this, Wanda. We'll learn together." Little Wanda took that moment to bang her spoon happily against the wooden table, her giggles echoing through the kitchen, surrounding them with the promise of family.

*****

Upstairs, Juanita pulled the sheets from her mother's single bed while Gordie cleaned up the kitchen and watched over the sleeping baby. Rolling the linens into a ball, she piled them next to the blanket and quilt heaped on the floor. She tugged the mattress free of the springs and hauled it across the room where she leaned it against the wall. Gordie would take the bed frame apart and the lot would be donated to Salvation Army.

The mattress sagged and slipped. Juanita caught it by the edge and as she struggled to prop it back up, she noticed a long cut in the ticking, at the top end. A safety pin held the sheared edges together, and a corner of what looked like a small book protruded from the tear. Excited, she removed the pin and pulled the book free. Her hands shook. The small hardcover book had a clasp with a lock, and the gold-painted word *DIARY* stamped across the front cover.

She went to her mother's jewelry box and rummaged through the simple costume pieces and childhood mementoes her mother had treasured enough to store in the satin-lined box. The diary key lay beneath a school picture of a very young Neva Sue Bently, her mom's best friend.

Key in hand, Juanita sank to the floor, pressed the tiny key into the lock and opened her mother's diary to the last entry.

June 7, 1965

Dear Diary,

I must leave Hilldale. He said he would use his bull whip on Papa and Ma before he killed them, if I don't do as he says. I'm scared. If I'm gone, my folks will be safe. I promised him I wouldn't tell about seeing him push Miss Sarah down the cellar steps all those years ago. But, Diary, I think he knows I know about how he hurts Neva Sue, how he's her boy's pa. Nobody's supposed to know about the boy, but she told me. Now the old man's after me, too. I have to leave. To protect Papa and Ma. To protect me. I asked Neva Sue to come with me, but she won't leave Gordie and she can't travel with him. There goes my prom, and Ma is sewing the prettiest turquoise dress, my favorite color. My backpack is ready, and as soon as I write a note to tell my folks not to come after me, I'm ready, too. I'm really scared, but I know I have to leave. This is it, Diary.

Sarah Elaine

Juanita let her fingers drift across the faded ink. Her mother left because of some man threatening her and her parents? All the years of hurt, abuse, feeling emotionally and physically abandoned, her mother's early, violent death from a drug overdose, all because someone in Hilldale threatened to take a bull whip...

Heat washed over her body. Her heart lurched and her stomached tightened. A bull whip! As the realization hit her, Gordie stepped into the bedroom and knelt down beside her.

"Little Wanda's asleep, and I got the dishes cleaned up, the food put away. What can I do to help? What did you find?"

Juanita looked into the face of the one man she trusted and loved with all her heart. She handed him her mother's diary and pointed to the passage she'd just read. "Here," she whispered, her voice catching on her pain, "read this part here."

Gordie took the small book and read, and as he did, she watched his face, knowing the sorrow the truth would bring to both of them. When he finished reading, he handed the book to her and looked into her eyes. "Grampa," he stated, his voice dull with the knowledge. Juanita nodded, silent before his pain. Gordie settled next to her, his shoulder touching hers.

"The bible says that the truth will set us free. Seems this here truth is tying me in knots and I don't feel real free, Wanda. My grampa—see, he was my pa, too—he sure brought a lot of pain and suffering wherever he went." He stopped and looked into Juanita's face. "How you going to get past this thing? What's it going to do to us? I feel bound up by that man's darkness and this truth ain't setting me free." Despair darkened his eyes, paled his cheeks.

217

Pat Jaeger

Juanita pulled away from him and folded her hands over the small book that shifted her whole world off center, changing everything she'd believed and experienced all her life, re-coloring it all with her mother's words. Silence lay heavy between the two young people and Gordie felt the weight of Sarah Elaine's words pressing the joy right out of his heart, out of his very life.

He couldn't fix it. There was no going back and undoing the damage done so long ago. The damage that had altered so many lives, and now had come full circle, back to him. Juanita's silence said it all. She couldn't forgive his grandfather, and she wouldn't be able to live with him knowing that he was the son of the man who'd destroyed her mother's life, and in so doing, brought such hurt to hers. His heart ached with the burden.

And then he felt her hand take his. He looked up into her beloved tear-stained face, framed with that wonderfully wild red hair, and into the eyes that once sparked their fury at him, at the world. Gordie caught his breath. Love for him shone from those eyes. Eyes dark with sorrow, but alive with love.

"The truth does set us free, Gordie, don't you see?" she said. "I've believed all my life that it was having me that made my mom so miserable. Because of me she wouldn't go back home, or see her parents. I believed she was so ashamed of having me that it drove her to do the drugs, that I deserved all the bad things that happened to me. Don't you see!" she cried, "It wasn't me after all." A sob escaped her throat and she threw herself into his arms. "It wasn't me," she wept, wrapping her arms around her husband's neck, as she let go of the terrible lie that had bound her all her life.

218

"But, Wanda, I'm his son. How can you stand seeing me every day, letting me be part of your life, part of Little Wanda's?" Gordie's voice shook with the fear of losing the two women he loved most.

Pulling away from him, Juanita swiped at her tears, leaned back and looked into his dear face. "Is that how you feel about Little Wanda? Every time you see her, hold her, you think of Eddie and his evil ways?"

"Land sakes, no!" Gordie said. "I love you, and that little girl is like my own flesh and blood, you know that." His agony sharpened his voice.

Smiling through her tears, his wife reached out and cupped his face in her hands. "Then why would I feel any differently about you? I love you. I love who you are, and it wasn't your fault what your father did any more than it was Little Wanda's fault what Eddie did. So see, we're both set free. We're free to love each other and to love our daughter. Gordie! I have to tell Grandma, right away. She's got to be set free, too." Joy lifted her voice and lit her eyes. Hugging her husband, she stood up, and clutching the diary to her chest, the two headed downstairs to their daughter.

FIFTY-FIVE

"Sarah Elaine didn't hate us," Wanda Harmon said, her voice soft with wonder. The diary lay open in her lap, the old woman's tears splattering the pages. Her sister-in-law had her arm around her shoulders, hugging her. Looking at Mary, then the two young people sitting at her feet, she continued, "All those years of hurting, believing we failed that child, her thinking we didn't love her, running off in the night, never coming home," her voice trailed off.

Mary patted her hand then spoke to the girl seated on the floor.

"What a blessing, to have found this," she looked at Juanita. "My dear, you have given us such a beautiful gift. You'll never know..." she stopped, seeing the expression on her niece's face. "Why, you do know, don't you, dear one." The two women held their arms out and Juanita leaned into them. Little Wanda studied the adults around her. She took that moment to push herself over to her back and kick her legs in the air, celebrating the freedom that saturated the room.

FIFTY-SIX

The house lay silent. Early morning light was just beginning to wash the walls with a soft rosy glow. Birds chittered and fussed, Kissy called to her calf who answered in his ever-deepening voice. Gordie opened his eyes, quickly halting the stretch he'd begun. On his pillow, almost nose-to-nose with him, lay his wife, freckles swimming across her sleep-flushed cheeks, curls, their fire absorbing the morning light, spilled around her face like a living halo, and her small hand pressed against his chest. Beautiful awake, to Gordie, Juanita was stunning in sleep. His heart squeezed hard in his chest causing him to catch his breath with the pain. How could love hurt so much?

Juanita and Little Wanda had stayed the night at Muley's, while the farmer slept at the Harmon place. Gordie had been surprised when Juanita had laid their daughter in the travel crib set up in the spare bedroom, then followed him to his room. He'd done his best to prepare it, scrubbing it clean, decorating the bed with new pillows, bedding, and a beautiful wedding ring quilt Miss Mary had given him when he'd explained his plans. Smiling at his flushed face, she'd reached up and kissed his cheek, then pushed the quilt into his arms.

"This was my wedding quilt. I made it from feed sack material my mother and I bought our flour and ground feed in, during the war years. It's never been used. A shadow crossed her face, then disappeared in another smile. You two are the closest thing to children I have, so it's yours now. I pray it covers you both in blessings."

Gordie's thoughts went back to his sleeping wife. After losing his mother, he thought he'd never suffer such agony again, but he knew, as he studied the beloved face next to him in the ever-brightening dawn, that this young woman and her baby girl were his life, and if he lost them, it would devastate him worse than he could imagine. As his silent prayer for his little family rose to the heavens, Juanita opened her eyes.

Smiling, Gordie planted a light kiss on her nose. The hand against his chest moved to his face and pinched his cheek. Whispering, Juanita stared at her husband. "That's what you get for being nice, your pillow invaded. I probably snored and drooled, and..." He hushed her with a gentle kiss.

"Shhhh," he whispered. "Listen." Frowning, Juanita pulled back and listened. Gordie grinned. "Guess who, for the very first time, slept through the night and ain't awake hollering for her breakfast?" Both listened to the peaceful breathing coming from the baby monitor resting on the night stand. They laughed softly, moving closer together as the rising sun shot arrows of light across their bed.

Book Club Questions

1. Do you identify with one or more of the characters? If so, how?

2. Juanita hitchhiked from Minnesota to Missouri. What could she have done differently to get to Hilldale?

3. Drugs and the abuse of alcohol are major factors in Sarah Elaine's demise. Have you had personal experience with a loved one who is struggling with addiction? Who's lost their life due to their addiction(s)?

4. Gordie and Juanita were at-risk children. Discuss ways of helping at-risk children and adults.

5. Discuss your ideas on what you think helped turn Juanita's life around.

6. Discover and share resources that help children like Juanita and Gordie.

7. Discover and share resources that help adults like Sarah Elaine.

Request for Reviews

Reviews are important to this author. If you would please take a few minutes to share on Amazon, it would be greatly appreciated. For contacting me, see the links below. Thank you!

Meet the Author

Pat Jaeger grew up in the Mid-West. The long cold winters made it perfect for reading books, playing guitar, and writing songs, poetry, short stories, and novels. Married with five grown children, a quiver full of grands and great-grands, she loves family get-togethers. Drawing from her mom's stories of life growing up in rural Mid-Missouri, as well as having lived there herself for nearly thirty years, Pat now lives and writes in southern Utah with her husband and two rascally rescue dogs.

patjaegerspages.com
patjaegerspages@yahoo.com

More Books by Pat Jaeger

DAN - Hilldale Missouri Series, Book 1

Made in the USA
San Bernardino, CA
12 June 2018